"If I take you, it will be because I want to."

The words made Deborah shiver. Did he want her? Want *her?* No one had ever wanted her like that. "And do you—want me?"

Looking round swiftly to check they were quite alone, Elliot pulled her to him, a dark glint in his eyes. "You are playing a very dangerous game, Deborah Napier. I would advise you to have a care, for if you dance with the devil, you are likely to get burnt. You may come with me, but only if you promise to do exactly as I say."

"You mean it!" *Oh God, he meant it!* She would be a housebreaker. A thief! "I'll do exactly as you say."

"Then prove it. Kiss me," Elliot said audaciously, not thinking for a moment that she would.

But she did. Without giving herself time to think, her heart hammering against her breast, Deborah stood on tiptoe, pulled his head down to hers and did as she was bid. Right there in Hyde Park in the middle of the day, she kissed him....

* * *

Outrageous Confessions of Lady Deborah
Harlequin® Historical #1100—August 2012

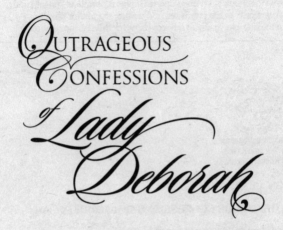

Outrageous Confessions of Lady Deborah

MARGUERITE KAYE

HARLEQUIN®
entertain, enrich, inspire™

Recycling programs
for this product may
not exist in your area.

ISBN-13: 978-0-373-29700-9

OUTRAGEOUS CONFESSIONS OF LADY DEBORAH

Available from Harlequin® Historical and
MARGUERITE KAYE

**Did you know that these novels are also
available as ebooks? Visit www.Harlequin.com.**

And in Harlequin Historical *Undone!* ebooks

Prologue

The murals were surprisingly well executed. Whoever had commissioned them certainly had eclectic taste, for Dionysius practiced his arts on one wall, with Sappho adjacent, and a selection of rather graphic and—in his lordship's opinion—physically impossible combinations of male and female were portrayed opposite. Upon the fourth wall was painted a rather interesting triumvirate which Charles Mumford, Third Marquess of Rosevale, would have liked to explore further. His current position, however, made this rather difficult.

'For pity's sake, Bella, have mercy, I beg of you.' The Marquess was a man most unused to pleading. In the normal run of things it was his expectation—indeed, he believed it was his inalienable right—to have his every instruction obeyed instantly. But the situation in which he currently found himself could by no stretch of the imagination be described as normal.

For a start he was trussed like a chicken, bound hand and foot to the ornate canopied bed in the cen-

tre of the room. His shirt having been ripped open and his breeches roughly pulled down, he was also shockingly exposed, excitingly vulnerable, from his neck to his knees.

Then there was the fact that he was being coolly appraised by quite the most exotic and alluring creature he had ever clapped eyes upon. Clad in a black velvet robe with a décolleté so daring it seemed to be held in place only by the sheer power of her considerable will, she was the stuff of every red-blooded man's fantasy. Dark silken tresses tumbled down her back. Her skin was the colour of whipped cream. Her lips were full, painted harlot red. Her countenance sultry. The black stock of the cat-o-nine-tails she stroked was thick and weighty. She was, overall, a perfect combination of the voluptuous and the vicious, which sent the blood surging to the Marquess's most prized piece of anatomy. Charles Mumford groaned. Whether in trepidation or anticipation only he could truly know.

Bella Donna allowed her eyes to wander languidly over the body of her captive. Despite the undoubted fact that he was an insufferable prig, more than deserving of whatever punishment she decided to mete out to him, the Marquess was a prime physical specimen, his lightly muscled body testament to his fondness for the noble art of fencing. A sheen of sweat glistened on his torso as he fought to free himself from his constraints. The muscles in his arms bulged like cords as they strained against the knots she had so expertly tied. A spatter-

ing of dark hair arrowed down from his chest, over the flat plane of his taut belly, and down. Bella's eyes widened as she followed its trail. His reputation was indeed well deserved. She flicked her tongue slowly over her rouged lips. Dispensing punishment did not preclude an element of pleasure. Especially hers.

Bella drew the whip slowly down the Marquess's body, watching his skin quiver as the leather thongs slid over him, giving his twitching member an expert and playful little tug.

His Lordship groaned. 'Devil take you, release me.'

Bella laughed. 'In your world your word may be law, but you are in my world now. The dark and erotic world of the night, where I am queen and you are my subject. I will release you when I have done with you and not before.'

'Curse you, Bella! Deadly Nightshade! You are well named. What have I done to deserve this?'

'You are a man. That is crime enough,' Bella hissed, noting with satisfaction that, despite his pleas, the Marquess's tumescence was burgeoning. She plied her whip once more, a little more decisively this time. A hiss as the leather thongs made contact, raising soft welts on the flesh, made her victim wince, made his jutting shaft stand up proudly. She shuddered with anticipation. They were ready. All three of them.

'Enough talk,' she said, as she hitched up her skirts and prepared to mount him. 'I have a notion for a midnight ride, and I see a stallion champing at the bit. Though I warn you,' she whispered into his ear, as she

began to sheath the thick pole of his rampant manhood, 'I will not hesitate to use the whip if you cannot maintain the gallop.'

The author put down her pen with a trembling hand. It was, she thought, quite the best and most outrageous scene she had written thus far.

'Goodnight, Bella,' she said as she slipped the sheaf of parchment into her desk and turned the key in the lock, 'I look forward to renewing our acquaintance tomorrow.'

Smiling with a satisfaction quite different from Bella's but no less deep, she snuffed out the candle and retired to her own rather more spartan bedchamber.

Chapter One

Sussex—February 1817

The mechanism which controlled the huge mantel clock jolted into action, the harsh grating sound shattering the blanket of silence, startling him into dropping his wrench. Elliot Marchmont melted back into the shadows of the elegant drawing room, taking refuge behind the thick damask window hangings. They were dusty. His nose itched. He had to quickly stifle a sneeze. Lady Kinsail, it seemed, was not an overly fastidious housekeeper.

The clock began to chime the hour. One. Two. Three. It was an old piece, Louis Quatorze by the looks of it, with an intricate face showing the phases of the moon as well as the time. Gold in the casing. Diamonds on the display. Valuable. There had been a similar one in a grand house he'd visited while in Lisbon. Elliot's lip curled. He doubted it was still there.

The chimes faded into the night and silence again

reigned. Elliot waited. One minute. Two. Only after five had elapsed did he dare move, for experience had taught him to be cautious while there was still a chance that someone in the household, disturbed by the sound, had awoken. But all was well. The coast was clear.

Outside, thin ribbons of grey cloud scudded over the luminous half-moon like wisps of smoke. Silent and stealthy as a cat, shading the light from his lantern with his kerchief, Elliot made his way over to the wall at the far end of the room on which the portrait was hung. The current Lord Kinsail glowered down at him in the dim light, a jowly man with hooded eyes and a thin mouth.

'Grave-robbing weasel,' Elliot hissed viciously. 'Callous, unfeeling prig.'

The likeness of the government minister who had, some years previously, been responsible for supplying the British army during the Peninsular War—or *not* supplying them, if you asked the man now gazing disdainfully up at him—remained unmoved.

Perched precariously on a flimsy-looking gilded chair, Elliot felt his way carefully round the picture, uttering a small grunt of satisfaction as the mechanism opened with a tiny click. The heavy portrait swung silently back on its hinges. He ducked, only just avoiding being clipped on the jaw by the ormolu corner of the frame.

Getting efficiently down to business, Elliot extracted his selection of picks from the capacious pocket of his greatcoat and carefully placed the wrench he used for leverage. Although the safe was old, the Earl had replaced the original warded lock with a more modern arrangement. Faced with four rather than the standard two separate lever tumblers to manipulate, it took Elliot almost twenty minutes to complete the delicate task. As the last tumbler lifted and the bolt finally slid back he eased open the safe door, breathing a sigh of relief.

Papers tied with ribbon and marked with the Earl's seal were crammed into the small space. Underneath them were a number of leather boxes which Elliot wasted no time in opening, rifling through the contents. The Kinsail jewels were, he noted, of excellent quality, if of surprisingly meagre quantity. The family coffers had obviously been seriously depleted at some point in the past. He shrugged. What these people did with their own property was none of his concern.

The item he was looking for was not in any of the boxes. He paused for a moment, one hand stroking his jawline, the rasp of his stubble audible in the smothering silence. Working his fingers quickly across the back wall of the safe, he found a loose panel which concealed a small recess in which sat a velvet pouch. Elliot's triumphant smile glinted in the moonlight as he unwrapped the prize he sought. The large blue diamond was strangely faceted and rectangular in shape. One hundred carats at least, he guessed, about half the size of the original from which it had been cut.

Slipping it into his pocket along with his picks, Elliot extracted his calling card and placed it carefully in the safe. A creak in the corridor outside made him pause in the act of opening the drawing-room door to make good his escape. It could simply be the sound of the timbers of the old house settling, but he decided not to risk exiting Kinsail Manor the way he had entered—through the basement—since this would require him to traverse the entire house.

Making hastily for the window, he pulled back the leaded glass and, with an agility which would have impressed but not surprised the men who had served under him, former Major Elliot Marchmont leapt on to the sill, grabbed the leaded drain which ran down the side of the building, said a silent prayer to whatever gods protected housebreakers that the pipe would support his muscular frame, and began the treacherous descent.

The stable clock chimed the half-hour as Lady Deborah Napier, Dowager Countess of Kinsail, passed through the side gate leading from the park into the formal gardens. In the time it had taken her to make her usual nightly circuit around the grounds of the Manor the skies had cleared. Shivering, she pulled her mantle around her. Made of turkey-red wool, with a short cape in the style of a man's greatcoat, it served the dual purpose of keeping her warm and disguising the fact that underneath she wore only her nightshift. An incongruous picture she must make, with her hair in its curl papers and her feet clad in hand-knitted stockings and sturdy boots—the staid Jacob, Lord Kinsail, would be appalled to discover that his late cousin's widow was accustomed to roam the grounds in such attire on almost every one of the long, sleepless nights of the annual visit which duty demanded of her.

As she passed through the stableyard, making her way across the grass in order to avoid her boots crunching on the gravel, Deborah smiled to herself. It was a small enough act of subversion when all was said and done, but it amused her none the less. Lord knew there was no love lost between herself and the Earl, who blamed her for everything—her husband's premature death, the debts he'd left behind, the shameful state of his lands and her own woeful failure to provide Jeremy with a son to take them on. Most especially Jacob blamed her for this last fact.

I suppose I should be grateful that he continues to acknowledge me, she mused, for, after all, an heiress whose coffers and womb have both proven ultimately barren is rather a pathetic creature—even if my empty nursery conferred upon Jacob a title he had no right to expect. But, alack, I cannot find it in me to be grateful for being invited to this house. I am, upon each visit, astonished anew that the damned man can think he is conferring a favour by inviting me to spend two torturous weeks in the very place where I spent seven torturous years.

She paused to gaze up at the moon. 'Is it any wonder,' she demanded of it, 'that I cannot find tranquil repose?'

The moon declined to answer and Deborah realised that she'd once again been talking to herself. It was an old habit, cultivated originally in the lonely years she'd spent after Mama and Papa had died, when she had been left largely to her own devices in her aged uncle's house. She had invented a whole schoolroom full of imaginary friends and filled page after page of the notebooks which should have contained her arithmetic with stories to tell them.

Deborah had no idea how long her elderly governess had been watching her from the doorway of the schoolroom that day, as she'd read aloud one of those tales of derring-do, stopping every now and then to consult her invisible companions on a point of plot, but it had been enough for that august lady to declare herself unable to cope with such a precocious child. To Deborah's delight, her governess had left and her uncle had decided to send her off to school.

'Little did she know,' Deborah muttered to herself, 'that she was conferring upon me the happiest five years of my life in all my eight-and-twenty.'

At Miss Kilpatrick's Seminary for Young Ladies, Deborah's stories had made her popular, helping her to overcome her initial shyness and make real friends.

As she'd grown from adolescence to young womanhood, her plots had progressed from pirates and plunder through ghosts and hauntings to tales of handsome knights fearlessly and boldly pursuing beautiful ladies. Love had ever been a theme—even in Deborah's most childish scribblings she had found new families for orphaned babes and reunited long-lost brothers with their loyal sister on a regular basis. But it was romantic love which had dominated her stories those last two years at the seminary—the kind which required her heroes to set out on wildly dangerous journeys and carry out impossible tasks; the kind which had her heroines defy their cruel guardians, risking life and limb and reputation to be with the man of their dreams.

Huddled around the meagre fire in the ladies' sitting room, Deborah had woven her plots, embellishing and embroidering as she narrated to her spellbound audience, so caught up in the worlds and characters she'd created that it had always been a jolt when Miss Kilpatrick had rapped on the door and told them all it was time for bed.

'Some day soon,' she remembered telling her best friend Beatrice, 'that will be us. When we leave here...'

But Bea—pretty, practical, a year older and a decade wiser, the eldest daughter of an extremely wealthy Lancashire mill owner—had laughed. 'Honestly, Deb, it's about time you realised those romances of yours are just make believe. People don't fall in love with one look; even if they did, you can be sure that they'd likely fall out of love again just as fast. I don't want my husband to kiss the hem of my skirt or clutch at his heart every time I walk into a room. I want to know that he'll be there when I need him, that he won't fritter my money away on lost causes and that he won't go off to fight dragons when we've got guests to dinner.'

Bea had married the eldest son of a fellow mill owner less than a year later, whom she'd declared, in one of her frank letters to Deborah, at that time once again incarcerated in her guardian's house, would *do very well.* Deborah's correspondence with her friend—with all of her friends—had been one of the many things Jeremy had taken from her. It was not that he had forbidden her to write, but that she had no longer been able to bear to paint a bright gloss on the dreadful reality of her own marriage. And now, though Jeremy had been dead two years, it was too late.

The melancholy which had been haunting her these last months and which had intensified, as ever, during her annual visit to Kinsail Manor settled upon Deborah like a black cloud. Jeremy's death had been far from the blessed release she had anticipated. Of late, she had come to feel as if she had simply swapped one prison for another. Loneliness yawned like a chasm, but she was afraid to breach it for she could not bear anyone to know the truth—even though that meant eventually the chasm would swallow her up.

She was not happy, but she had no idea what to do to alter that state—or, indeed, if she was now capable of being anything else. Isolated as she was, at least when she was alone she was safe, which was some consolation. No one could harm her. She would not let anyone harm her ever again.

A breeze caught at her mantle, whipping it open. Goosebumps rose on her flesh as the cool night air met her exposed skin. She had been lost in the past for far too long. She would not sleep, of that she was certain, but if she did not get back into the house she would likely catch a cold and that would of a surety not do. It would give Lady Margaret, the Earl's downtrodden wife, whose desperation made her seek any sort of ally, an excuse to beg Deborah to prolong her stay.

Head down, struggling to hold her cloak around her, Deborah made haste towards the side door to the east wing and was directly under the long drawing room when a scuffling noise gave her pause. She had no sooner looked up and caught sight of a dark, menacing figure, seemingly clinging to the sheer wall of the Manor, when it fell backwards towards her.

The bracket holding the drainpipe loosened as he was still some fifteen feet or so from the ground. Deciding not to take a chance on the entire thing coming away from the wall, Elliot let go, trusting that his landing would be cushioned by the grass. He did not expect his fall to be broken by something much softer.

'Oof!'

The female's muffled cry came from underneath him. Her ghostly pale face peered up at him, her eyes wide with shock, her mouth forming a perfect little 'o' shape.

Elliot felt the breath he had knocked out of her caress his cheek before he quickly covered her mouth with his hand. 'Don't be afraid, I mean you no harm, I promise.'

Delicate eyebrows lifted in disbelief. Heavy lids over eyes which were—what colour? Brown? He could not tell in this light. Fair brows. Her hands flailed at his sides. Her body was soft, yielding. He was lying on top of her—quite improperly, he supposed. At the same moment he realised that it was also quite delight-

ful. She seemed to be wearing nothing but a shift beneath her cloak. He could feel the rise and fall of her
breasts against his chest. Her mouth was warm against
his palm. For a second or two he lay there, caught up
in the unexpected pleasure of her physical proximity
before several things occurred to him at once.

She was most likely the Countess of Kinsail.

She would definitely raise the alarm as soon as she
possibly could.

If he was caught he would go to the gallows.

He had to leave. Now!

In one swift movement Elliot rolled on to his feet,
pulling the distracting female with him. Still with one
hand covering her mouth, he put his other around her
waist. A slim waist. And she was tall, too, for a lady.
The Earl was a fortunate man, damn him. 'If I take my
hand away, do you promise not to scream?' he asked,
keeping his voice low.

A lift of those expressive brows and an indignant
look which could mean no or it could mean yes.

Elliot decided to take the risk. 'Did I hurt you? I
wasn't expecting you to be there—as you can imagine,' he said.

'That makes two of us.'

Her voice was husky—but then it would be, for he'd
just knocked the wind out of her. She had an unusual
face, an interesting face, which was much better than
beautiful. A full mouth with rather a cynical twist to
it. No tears nor any sign of hysterics, and her expres-

sion was rather haughty, with a surprising trace of amusement.

Elliot felt the answering tug of his own smile. 'Delightful as it was—for me, at least—I did not intend to use you to soften my landing.'

'I am happy to have been of value.' Deborah looked at him through dazed eyes. 'What on earth were you doing?' she asked, realising as she did so that it was an amazingly foolish question.

But he didn't look like a common housebreaker— not that she knew what housebreakers looked like! She should surely be screaming out for help. Of a certain she should be afraid, for she held his fate in her hands and he must know it, yet she felt none of those things. She felt—a dreadful, shocking realisation, but true—she felt intrigued. And unsettled. The weight of him on top of her. The solid-packed muscle of his extremely male body. The touch of his hand on her mouth.

'What were you doing, halfway up the wall of the Manor?'

Elliot grinned. 'Exactly what you suspect I was doing, I'm afraid, Lady Kinsail.'

Now was definitely the time to cry for help, yet Deborah did not. 'You know me?'

'I know of you.'

'Oh.' Conscious of her curl papers and her nightshift, she struggled to pull her mantle back around her. 'I didn't dress for—I did not expect to meet anyone,' she said, feeling herself flushing, trusting to the gloom that it would go undetected.

'Nor did I.'

The housebreaker chuckled. A low, husky growl of a laugh, distinctively male, it sent shivers over Deborah's skin. He had a striking face, strong-featured, with heavy brows, deep grooves running down the side of his mouth, and eyes which looked as if they had witnessed too much. A fierce face with a discernible undercurrent of danger. Yet those eyes suggested compassion and even more improbably, given the circumstances, integrity. A memorable face, indeed, and an extremely attractive one. She met his gaze and for a few seconds the air seemed to still between them. A connection, a *frisson*, something she could not name, sparked.

'I'm sorry to have alarmed you,' he said finally, 'but if you must blame anyone for my presence here you must blame your husband.'

Deborah began to wonder if perhaps she was dreaming. 'But Jeremy—my husband—is...'

'A most fortunate man,' Elliot said with a twisted smile. 'I must thank you for not calling out. I am in your debt.' He knew he should not, but he could not resist. 'Let me demonstrate my gratitude.' When he pulled her to him she did not resist. The touch of her lips on his was warm, sweet and all too fleeting. He released her extremely reluctantly. 'I must go,' he said roughly. 'And you, madam, must do as you see fit.'

'Wait a minute. I don't even know what your name is.'

The housebreaker laughed again. 'I could tell you, but then I'd have to kill you.'

He was already fleeing across the lawn. Staring after him in utter bemusement, Deborah remained stock still, watching the shadowy figure melt into the darkness. The stable clock chimed the hour. Above her, she could hear the sharper chimes of another clock. Looking up, she saw the window of the long drawing room was wide open. The French clock—it must be that she could hear. She touched her fingers to her mouth where the house-breaker had kissed her. Kissed her! A common thief!

No. Housebreaker he might be, but he was most certainly not common. His voice was that of an educated man. He had an air about him of someone used to command. The greatcoat which enveloped him was of fine wool. And, now she thought about it, his boots were of an excellent cut and highly polished. He smelled of clean linen and fresh air and only very slightly of sweat and leather and horse. She supposed he must have tied his steed up somewhere close by. She listened intently, but could hear nothing save the rustle of the breeze as it tugged at the bare branches of the trees.

She should wake the Earl. At the very least she should alert the servants. Deborah frowned. Whatever the man had stolen must have been concealed about his person, for he'd carried no sackfull of loot. Papers, perhaps? Despite the arduous task of setting Jeremy's estates to rights—a task which his cousin never ceased to complain about—Lord Kinsail continued to play an active role in the government. Was the housebreaker a spy? That certainly made more sense, though the war was so long over there was surely no need for such subterfuge. And he had neither looked nor sounded like a traitor.

Deborah's laugh, quickly stifled, had an unwelcome note of hysteria in it. She had no more idea of what a spy should look like than a housebreaker.

None of it made sense. It occurred to her rather be-latedly that the thing which Lord Kinsail would con-sider made least sense of all was her own presence in the grounds, in her night clothes, at four in the morn-ing. He'd want to know why she'd made no attempt to raise the alarm immediately—what could she say when she didn't know the answer to that question herself? It wasn't as if the thief had threatened her. She hadn't felt scared, exactly, more…what?

The thought of having to suffer Jacob's inquisition made up her mind. She would not give him any more reason to treat her with disdain. In fact, Deborah de-cided, making her way hurriedly to the side door, the time had come to break free from Lord Kinsail and this blighted place. Small consolation—very small—but her failure to provide Jeremy with an heir had one advan-tage. She had no real obligation to maintain close ties with his family. Lord Kinsail might grudge her every penny of the miserly widow's portion which he doled out irregularly, and only after several reminders, but she doubted he could ultimately refuse to pay it. In any case, she was determined to find a way to survive with-out it. This would be her last visit to Kinsail Manor and damn the consequences!

Feeling decidedly better, Deborah fastened the door

carefully behind her and fled up the stairs to her chamber on the third floor. Whatever it was the bold housebreaker had taken would be discovered in the morning. He was already gone, and her rousing the household now would not bring him back.

She yawned heavily as she discarded her mantle and unlaced her muddy boots, pushing them to the back of the cupboard out of sight of the inquisitive maid. Catching a glimpse of herself in the mirror, she made a face. Despite her hair curlers, that look on the housebreaker's face just before he kissed her had been unmistakable. Not that she was by any stretch of the imagination an expert, but she was sure, none the less. He had wanted her.

Heat washed over her. What would it be like to submit to someone like that? Deborah pulled the bedclothes up around her, too beguiled by this thought to notice the cold. Desire. She wrapped her arms around herself, closed her eyes and recalled the velvet touch of his lips on hers. Beneath her palms her nipples budded. Behind her lids wanting flared the colour of crimson. Desire. Sharpened by its very illicitness. Desire of the dark, venal kind which roused Bella Donna, the heroine of the novels which were currently scandalising the *ton*, to shocking heights of passion. Desire such as she had never shared.

Desire. Deborah slipped down into the welcoming dark embrace of the bed, her hands slipping and sliding down over the cotton of her nightdress. And down.

Closing her eyes tighter, she abandoned herself to the imagined caresses of a virile and skilled lover.

She awoke much later in the morning than usual, dragging herself up from the depths of slumber to the hue and cry of a household in a state of pandemonium. Slipping into a thick kerseymere gown, for Kinsail Manor, owing to a combination of its age and its current incumbent's frugality, was an uncomfortably draughty place, Deborah sat at her mirror to take out her curl papers. Her straitened circumstances meant she could not afford the luxury of a personal maid, and, though Lady Kinsail had begged her to make use of her own dear Dorcas, Her Ladyship's 'own dear Dorcas' was in fact an exceedingly dour creature, who believed a widow's hair should be confined under a cap and kept there with a battalion of hairpins—the sharper the better.

Since she had perforce been attending to her own *toilette* for most of her adult life, Deborah made short work of gathering her long flaxen tresses high on her head and arranging her curls in a cluster over one shoulder. Her gown she had fashioned herself, too, in plain blue, with not a trace of the French work, furbelows and frills so beloved of *Ackerman's Repository.*

She had resented her blacks when Jeremy died, resented the way they defined her as his relic, but it had taken her a full six months after the designated year of mourning to cast them off all the same, for she had come to appreciate the anonymity they granted her. It was then she had discovered that she lacked any identity at all to fill the gap. Like the anonymous gowns of blues and browns and greys she now wore, neither fashionable nor utterly dowdy, she felt herself indeterminate, somewhat undefined. Like an abandoned canvas, half painted.

An urgent rap at the door interrupted this chastening thought. 'Please, Your Ladyship, but His Lordship asks you to join him in the long drawing room urgently.' The housemaid, still clad in the brown sack apron she wore to lay the morning fires, was fairly bursting with the important news she had to impart. 'We've all to assemble there,' she informed Deborah as she trotted along the narrow corridor which connected the oldest—and dampest and coldest—wing of Kinsail Manor with the main body of the house, built by Jeremy's great-grandfather. 'The master wants to know if anyone heard or saw him.'

'Heard who?' Deborah asked, knowing full well that the girl could only mean the housebreaker.

She should have woken Jacob, she knew she should have, but she could not find it in her to regret this oversight. If she was honest, there was a bit of her—a tiny, malicious, nothing-to-be-proud-of bit of her—which was actually quite glad. Or, if not glad, at least indifferent. Jacob had taken everything from her that Jeremy had not already extorted. Whatever precious thing had been stolen, she could not care a jot. What was more, she decided on the spur of the moment, she was going to continue to keep her mouth firmly shut. She would not admit to wandering the grounds. She would not provoke one of his sermons. She would not!

'I'm sorry—what were you saying?' Deborah realised the maid had been talking to her while her thoughts had been occupied elsewhere. They were outside the drawing room now. The door stood wide open, revealing the gathered ranks of Lord Kinsail's household. At the head of the room, under his own portrait, stood the man himself.

'Best to go in, My Lady,' the maid whispered. 'We're last to arrive.' She scuttled over to join the rest of the maidservants, who were clustered like a nervy flock of sheep around the housekeeper. Mrs Chambers, a relic from Deborah's days as chatelaine, cast her a disapproving look.

Inured to such treatment, Deborah made her way to the top of the room to join the Earl. The frame of the portrait swung open on its hinge to reveal the safe. Her lips twisted into a bitter smile. Jeremy had shown it to her when they were first married, though in those days it had been concealed behind a portrait of his father.

'Empty coffers,' Jeremy had said to her. 'Though not for much longer—thanks to you, my darling wife.'

The revelation that the terms of her inheritance would force him to wait several years for her to attain her majority and gain the larger part of her fortune had not been the beginning of his change in attitude towards her, but after that he'd ceased to pretend.

She should never have married him. But there was no time for her to become entangled in that morass yet again. Lady Kinsail, even more palely loitering than ever, was seated on a gilt chair almost as frail as herself. Deborah went to her side.

'Cousin Margaret,' she said, squeezing Her Ladyship's cold hand between her own. Though she persistently refused to grant Lord Kinsail the appellation of cousin, she had conceded it to his wife. They were not related, but it rescued them from the hideous social quagmire of having two Countesses of Kinsail in the one household. 'What, pray, has occurred?'

'Oh, Cousin Deborah, such a dreadful thing.' Lady Kinsail's voice was, like her appearance, wraith-like. 'A common housebreaker—'

'No common housebreaker,' her lord interrupted. Under normal circumstances Lord Kinsail's complexion and his temper had a tendency towards the choleric. This morning he resembled an over-ripe tomato. 'I don't know what time you call this, Cousin,' he fumed.

'A quarter after nine, if the clock is to be trusted,' Deborah replied, making a point of arranging her own chair by his wife and shaking out her skirts as she sat down.

'Of course it's to be trusted. It's Louis Quatorze! Say what you like about the French, but they know how to turn out a timepiece,' Lord Kinsail said testily. 'I have it upon good authority that that clock was originally made for the Duc d'Orleans himself.'

'A pity, then,' Deborah said tightly, 'that such an heirloom is no longer in his family. I abhor things being taken from their rightful owners.'

Lord Kinsail was pompous, parsimonious, and so puffed-up with his own conceit that it was a constant surprise to Deborah that he did not explode with a loud pop. But he was no fool.

He narrowed his eyes. 'If you had served my cousin better as a wife, then the estates which you allowed him to bring to ruin upon that ill-fated marriage of yours would not now be my responsibility, but your son's. If you had served my cousin better as a wife, Cousin Deborah, I have no doubt that he would not have felt the need to seek consolation in the gaming houses of St James's, thus ensuring that his successor had hardly a pair of brass farthings to rub together.'

Deborah flinched, annoyed at having exposed herself for, cruel as the remarks were, there was a deep-rooted part of her, quite resistant to all her attempts to eradicate it, which believed them to be true. She had made Jeremy about as bad a wife as it was possible to make. Which did not, however, mean that she had to accept Jacob's condemnation—she was more than capable of condemning herself. And she was damned if she was going to apologise for her remark about the clock!

'Don't let me hold you back any further, Jacob,' she said with a prim smile.

Lord Kinsail glowered, making a point of turning his back on her and clearing his throat noisily before addressing the staff. 'As you know by now, we have suffered a break-in at Kinsail Manor,' he said. 'A most valuable item has been taken from this safe. A safe which, I might add, has one of the most complex of new locks. This was no ordinary robbery. The brazen rogue, a menace to polite society and a plague upon those better off than himself, was no ordinary thief.'

With a flourish, His Lordship produced an object and waved it theatrically in front of his audience. There was a gasp of surprise. Several of the male servants muttered under their breath with relief, for now there could be no question of blame attaching itself to them.

At first Deborah failed to understand the import of the item. A feather. But it was a most distinctive feather—long with a blue-and-green eye. A peacock feather. The man who had dropped from the sky on top of her last night must have been the notorious Peacock!

Good grief! She had encountered the Peacock—or, more accurately, the Peacock had encountered her! Deborah listened with half an ear to Jacob's diatribe against the man's crimes, barely able to assimilate the fact. She watched without surprise as in turn every one of the servants denied hearing or seeing anything out of the ordinary, just as the servants in every one of the Peacock's other scenes of crime had done. No one had ever disturbed him in the act. No one had ever caught so much as a fleeting glance of him leaving. Private investigators, Bow Street Runners—all were completely flummoxed by him. He came and went like a cat in the night. For nigh on two years now, the Peacock had eluded all attempts to capture him. No lock was too complex for the man, no house too secure.

With the room finally empty of staff, Lord Kinsail

turned his attentions back to Deborah. 'And you?' he demanded. 'Did you see anything of the rogue?'

She felt herself flushing. Though God knew she'd had opportunity aplenty, she had never grown accustomed to prevarication. 'Why would I have seen anything?'

'I know all about your midnight rambles,' Lord Kinsail said, making her start. 'Aye, and well might you look guilty. I am not the fool you take me for, Cousin Deborah.' He permitted himself a small smile before continuing. 'My head groom has seen you wandering about the park like a ghost.'

'I have never taken you for a fool, Jacob,' Deborah replied, 'merely as unfeeling. I take the air at night because I have difficulty sleeping in this house.'

'Conscience keeps you awake, no doubt.'

'Memories.'

'Spectres, more like,' Lord Kinsail replied darkly. 'You have not answered my question.'

Deborah bit her lip. She ought to tell him, but she simply could not bring herself to. All her pent-up resentment at his quite unjustified and utterly biased opinion of her, combined with her anger at herself for lacking the willpower to enlighten his ignorance, served to engender a gust of rebelliousness. 'I saw nothing at all.'

'You are positive?'

'Quite. You have not said what was stolen, Jacob.'

'An item of considerable value.'

Alerted by his decidedly cagey look, Deborah raised an enquiring brow. 'Why so close-mouthed? Was it government papers? Goodness, Jacob,' she said in mock horror, 'don't tell me you have you lost some important state secret?'

'The item stolen was of a personal nature. A recent acquisition. I do not care to elaborate,' Lord Kinsail blustered.

'You will have to disclose it to the Bow Street Runners.'

'I intend to have the matter investigated privately. I have no desire at all to have the Kinsail name splashed across the scandal sheets.'

Deborah was intrigued. Jacob was looking acutely uncomfortable. A glance at Margaret told her that Her Ladyship was as much in the dark as she was. She was tempted—extremely tempted—to probe, but her instinct for caution kept her silent. That and the fact that she doubted she would be able to sustain her lie if interrogated further.

The sensible thing to do would be to make good her escape while Jacob was distracted, and Deborah had learned that doing the sensible thing was most often the best.

Getting to her feet, she addressed herself to Lady Kinsail. 'Such a shocking thing to have happened, Cousin Margaret, you must be quite overset and wishing to take to your bed. In the circumstances, I could not bear to be a further burden to you. I think it best that I curtail my visit. I will leave this morning, as soon as it can be arranged.'

'Oh, but Cousin Deborah, there is no need—'

Lord Kinsail interrupted his wife. 'I trust you are not expecting me to foot the bill if you decide to travel post?'

'I shall go on the afternoon stage,' Deborah replied coldly. 'If you can but extend your generosity to providing me with transport to the coaching inn…'

'Cousin Deborah, really, there is no need…' Lady Kinsail said, sounding just a little desperate.

'If that is what Cousin Deborah wants, my dear, then we shall not dissuade her. I shall order the gig.' Lord Kinsail tugged the bell. 'In one hour. I trust you will not keep my horses waiting?'

'I shall make my farewells now to ensure that I do not,' Deborah replied, trying to hide her relief. 'Cousin Margaret.' She pressed Her Ladyship's hand. 'Jacob.' She dropped the most marginal of curtsies. 'I wish you luck with recovering your property. Thank you for your hospitality. I must make haste now if I am to complete my packing in time. Goodbye.'

'Until next year,' Lady Kinsail said faintly.

Deborah paused on the brink of gainsaying her, but once again caution intervened. If there was one thing the Earl loathed more than having his cousin's widow as a house guest, she suspected it would be having his cousin's widow turn down his hospitality.

'So much can happen in a year,' she said enigmatically, and left, closing the door of the long drawing room behind her for what was, she fervently hoped, the very last time.

Chapter Two

London, three weeks later

Elliot stifled a yawn and fished in his waistcoat pocket for his watch. Five minutes off two in the morning and his friend Cunningham was showing no inclination to leave. The atmosphere in the gambling salon of Brooks's was one of intense concentration disturbed only by the chink of coin, the glug of a decanter emptying, the snap of cards and soft murmurings as the stakes were raised. The gamblers were much too hardened to betray anything so crass as emotion as the stack of guineas and promissory notes shifted across the baize from one punter to another.

Some of the cardplayers wore hats to shield their faces. Others tucked the ruffles of their shirt sleeves up under leather cuffs. Elliot, who had been used to gambling with his life for far higher stakes, could not help finding the whole scene slightly risible. He had placed a few desultory bets at faro earlier, more for form's sake than anything, but the last hour and a half had been spent as a spectator.

Restlessly pacing the long room, with its ornately corniced concave ceiling from which a heavy chandelier hung, the candles in it guttering, he called to mind the many similar reception rooms across Europe he had visited. Cards were not the game which had attracted him to such places. In the midst of war, cards were a means for his men to while away the long hours between battles. Civilians didn't understand the boredom of war any more than they understood its visceral thrill. He had no idea why Cunningham could ever have thought he would be amused by a night such as the one they had just spent. Carousing and gambling left Elliot cold. No doubt when Cunningham rose from the tables he would be expecting to indulge in that third most gentlemanly pursuit, whoring—another pastime which held no interest for Elliot. He was a gentleman now, perforce, but he was, first and foremost his own man, and always had been—even in the confines of his uniform. Elliot had had enough.

'I find I have had a surfeit of excitement, my dear Cunningham,' he said, tapping his friend lightly on the shoulder. 'I wish you luck with the cards. And with the ladies.'

'Luck doesn't come into it, Elliot. You of all people should know that. Never met a devil more fortunate with the fairer sex than you.'

'Never confuse success with good fortune, my friend,' Elliot replied with a thin smile. 'I bid you goodnight.'

He collected his hat and gloves and headed out into St James's, doubting he'd be making much use of his new club membership in the future. It was a cold night, dank and foggy, with only a sliver of moon. A house-breaker's kind of night, though it was much too soon to be thinking about that.

Kinsail's diamond had proved rather difficult to dispose of. Elliot's usual fence had refused to have anything to do with such a distinctive stone, forcing him into an unplanned trip to the Low Countries where he had, reluctantly, had it cut and re-faceted before selling it on. The resultant three diamonds had garnered far short, collectively, of what Lord Kinsail was rumoured to have paid for the parent. But then, Kinsail had paid the inflated premium such contraband goods commanded, so Elliot's thief-taker had informed him. More important—far more important—was the price Kinsail was now paying for his dereliction of duty to the British army.

Not that he knew that, of course, any more than he really understood the price paid by that army for his ne-glect. Men such as Kinsail saw lists demanding horses, mules, surgeons. Other lists requiring field guns, can-nons, rifles, vied for their attention, and more often won. But what use was one of the new howitzers when there were no horses to haul it into battle? What use were muskets, Baker rifles, bayonets, when the men who would wield them lay dying on the battlefields for want of a horse and cart to carry them to a field hospi-tal? For want of a surgeon with any experience to tend to them when they got there? What did Kinsail and his like know of the pain and suffering caused by their penny-pinching. The ignorance which led them to put guns before boots and water and bandages?

Elliot cursed, forced his fists to uncurl. Even now, six years later, Henry's face, rigid with pain, haunted him. But what did Kinsail and his like know of that? Nothing. Absolutely nothing. And even if he could, by some miracle, paint the picture for them, it would give them but a moment's pain. Far better to hit them where it hurt—to take from them what they valued and use it to fund what really mattered. Those diamonds, even in their cut-down form, would make an enormous difference. That miserly bastard Kinsail would never know that his jewel had, by the most dubious and complex route, gone some way to make reparation for his war crimes.

As ever, following what he liked to think of as a successful mission, he had scoured the newspapers for word of the robbery, but Lord Kinsail had, unsurprisingly, declined to make public his loss. For perhaps the hundredth time since that night Elliot wondered what, if anything, Lady Kinsail had said about their encounter. For what seemed like the thousandth time the memory of her pressed beneath him flitted unbidden into his mind. The feel of her mouth on his. The soft, husky note to her voice. That face—the haughty, questioning look, the big eyes which had shown not one whit of fear.

He should not have kissed her. He had thought, as he fled the scene of his crime, that she had kissed him back, but had come to believe that mere wish fulfilment. She had simply been too startled to resist. After all, as far as she was concerned he was a thief. But why had she not cried foul?

The bright gas lighting of Pall Mall gave way to the dimmer and appropriately shadier braziers around Covent Garden. Thin as London was of company this early in the year, there seemed to be no shortage of customers for the wretches forced to earn their living on the streets. A scuffle, a loud cry, then a cackle of laughter rent the air as a man was dumped unceremoniously on to the steps of a brothel. Shaking his head at a questioning pock-marked street walker, Elliot pressed a shilling into her filthy hand and made haste across the market square, ignoring her astonished thanks.

The stark contrast between the homes of the gentlemen who frequented the privileged clubs of St James's and the hovels and rookeries which were home to London's whores, whom those same gentlemen would visit later, made him furious. He had seen poorer and he had seen sicker people abroad, but this—this was home, the country he had served for nigh on sixteen years. It shouldn't be like this. Was this what twenty-odd years of war had won them?

In the far corner of the square he spied something which never failed to make him heartsick. Just a man asleep in a doorway, huddled under a worn grey blanket, but the empty, flapping ends of his trousers told their story all too well. The low wooden trolley against which he rested merely confirmed it. To the callused, scarred

legacy of guns and gunpowder on his hands would be
added the scraping sores caused from having to propel
himself about on his makeshift invalid cart. He stank,
the perfume of the streets overlaid with gin, but to Elliot what he smelled most of was betrayal.

'May God, if God there be, look down on you, old
comrade,' he whispered.

Careful not to disturb the man's gin-fuelled slumber,
he slipped a gold coin into the veteran's pocket, along
with a card bearing a message and an address. To many,
charity was the ultimate insult, but to some—well, it
was worth trying. Elliot never gave up trying.

Weary now, he made his way towards Bloomsbury,
where he had taken a house. 'The fringes of society,'
Cunningham called it, 'full of Cits.' He could not understand Elliot's reluctance to take a house in Mayfair, or
even a gentleman's rooms in Albemarle Street, but Elliot
had no desire to rub shoulders with the *ton* any more
than he desired to settle down, as his sister Elizabeth
said he ought. Said so regularly and forcefully, Elliot
thought with a smile as he passed through Drury Lane.

They were surprisingly alike, he and his sister. Almost twelve years his junior, Lizzie had been a mere
child when Elliot joined the army. He had known her
mostly through her letters to him as she was growing
up. As their father's health had declined and war kept
Elliot abroad, Lizzie had shouldered much of the responsibility for the overseeing of the estate as well as
the care of her fast-failing parent. Knowing full well
how much her brother's career meant to him, she had

refrained from informing him of the true nature of affairs back home until their father's demise had become imminent. Touched by her devotion, Elliot had been impressed and also a little guilt-ridden, though Lizzie herself would have none of that, when he had finally returned for good after Waterloo.

'I have merely done my duty as you did yours. Now you are home the estates are yours, and since Papa has left me more than adequately provided for I intend to enjoy myself,' she'd told him.

She had done so by marrying a rather dour Scot, Alexander Murray, with rather indecent haste, after just three months of mourning. The attachment was of long standing, she had informed her astonished brother, and while her dearest Alex had agreed that she could not marry while her papa was ailing, she'd seen no reason for him to wait now that Papa had no further need of her. Lizzie had emerged from her blacks like a butterfly from a chrysalis—an elegant matron with a sharp mind and a witty tongue, which made her a popular hostess and an adored wife. Matrimony, she informed her brother at regular intervals, was the happiest of states. He must try it for himself.

Russell Square was quiet. Bolting the door behind him, Elliot climbed wearily up to his bedchamber. After tugging off his neckcloth, neatly folding his clothes—an old military habit, impossible to shake—Elliot yawned and climbed thankfully between the cool sheets of his bed. Another hangover from his military days: to have neither warming pan nor fire in the room.

He had no wish to be manacled in wedlock. It was not that he didn't like women. He liked women a lot, and he'd liked a lot of women. But never too much, and never for too long. In the courts of Europe loyalty to one's country came before loyalty to one's spouse. In the courts of Europe the thrill of intrigue and adventure, legitimised by the uncertainty of war, made fidelity of rather less import than variety.

'Living in the moment,' one of his paramours, an Italian countess, had called it. Voluptuous Elena, whose pillow talk had been most enlightening, and whose penchant for making love in the most public of places had added an enticing element of danger to their coupling. That time in the coach, coming back from the Ambassador's party…Elliot laughed softly into the darkness at the memory. It had been later, in another country, in another coach and with another woman—this one rather less inclined to court public exposure—that he had realised how practised had been Elena's manoeuvres. Her ingenious use of the coach straps, for example. He had obviously not been the first and he was without a doubt that he had not been her last.

He wondered what Elena was doing now. And Cecily. And Carmela. And Gisela. And Julieanne. And—what was her name?—oh, yes, Nicolette. He could not forget Nicolette.

Except he could hardly remember what she looked like. And the others, too, seemed to merge and coalesce into one indistinct figure. He missed them all, but did not miss any one in particular. What he really missed was the life, the camaraderie. Not the battles, for the thrill of the charge was paid for in gore and blood. Nor the pitiless reality of war either—the long marches, the endless waiting for supplies which did not come, his men stoically starving, clad in threadbare uniforms, footwear which was more patches than boot. Killing and suffering. Suffering which continued still.

Elliot's fists clenched as he thought of the old soldier in Covent Garden. One of thousands. No, he'd had more than enough of that.

What he missed was the other, secret part of his army career, as a spy behind enemy lines. The excitement of the unknown, pitting his wits against a foe who did not even know of his existence, knowing that before he was ever discovered he would be gone. The transience of it all had made living in the moment the only way to survive. The pulsing, vibrant urgency of taking chance upon chance, the soaring elation of a mission pulled off against the odds. He missed that. The pleasure of sharing flesh with flesh, knowing that, too, was transient. He missed that also. Since coming home he had taken no lover. He would not take a whore, and somehow, in England, taking the wife of another man seemed wrong.

Abstinence had not really troubled him. He had encountered no woman who had stirred him beyond vague interest until his encounter with Lady Kinsail.

Elliot sighed as her face swam into his mind again and his body recalled hers. Between his legs, his shaft stirred. *Dammit,* he would never sleep now! That smile of hers. That mouth. His erection hardened. What would it feel like to have that mouth on him, licking, tasting, sucking, cupping? Elliot closed his eyes and, wrapping his hand around his throbbing girth beneath the sheets, gave himself over to imagining.

Deborah stood undecidedly on the steps of the discreet offices of Freyworth & Sons in Pall Mall. It was early—not long after ten—a pretty day for March, and she longed to stretch her legs and mull over the rather worrying things which Mr Freyworth had said. It was true, her writing had of late become more of a chore than a pleasure, but she had not been aware, until he had pointed it out, that her general ennui had transferred itself on to the page. Stale. That was how her publisher had described her latest book. Knitting her brow, Deborah was forced to acknowledge the truth of what he said. Perhaps her imagination had simply reached its limit?

Across from her lay St James's Park, and a short way to the left was Green Park. There would be daffodils there. Not the sort of freshness Mr Freyworth was demanding, but perhaps they would help inspire her. She could walk over Constitution Hill, then carry on into Hyde Park and watch the riders.

Even at the end, when money had been as scarce as hens' teeth at Kinsail Manor, Jeremy had found the funds to keep his horses. Riding had always been a solace to Deborah, though these days it was, as with most things, a pleasure she could only experience vicariously.

She had no maid to accompany her, which when she was married would have been a heinous crime, but a

combination, she believed, of her widowhood, her im-
poverished state and the bald fact that she possessed
no maid, had allowed her a relative freedom which she
cherished. In fact it was rather her self-possessed air,
the invisible wall which she had built around herself,
which made it only very occasionally necessary for
Deborah to rebuff any man who approached her. For
her charms were not so recondite as she imagined, and
nor was she anywhere near so old, but of this she was
blissfully unaware.

In the Green Park, the fresh grass of the gently rolling meadows made her feel as if she was far from the
metropolis. Her mind wandered from her business meeting back to *that* night, as it had done on countless oc-
casions in the days which had elapsed since. Though
she had scoured both *The Times* and the *Morning Post*
on her visits to Hookham's circulating library in Bond
Street, she had found no mention of the theft from Kinsail Manor. Jacob had been as good as his word.

The shifty-eyed investigator who had come calling
at her lodgings in Hans Town had been equally reticent.
She had absolutely no idea what had been stolen save
that it was small, definitely not papers, and definitely
extremely valuable. *What?* And *why* was Jacob so intent on silence? And *how,* when he was so intent, had
the housebreaker discovered the presence of whatever
it was in the safe when even Jacob's wife had no idea
of its existence?

The housebreaker who had kissed her.

Deborah paused to admire a clump of primroses, but

her gaze blurred as the cheerful yellow flowers were replaced by a fierce countenance in her mind's eye. Try as she might, she had been unable to forget him. Unable and unwilling, if she was honest. In the secret dark of night he came to her and she seldom had the willpower to refuse him. Never, not even in the early days with Jeremy, before they were married, when she had been so naïvely in love, had she felt such a gut-wrenching pull of attraction. *Who and why? And where was he now?* She had no answers, nor likely ever would, but the questions would not quit her mind. His presence had fired her imagination.

Reaching the boundary of the Green Park, she made her way across the busy thoroughfare of Piccadilly towards Hyde Park, with the intention of walking along Rotten Row to the Queen's Gate. Carriages, horses, stray dogs, urchins, crossing sweepers and costermongers made navigating to the other side treacherous at the best of times, but Deborah wove her way through the traffic with her mind fatally focused elsewhere.

The driver of an ale cart swerved to avoid her.

She barely noticed the drayman's cursing, but on the other side of the road Elliot, emerging from Apsley House where he had been petitioning Wellesley—he never could think of him as Wellington—froze. It was her! He was sure of it—though how he could be, when he had not even seen her in daylight, he had no idea.

But it was most definitely Lady Kinsail and she was headed straight for him—or at least for the gates to the park. She was dressed simply—even, to his practised eye, rather dowdily for a countess. The full-length brown pelisse she wore over a taupe walking dress was bereft of trimming, lacking the current fashion for flounces, tassels and ruffles. Her hair, what he could see of it under the shallow poke of her bonnet, was flaxen. She was tall, elegant and slender, just as he remembered. In the bright sunlight, her complexion had a bloom to it, but her expression was the same: challenging, ironic, a little remote. Not a beautiful woman—she was too singular for that—but there was definitely something about her, the very challenge of her detachment, that appealed to him.

He should go. It would be madness to risk being identified. But even as he forced himself to turn away he caught her eye, saw the start of recognition in hers and it was too late.

Elliot, who had in any case always preferred to court trouble than to flee from it, covered the short distance between them in several quick strides. 'Lady Kinsail.' He swept her a bow.

'It *is* you!' Deborah exclaimed. She could feel her colour rising, and wished that the poke of her bonnet were more fashionably high to disguise it. 'The housebreaker. Though I have to say in the light of day you look even less like one than when you—when I...'

'So very kindly broke my fall,' Elliot finished for her. 'For which I am most grateful, believe me.'

Deborah blushed. 'You expressed your gratitude at the time, as I recall.'

'Not as thoroughly as I'd have liked to.'

'I didn't tell,' she blurted out in confusion.

'That I kissed you?'

'No. I mean I didn't report you. I should have. I know I should have. But I didn't.'

'Well, I'll be damned!' Elliot stared at her in astonishment.

Her eyes were coffee brown, almost black, with a sort of hazel or gold colour around the rim of the iris. A strange combination, with that flaxen hair. The pink tip of her tongue flicked out along the full length of her lower lip to moisten it.

He dragged his eyes away. They were in danger of making a show of themselves, standing stock still at the busy entrance gates. Taking her arm, he ushered her into the park. 'Let's find somewhere more private, away from the crowds.'

Deborah tingled where his fingers clasped her arm. It was most—strange. In a nice way. So nice that she allowed herself to be led down one of the more secluded paths without protest.

He was taller than she remembered. In daylight his countenance was swarthy, the colour of one who had spent much time in the sun. The lines around his eyes, too, which gave him that fierce quality, looked as if they came from squinting in bright light. Snatching a glance up at him, she noticed a scar slicing through his left eyebrow, and another, a thin thread on his forehead just below the hairline. A soldier? Certainly it would explain his bearing, the upright stance, the quick stride which even her long legs were struggling to keep up with.

He was exceedingly well dressed, in a rich blue double-breasted tailcoat with brass buttons, and the snowy white of his cravat was carefully tied, enhancing the strong line of his jaw, the tanned complexion. Brown trousers, black boots, a single fob, a beaver hat—though the crown was not tall enough to be truly fashionable. His *toilette* was elegant but simple. Like herself, he eschewed ostentation, though unlike herself his reason did not appear to be lack of funds. Housebreaking must be a lucrative profession.

No, she could not bring herself to believe that he stole in order to dress well. Whatever reason he had for breaking into houses, it was not avarice. It appealed to her sense of irony that the famous Peacock was decidedly no peacock. Maybe his choice of calling card was deliberately self-mocking.

'What is so amusing?' Elliot brought them both to a halt by a rustic bench facing the sun.

'Just an idle thought.'

'We can sit here awhile,' he said, after carefully wiping the wood down with his kerchief. 'As long as the sun prevails we shall not get cold.'

Obediently, Deborah sat down. There were so many things she wanted to ask, but as she stared up at him she was too overwhelmed by the reality of him, which was so much *more* than the memory of him, to order her thoughts properly. 'Are you really the Peacock?'

A word from her in the right ear and he would be dancing on the end of a rope at Tyburn. Though so far she had of her own admission said nothing. 'Yes,' Elliot replied, 'I really am the Peacock.'

'When I saw Jacob holding up the feather I could scarcely believe it.'

It was a small bench. Elliot's knees touched her leg as he angled himself to face her. A spark of awareness shot through him at the contact. He remembered the way she'd felt beneath him. He remembered, too, the things he'd imagined her doing to him since and prayed none of it showed on his face. He had to remind himself that she was married. *Married!* In England, that mattered.

'Why?' he asked abruptly. 'Why did you say nothing to your husband?'

'You mentioned him during our first conversation— if it could be called a conversation,' Deborah said with a frown. 'You said that I must blame him, or some such words. Blame him for what? What has Jeremy to do with your breaking into Kinsail Manor?'

Jeremy! It had slipped his mind, but he remembered now that was the name she'd given Kinsail. 'You mean Jacob, surely?' Elliot said, also frowning. 'Jacob, the Earl of Kinsail. Your husband.'

Her eyes widened with surprise and she burst into a peal of laughter, brimming with amusement like a champagne flute full of bubbles. Then, as if she was quite unused to the sound, she stopped abruptly. 'I am not the current Lady Kinsail. Jacob is my husband's cousin, the Fifth Earl. Jeremy was the fourth.'

'Was? You're a widow?' *She was a widow!*

'Of some two years' standing,' the widow replied.

'I can't tell you how pleased I am to hear that.' The words were out before he could stop them.

'I doubt very much that the pleasure you take from my status could rival mine.'

'That, if you don't mind my saying so, was an even more telling remark than my own.'

Deborah coloured. 'I am aware of that.'

'It was not a love-match, then, I take it?'

'No. Yes. I thought it was. I was just eighteen when we met—my head stuffed full of romantic fancies, as foolish and unworldly as it's possible to imagine a person could be—and Jeremy was…seemed to be…well, he swept me off my feet, to put it in the sort of terms I'd have used myself then,' Deborah said with a twisted smile. 'When Jeremy proposed I thought all my birthdays had come at once. My guardian—my uncle—my parents died when I was very young—was only too glad to be able to wash his hands of me, so we were married three months after we met. I thought myself wildly in love, but it was all a sham. Jeremy was only interested in my money. Pathetic, isn't it? I don't know why I have told you all this, but you did ask.'

'I think it's sad, not pathetic. Were you very unhappy?'

Deborah shrugged. 'I was very naïve and very set upon the match. I was not the only one who suffered as a result. I should never have married him. You know, this is all rather boring. Do you mind if we change the subject?'

Her husband sounded like a complete bastard. Elliot couldn't understand why she was so determined to lay the blame on herself but, much as he wished to probe deeper, her closed look was back. He doubted he would get anywhere. 'I beg your pardon,' he said. 'I didn't mean to upset you.'

'You didn't,' Deborah replied, tilting her chin and sniffing.

He wanted to kiss her then, for that defiant little look. Actually, he'd wanted to kiss her before that. 'You know, you don't look a bit like a dowager,' Elliot said lightly. 'Not a trace of grey hair, you don't dab at your eyes with a black lace kerchief, or sniff at your smelling salts, and I've seen not a trace of an obnoxious little lap dog—unless he's too precious to be allowed outside in the cold. The Dowager Countess of Kinsail.' He shook his head. 'No, it's just not you.'

He was rewarded with a weak smile. 'I prefer not to use the title. It's Deborah Napier. And if I don't look like a dowager you look even less like a housebreaker.'

'Deborah. Now, *that* suits you. I am Elliot Marchmont, known to a very select few as the Peacock.'

'What was it you stole, may I ask? Only Jacob has not let on, for some reason.'

'For a very good reason,' Elliot said drily. 'I suppose there is no harm in telling you, since you already have my fate in your hands. It was a diamond. A large blue diamond, reputedly cut from the original French crown jewels. Kinsail came by it in what one might call a rather roundabout and unorthodox manner.'

'You mean illegally? Jacob?' Deborah squeaked.

'Why do you look so surprised?'

'Because he's a sanctimonious, parsimonious prude who is never happier than when condemning others for lack of principles or morals or—well, anyway—' She broke off, realising she had once again forgotten her golden rule of keeping her feelings strictly under wraps. This man unsettled her. 'How did you know about it?'

'I have my sources.'

'Goodness. Do you mean those people they call fences? The ones who live in the Rookeries?' Deborah asked, using with relish the cant she had only ever written.

'I have to say, for an upstanding member of the aristocracy you seem to have an unhealthy interest in the seamy underbelly of society.'

'I prefer to attribute it to a vivid imagination. Is it true what they say? That there is not a safe in England you cannot break?'

'I have not yet encountered one,' Elliot said, rather taken aback by her reaction, which seemed to be fascination rather than disapproval.

She was sitting on a bench in Hyde Park in broad daylight with the notorious Peacock. She should be calling the authorities. But instead of being in fear for her life she looked intrigued—excited, even. He had the distinct feeling that he had in Deborah Napier, Dowager Countess of Kinsail, met someone almost as subversive as he was himself.

'I wish you would tell me all,' she said, as if to confirm his thoughts. 'Why do you do it? What is it like to pit your wits against the world as you do? Are you ever afraid of being caught?'

She had not asked him what he'd done with the diamond. Surely that was the first question any woman would have asked? But she seemed to have no real interest in the outcome, only the method. Just like him—well, at least in part.

'There's always a chance,' Elliot replied, beguiled by the way her eyes lit up. 'But if it was no risk it would not be worth doing. That is part of it for me—the excitement, knowing that one false move could be an end. There's nothing like it. Not since…'

'The army?'

'How did you know that?'

'The way you walk. The scars on your face.' Deborah touched his brow, felt a jolt at the contact and drew her hand away quickly. 'The first time I met you I thought you were a man used to being in command. Were you a soldier for long?'

'Sixteen years. We ran off when I was just fifteen, me and my school friend Henry. Like you, he was orphaned, only his father had made no provision for him. In the same week he lost his family and his place at school. He was to be apprenticed to a lawyer.' Elliot laughed. 'Henry—a lawyer. Nothing could be more unlikely. He decided he would enlist instead, and I decided to go with him because by then I'd had enough of school and the notion of returning to the family estates and learning from my father how to take up the reins sounded like purgatory. So we ran off together, lied about our ages.'

'What about your parents?'

'My mother was dead. My father was not particularly happy, but we were not yet at war at that point, and I persuaded him that it would be good for me to learn some independence and some discipline. He bought me my first commission. Then the wars with Napoleon came, and by that time I'd discovered I had a talent for soldiering. The army was my family. In a way it was selfish of me, but by that time my loyalty to my men was such that—to be frank—I could not have left while there was a war to be won. To his enormous credit, my father supported me in that. I was a major when I resigned my commission after Waterloo. My only regret is that my father died just six months after I returned home.'

'It must have been very difficult for you to adjust to civilian life after all that time.'

'Yes, it was. Very.' Her perception surprised Elliot. 'People don't really see that.'

'People never do. I was nineteen when I married. When Jeremy died I found I had no idea who I was. Two years later I'm still not sure.'

'I came home to take up the mantle of my family estates, to settle down into the quiet country life I'd joined up to avoid in the first place. Not much more than two years ago and I'm still not sure, either, who I am. I'm not a soldier any more, but I'm pretty damn sure that I'd die of boredom as a country squire.'

'So you've taken up housebreaking instead? Is that it?' Deborah asked, looking amused.

'Partly.'

'I wish I'd thought of something as exciting, but I lack the skills. How came you to acquire them? Is it part of basic army training, lock-picking?'

Elliot laughed. 'No, but the British army is made up almost entirely of volunteers, you know. You'd be astonished at the skills one can learn from the men.'

'Is that how you came about your contacts, too?' Deborah chuckled. 'I do not recall reading in the newspapers that the war against Napoleon was won by fences and pickpockets and the like.'

'The war was won by poor bastards from all walks of life who enlisted because they had the misguided belief that at the end of it they would have made a better life for themselves and their families,' Elliot said grimly. 'The same poor bastards you see begging on the streets now—those of them who made it home.'

'I'm sorry,' Deborah said, taken aback by the sudden change in him. 'I did not mean to make light of it. You must have lost some good friends.'

'Yes.' Surprised by the urge to confide in her, Elliot took a deep breath. 'Sorry.'

'You have no need to be. I should have known better. Time makes no difference with such scars, does it? A year, two—people think you should have forgotten.'

'I won't ever forget.'

'Nor I,' Deborah said softly.

She recognised that tone. And the look in his eyes—

the darkness, suffering, guilt. She wondered what it was that had put it there. It went too deep to be solely down to the horrors of war. But though she was tempted to ask, she did not. Something about him—a shuttered look, a reticence—warned her off. Besides, questions begat questions. She did not wish to reveal why it was she understood him.

'What do you do with your time?' Elliot asked. 'Despite what you said, you don't give the appearance of one who is enjoying her widowhood.'

'I am still becoming accustomed,' Deborah said with a shrug. 'It is not what I expected—not that I was actually planning for it, because Jeremy was only six-and-thirty. I mean, I did not murder him or anything like that.'

'But you thought about it?'

'Well, only by way of diversion when I was…' *Writing my first book,* she had been about to say.

Deborah stared at Elliot, aghast. He was trying not to smile. The corner of his mouth was quivering with the effort of restraining his laughter.

'It's not funny. That was a shocking thing to make me say,' she said, trying to hide the quiver in her own voice.

'I did not *make* you say anything.'

'You know, I wish you would take me with you,' Deborah said impulsively.

'I'm sorry?'

'Just once. I wish I could accompany you—the Peacock. It would be—I don't know—marvellous.' *And perhaps inspiring,* Deborah thought.

Elliot burst out laughing. 'Marvellous! I've heard my escapades described in many ways, but marvellous has never been one of them. You are the most original woman I have ever met.'

'Yes? I take that as a huge compliment, I think. Have you met many women?'

'Many. They've asked me many things, too,' Elliot said wickedly. 'But not one of them has shown an interest in housebreaking.'

'Well, I am very interested in housebreaking,' Deborah said, trying not to think about the many voluptuous and experienced women Elliot had met. 'Will you consider it?'

'Consider—good God. You are not serious?'

She could not quite believe it herself, but it seemed she was. For one night, she would step out of her shadow, cast off the ghosts which haunted her and act as boldly as her literary alter ego. In fact, she would *be* Bella. It was perfect. Just exactly the boost her writing needed to stop it from stagnating.

Deborah's eyes positively sparkled. 'You have no idea how much,' she said.

Elliot seemed to find her enthusiasm amusing. He was laughing—a deep, gruff sound which shivered over her skin. She found herself staring at his mouth. His knee pressed into her thigh through the cambric of her dress. Little ripples of heat spread from the contact. Up.

'Will you take me?' she asked, half-joking, half-something else she chose not to acknowledge.

Elliot couldn't take his eyes off her mouth. She smelled of spring and flowers and something more elusive. He leaned closer. There were just the tiniest traces of lines around her eyes. He'd thought her three-or four-and-twenty, but she must be older. That darkness that lurked at the back of her eyes was experience. She was a widow. He couldn't possibly kiss her here, in the park. But she was a widow. So not married. Or not any more. He wanted to kiss her. He wanted to do a lot more than that.

'Elliot, will you take me?'

She was serious! He sat back, blinked, pulled his hat from his head, looked at it, put it back again. 'Don't be ridiculous.'

'It's not ridiculous,' Deborah said, too taken up with the outrageous idea to care how wild it sounded, to notice the reckless edge to her voice. This was what she wanted. This was what she'd been waiting for. Excitement—enough to jolt her out of her melancholy. And experience. The authenticity it would lend to her story would give Bella Donna a new lease of life. 'Please, Elliot.'

Her hand was on his coat sleeve. Her gloves were worn. His own were new. He hated wearing gloves. He wanted to feel her skin. 'No,' he said, shaking her hand away. 'I could not possibly…'

'Why not? Are you afraid I would mess things up

for you? I would not, I promise, I would do only as you instructed.'

For a few wild seconds he imagined it—the pair of them in cahoots. Her presence would lend a wholly new edge to the thrill of the escapade. What the devil was he thinking? 'Madness,' Elliot exclaimed, leaping to his feet. 'You don't know what you're asking. To risk the gallows…'

'It would not come to that. It never has yet—you are too clever for that.' She couldn't understand why, but she *had* to persuade him. 'Please. My life is so—you have no idea. I can't explain, but if I could just—I want to feel alive!'

Elliot had no difficulty in recognising that particular sentiment. It was still madness and he still had no intention of agreeing, but he couldn't help empathising with what she said. 'Deborah, it's impossible,' he said gently.

'It's not.' Desperation made her ruthless. 'I want to come with you the next time. In fact, I am determined to come with you; if you do not agree I will inform upon you.'

This he had not anticipated. God dammit, he couldn't help admire her daring. She must want this very badly. He wondered why. That fatal curiosity of his. Elliot tried valiantly to stifle it. 'You would be unwise to do so. By your silence, you have already implicated yourself. I could say that you were my accomplice.'

'Oh!' The wounded look Deborah gave him was almost comical. The resolute set to her mouth which followed, the straightening of her shoulders, was not. 'It is a risk I'm prepared to take.'

'It seems to me that you're prepared to take a great many risks.'

'You think so? You don't know me very well.'

The light went out of her so quickly it was almost like looking at a different person. One minute she was sparkling, the next bleak. He recognised the edge of desperation which made her reckless. She was a fascinating mixture.

It would be madness to consider doing as she asked. He was only thinking about it because he wanted her. He wanted her a lot. And she wanted him too—though she would no more acknowledge it than her real reasons for wishing to break into a house with him. If he did not take her, what then? He could not possibly be considering this.

Slowly, he began to shake his head.

'No! Please, don't say no. I mean it, Elliot—if you say no I will inform on you.'

Really, he could not imagine a more original female. She was quite as ruthless in her own way as he was. Elliot's smile was a slow curl, just the one side of his mouth. His finger traced her determinedly set lips. The pulse at her throat fluttered. He felt the shallow intake of her breath, but she did not flinch. Ridiculous, but what he thought he saw in her was a kindred spirit. One who stood on the edge of society. It was absolute madness even to be considering doing as she asked.

'You won't persuade me with threats,' he said softly. 'If I take you, it will be because I want to.'

The words made Deborah shiver. Did he want her? Want *her?* No one had ever wanted her like that. 'And do you—want me?' she asked. Because it was exactly what Bella Donna would have said, and because if she let herself think like Deborah she'd turn tail and flee and regret it for the rest of her days, and she was sick, sick, sick of regrets.

Looking round swiftly to check they were quite alone, Elliot pulled her to him, a dark glint in his eyes. 'You are playing a very dangerous game, Deborah Napier. I would advise you to have a care. For if you dance with the devil you are likely to get burnt. You may come with me, but only if you promise to do exactly as I say.'

'You mean it!' *Oh, God, he meant it!* She would be a housebreaker. A thief!

Since this rather vital aspect hadn't actually occurred to her until now, Deborah wavered. But her failing to take part would not avert the crime. And if their victim was like Jacob most likely he would deserve it anyway, or could easily afford the loss. And Bella needed this, and she needed Bella, and Elliot was waiting for an answer. She would never get another chance. Never!

'I promise,' she said. 'I'll do exactly as you say.'

'Then prove it. Kiss me,' Elliot said audaciously, not thinking for a moment that she would.

But she did. Without giving herself time to think, her heart hammering against her breast, Deborah stood on tiptoe, pulled his head down to hers, and did as she was bid. Right there in Hyde Park, in the middle of the day, she kissed him.

She meant it as a kiss to seal their bargain, but as soon
as her lips there to look. Well, sought to enter the
village stood nine.

Chapter Three

She meant it as a kiss to seal their bargain, but as soon
as her lips touched his memories, real and imagined,
made the taste of him headily familiar. Elliot's hands
settled on her hips, pulling her closer. Deborah linked
her gloved hands around his neck, enjoying the lean
length of his body hard against hers, just as before, in
the dark of night, when he had landed on top of her.

His lips were warm on hers, every bit as sinfully delicious as she'd imagined, coaxing her mouth to flower
open beneath his, teasing her lips into compliance, heat-
ing her gently, delicately, until his tongue touched hers.
She shuddered, felt rather than heard his sharp intake of
breath. The kiss deepened, darkened, and Deborah forgot all about her surroundings as Elliot's mouth claimed
hers, as he pulled her into the hard warmth of his body,
so close that she could feel the fob of his watch pressing into her stomach, smell the starch on his neckcloth.

It was a kiss like none she had ever tasted, heated
by the bargain it concluded, fired by the very illicit-

ness of their kissing here in a public space, where at any moment they could be discovered. She could not have imagined, could not have dreamed, that kissing—just kissing—could arouse her in this way. She had not thought it possible—had not even attributed such an awakening to Bella Donna.

The clop of a horse passing on the other side of the high hedge penetrated the hazy mists of her desire-fuelled mind. Deborah wrenched herself free even as Elliot released her. They stared at each other, breathing heavily. He tugged at his neckcloth as if it were constricting him. Her gloved hand touched her lips. They felt swollen.

Elliot picked his hat up from the ground where it had fallen, striving for a nonchalance he was far from feeling. The reality of Deborah Napier's kisses made a poor shadow of his fantasies. It was complete folly, unbelievably risky, but if this intriguing creature wanted to join forces with his alter ego he could not refuse her.

He wanted her. He wasn't sure what he was going to do about that, but he was sure he wanted to do something. Not that that was why he was going to agree to this madness. He was doing it for her. To relieve the darkness behind those beguiling eyes. To release her, if only temporarily, from the emotional embargo she seemed to have placed upon herself. That was the only reason. The main one, certainly.

'Are you quite sure you want to do this?' he asked.

Still dazed and confused by the delights of lip on lip, tongue on tongue, struggling to tamp down the shocking and wholly new passion which their kiss had lit, Deborah was not at first sure what he was asking. Then the meaning of his question sank home, and she smiled. It was not the tight, polite smile behind which she usually hid, but a wide, true smile which lit her eyes, wiping the haughty expression from her face and with it several years.

'Oh, yes,' she said, 'I'm sure.'

A week went by before she heard from him again. A week when sanity took hold in the light of day and Deborah wondered what on earth had possessed her to suggest this wild escapade.

Housebreaking and stealing—the simple fact that they were illegal should be suffice to prevent her even contemplating them. Her conscience told her so several times a day, her head warned her of the possible consequences, yet her heart would listen to none of it. Whether she accompanied him or not, the Peacock would commit the crime. He was never caught. And even if she was discovered, there was the sad, indisputable fact, that she couldn't make herself see the difference between the prison she already inhabited and gaol, no matter how often she told herself there was an enormous difference.

Had her doubts been more constant they would have prevailed, but the problem was they were fickle things, dissolving whenever she took up her pen, or played out her encounter with Elliot again, or with the coming of dusk. Excitement took hold of her then. Jagged and dangerous like one of the saw-toothed swords she had seen in an exhibition at Bullock's Museum in Piccadilly, it was fatally enticing. For the first time in a very long time, she really *wanted* something.

She knew what she contemplated was reckless beyond belief, but still the logic of this failed to take root. She wanted the visceral thrill. She wanted to feel her blood coursing through her veins. She wanted to feel alive. And besides, she owed it to Bella, whose existence had seen her through the darkest of days, to gild her latest story with as much authenticity as possible.

In truth, when Deborah's heart quailed at the prospect of aiding and abetting the Peacock, it was Bella's ruthless courage which bolstered her. It was through Bella's eyes that she peered out into the dimly lit street from her drawing-room window some eight days after that encounter in the park, her heart fluttering with fear—not of what was to come, but of what she would feel if Elliot did not turn up.

His promise, so reluctantly given, could so easily be reneged upon. She knew nothing of him, after all, and despite his having surrendered his name, she had made no enquiries, having neither trusted friends nor trusted servants. Had he been similarly reticent? It hadn't occurred to her until now that he might ask about her, though it should have. Jeremy's title meant nothing to her; the penurious state in which he had left her made it easy for her to fade into the background of a society she had never really been permitted to inhabit even when he was alive, but she was still, unfortunately, the

Dowager Countess of Kinsail. And though Jeremy had been gone two years, the scandal of his debts, his premature death, were not so easily buried as his corpse.

Deborah clenched her fists inside the pockets of the greatcoat she wore. Elliot would not judge her. It wasn't possible—no one knew the murky details of her marriage. He would come. He had given his word and he had not the look of a man who would break a promise. Casting a quick glance out at the empty street, she retrieved the note from behind the clock, scanning the terse content by the light of the single candle.

It is set for tonight. I will call for you at fifteen minutes past midnight. If you have changed your mind, send word with the boy.

No signature. No address. The boy referred to was the street urchin who had delivered the note earlier in the day. Surely, surely, surely, if Elliot Marchmont had reservations about her, he would not have sent such a note? After all, even if she did know where he lived— which she did not—she was hardly likely to come hammering on his door, demanding that he fulfil his promise. It had been a test, this silence, a test of trust, and she had not failed. He would come, she told herself. He cared naught for her past, and why should he? Besides, she thought defiantly, returning to her vigil at the window, it was not Deborah, Dowager Countess of Kinsail, who would be his aider and abettor, any more than it was Elliot Marchmont who would commit the crime. Tonight it was the Peacock and Bella Donna.

She smiled into the darkness and let go the last of

her doubts as the clock chimed the hour. Midnight. The witching hour. The hour of transformations and magic. Bella's hour. Deborah's reservations must bide their time until morning.

She was waiting for him on the doorstep. He saw the pale glimmer of her hair, stark against the dark of her clothing, as he rounded the corner. Elliot was not sure whether to be glad or sorry. No, that was a lie, he knew perfectly well how he felt, and it was the direct opposite of what he *ought* to. Something like a ripple shimmered through his blood as he strode quickly across the street. Reckless, foolish, crazy as it was to be taking her with him, it was what he wanted. It wasn't just that he was curious, and it wasn't just that he desired her either— not wholly, though that was part of it. He didn't know what it was. The unknown, maybe? Something different? Something more? He didn't care. What mattered now, at this moment, was that she was here and her very presence made everything sharper, more attenuated.

She was wearing some sort of greatcoat. Her smile was tremulous. No gloves. Her hands, when he took them in his, were icy. 'It's not too late, you can still change your mind,' Elliot said softly, but Deborah shook her head, gave him that look, that haughty, determined one. Did she know what a challenge it was? He doubted it. 'Are you sure?'

'You sound as if you're the one who's having second thoughts.'

'I should be, but I'm not,' Elliot replied.

Looking up at him, Deborah felt that kick-in-the-stomach pull of attraction. He was not handsome, his face was too hard for that, but he was charismatic. She pulled her hand from his. 'Where are we going?'

'You'll see.'

'Have you a carriage? A horse?'

'It's not that far.'

Deborah sucked in her breath. 'You mean we're going to—here, in town? But isn't that…'

'Risky? Wasn't that rather the point?'

She shivered. She had imagined a house like Kinsail Manor. The dark of night. The silence of the country. For a few seconds, reality intruded. Streetlamps. Night watchmen. Late-night revellers. And surely more locks, bolts and servants to contend with.

'Having second thoughts, Lady Kinsail?'

His mocking tone made her stiffen. 'No. And don't call me that.'

'Deborah.'

The way he said her name, giving it a dusky note it had never contained before, made her belly clench. His nearness threatened to overset her. She pushed back her greatcoat in an effort to distract herself. 'What do you think of my clothing? Is it appropriate for a house-breaker?'

The breeches and boots revealed long, long legs. Blood rushed to Elliot's groin. He tried not to imagine what her *derrière* would look like, tried not to picture those fabulous legs wrapped around him. Was she wearing corsets beneath that coat? 'It's very…' Revealing?

Erotic? Stimulating? Dear God! 'Very practical,' he said, dragging his eyes away. 'If I didn't know better, I'd say you'd done this before.'

'I found the clothes in a trunk in the house when I moved in. They must have belonged to the previous tenant. I kept them, but he never came back for them. He must have been quite a small man, for they are a perfect fit, don't you think?'

She pushed the greatcoat further back and posed for his inspection, quite oblivious of the effect her display of leg was having on him. 'I think we had best make tracks,' Elliot said brusquely.

Pulling the greatcoat back around her and jamming her hat on to her head, Deborah hurried after him as he crossed the road. 'Where are we going? What are we going to steal? Whose house is it?' Her questions were breathless for she was struggling to keep pace with him as they skirted the beginnings of the new buildings to the east of Hans Town, avoiding the main thoroughfares, heading towards Hyde Park.

'The less you know the better,' Elliot replied.

Her booted feet stumbled on the mix of cobbles and mud as they wended north along mews and through stables. The houses grew grander as they passed Berkeley Square. Crossing Mount Street and into another mews, Deborah's nerves began to take hold. When Elliot pulled her down a shallow flight of steps and into the shelter of the basement wall, she looked up and up and up at the massive building in front of which they stood, and thought she might actually be sick. 'This is Grosvenor Square,' she whispered.

Elliot nodded. She caught the gleam of his smile and remembered her first impression of him. Dangerous. Her fear was dissipated by anticipation, pounding through her veins in a rush. 'Is this *it?*' she asked, looking with awe at the elegant town house, the rows of windows like blank, sleeping eyes.

'This is your last chance to change your mind. After this there is no going back, do you understand?'

He was standing close enough for her to sense his excitement. It was contagious. Her stomach felt as if it were tied in a knot. Deborah nodded.

Elliot's laugh, the low growl she had first heard in the grounds of Kinsail Manor, quivered over her. 'Very well,' he said, 'now listen very carefully.'

Slowly, methodically, he went over the details of his plan, details she realised he could only have compiled as a result of thorough observation and reconnaissance. He had an impressive eye for minutiae. She understood now why it had taken him over a week to contact her. She listened so carefully she scarcely dared breathe before reciting each step back to him slowly, painstakingly, a frown furrowing her brows, determined to miss nothing, to prove herself worthy.

'Good. You have an excellent memory,' Elliot said, when she had repeated it a second time.

'You are impressively well prepared,' Deborah returned with a grin.

'Know your territory. I've had plenty of practice.'

'Another unexpected bonus of your army training, no doubt. If only they knew.'

'And yet another is that I expect to be obeyed. Remember that.'

He spoke lightly, but she was in no doubt that he meant it, nor in any doubt that he had always achieved absolute obedience. It was not fear of retribution, but implicit trust that would have inspired the same loyalty in his troops which she felt stirring her courage. A determination not to let him down, to live up to the expectations he had of her. 'Understood,' Deborah said, with a mock salute which made him smile.

The watch called the hour from the other side of the mews. Across the way, a candle flame reflected in the dimpled glass of a window pane was snuffed out. Above, the town house was in complete darkness. 'They are early to bed, our occupants,' Elliot whispered. 'And early to rise too.' When he awoke tomorrow, the Minister would be the poorer and the men he had deprived would be his beneficiaries. Justice of the sort which the government seemed incapable of delivering would be served. The glow of satisfaction warmed him. 'Ready?' he asked Deborah.

She nodded. Her eyes glittered in the dim light. He leaned towards her, pressing a swift kiss to her icy lips. 'Let's go.'

Though the lock was easily picked, the door on to the mews was bolted on the inside, as he had expected. The lower windows were barred. The wave of crime which the upright citizens of London blamed on the soldiers

they had once revered had weighted the coffers of lock-
smiths and ironmongers, who did a roaring trade these
days in providing protection against the poor wretches
who had perforce resorted to theft. Nodding to Deborah to assume her post as lookout at the top of the steps
on to the mews, Elliot untied the length of rope from
his waist and attached the little hook which had been
made by the regiment's smithy to his own design. The
cotton which was wrapped around it muffled the report
as the hook found its mark on the first throw. Testing it
with a sharp tug, Elliot climbed swiftly to the second
floor. The lock on this window gave way to his jemmy.
It was the work of moments to pull in the rope, detach
the hook, close the window, jump lightly down from
the sill and make his way stealthily back down into the
bowels of the house.

Deborah was waiting at the door as he slid the bolts
back. She slipped silently into the narrow corridor
and followed him back through the flagstoned kitchen
where the banked fire provided a modicum of light, into
the gloom of the servants' staircase and up.

He dared not use his lantern. Behind him, Deborah,
obviously as able to see in the dark as he was, did not
stumble. He was impressed by her courage and excited
by her presence there in his shadow.

The painting was in the study, at the back of the
house adjacent to the room he had first entered. 'An
early study of Philip the Fourth,' Elliot whispered to
Deborah. 'It's bigger than I remember. But then, the last
time I saw it, it was hanging in a rather larger house.'

She stared at the decidedly ugly subject, resplendent in black and silver. She could see it was beautifully executed, but she could not like it. 'You said you've seen it before?'

'In Madrid. In the house of one of our senior Spanish allies.'

'Then how did it get here?'

Elliot shrugged. 'Plunder. A gift. A bribe. I don't know,' he said, pressing the button which released the blade of his knife. Quickly, he cut the painting from its heavy frame and rolled it up before handing it to Deborah.

She took it gingerly. 'How did you know where to find it?'

'I have my sources.'

'You said that before.'

He caught her wrist and pulled her close. 'This may well be a game to you, but you have to realise, you're playing with fire. If we are caught...'

'We won't be. You're the Peacock, you never have been yet.'

Her utter confidence in him was flattering, there was no denying it, but a tiny noise outside the door distracted him. Quickly, Elliot pulled Deborah towards the cover of the window curtains. 'Hush!'

His hand covered her mouth. Her back was pressed into his body. Her heart thudded much too loud. She listened hard, but could hear nothing save the rasp of her own breathing, the softer whisper of his. The curtains smelled musty. They waited, motionless, for what seemed like aeons. Her nose tickled. She was acutely conscious of him, tensed behind her. She was inappropriately conscious of her legs, her bottom, her back, moulded against the front of his body. Everything felt stretched, more real, and yet unreal. The air crackled with tension. Between them, an invisible cord of awareness. She had never felt more alive.

She felt him relax before he moved his hand from her mouth. 'What…?'

He turned her around. She caught the gleam of his smile, heard the little huff of his chuckle. 'I thought I heard someone, but it must have been a rat.'

Deborah shuddered. 'I hate rats.' Elliot laughed again. She felt it this time, vibrating in his chest against hers. 'What's so funny?'

'You follow me across London in the middle of the night dressed as a man, break into a house and steal a priceless painting with barely a tremble, but a rat makes you shiver. Would you rather we'd encountered the master of the house? He is a rat of an altogether different order.'

'I'd rather we didn't encounter anyone.'

'Then we should make haste.' From his pocket, Elliot produced the feather and handed it to Deborah. 'My calling card. Will you do the honours?'

She placed it carefully on the ledge of the empty frame. 'You made this seem so easy,' she said.

Elliot, who had been in the process of retrieving his grappling hook from the floor, heard the note of disappointment in her voice. It was ridiculous to add danger to risk, but he sensed it was danger she craved. Hastily, he cut his grappling hook free of its rope and crammed it into his pocket, before securing the long cord by twisting it around the gilded legs of the heavy marble-topped table which filled the window embrasure. 'Give me the painting,' he said.

Deborah handed over the rolled canvas. 'Aren't we going back down the stairs?'

'You'll get a more authentic experience leaving this way. If you dare, that is,' Elliot replied. They were two storeys up, nothing for one so used to shimmying up and down ropes, but as Deborah leaned cautiously out of the window and peered down, he saw the sheer drop through her eyes. 'We'll use the stairs,' he said, making to pull the rope in.

She stayed his hand. 'Absolutely not! You're quite right, what is the use in half an experience?' she said. 'Just show me what to do.'

'You could be badly hurt if you fall.' Elliot was already regretting having teased her. He should have known she would rise to the challenge.

'I could hang if we're caught,' Deborah retorted. 'I'll take my chances.'

She was deliberately courting danger. He recognised that, because he did it so often himself. The tilt of her chin, the determination in her voice made it impossible for him to deny her, much as he knew he ought. She seemed always to have this effect on him. A connection between them crackled and briefly flared. 'Very well,' Elliot said, tearing his eyes away, 'I'll go first, that way

I can catch you if you fall. Watch what I do. Wait until I'm on the ground before you come out.'

A clock chimed in the hallway outside the room, making Deborah jump. 'What if someone comes?'

Elliot picked up her hat and jammed it back on her head. 'They won't. You're perfectly safe, you're with the Peacock, remember? Now pay attention. It's all in the way you hold the rope.'

Deborah watched, heart drumming, as he showed her what to do with her hands and feet. Her palms were damp as she leaned out, seeing him disappear swiftly down, making it seem effortless. It was a long way. If she fell—but she would not fall. She cast another glance over her shoulder at the door. She listened hard, but could hear nothing. The room seemed larger, darker, much more sinister without Elliot's presence. Fear crept stealthily up from her booted feet, winding its way like a vine, making her legs shake, her hands too. The urge to turn tail, to flee out of the door, down the servants' staircase to the kitchen, was almost overwhelming. Only the stronger fear, that without Elliot to guide her she would be lost, overturn something, rouse the household, kept her rooted to the spot. Right at this moment, she effectively held his life in her hands. She would not let him down. *She would not!*

Determination to prove herself worthy uprooted her feet. Deborah's heart still pounded so hard and fast she felt faint, but she bit her lip hard, wiped her damp palms on her breeches and sat gingerly on the edge of the sill.

Elliot was already on the ground, looking up anxiously. She waved. The ground swam. *Don't look down!*

She grasped the rope as he had shown her. She edged out. Her legs dangled in the air. Breathing quickly to still the panic, she floundered for the rope with her feet, found it, gripped it tight between her thighs. Her arms were surely too frail to support her. She dangled, half in, half out of the window, for a dreadful moment. Then she kicked away from the ledge and began to descend. Slowly she went, shakily, her hands burning on the rope, losing it, retrieving it, gripping tighter. Her shoulders ached. Her thighs, too. Down. Slowly down, looking neither up at the window nor towards Elliot. One floor. If she fell now, she would probably survive. A broken limb or so. Small consolation. Don't think about falling. Down. Her arms felt as if they would part company with her shoulders. Thank heavens she wore breeches. Even so, she would be bruised. Down.

'Not far to go now. Hold on.'

Elliot's voice sounded strained, for the first time that night. Deborah risked a downward glance. Her foot dangled about a yard from his upturned face. Relieved and triumphant, she grinned. 'Did you think I would fall on you? As you did at Kinsail Manor?'

Elliot grabbed her ankle. 'It crossed my mind!'

She covered the final few feet quickly, safe in the knowledge that he had her. If he had not held her when she landed, she would have sunk to the cobbles, for her legs felt as if the bones had been removed. 'Sorry.' She clutched at Elliot's coat. 'I just need…'

Anxiously casting a glance to the end of the mews where the rumbling of a carriage slowed, Elliot put his arm around her waist. 'We must make haste. If anyone comes—that rope is rather a giveaway, I'm afraid.'

Guiltily, Deborah realised she hadn't even closed over the window. It gaped, wide and betraying, the rope hanging like a declaration. 'I'm fine,' she said, straightening, ignoring the pain shooting through her legs and taking a stumbling step towards the other end of the mews. Gritting her teeth, she forced herself to walk.

'Not too fast, or we will draw unwanted attention. Push your hat down over your face.' Elliot caught up with her, put his arm through hers. His grip tightened.

They walked together back to Hans Town through streets blanketed in silence. Now that it was over, Elliot was astounded at himself for placing Deborah in such danger. 'I should not have brought you.'

She turned the key in her door and pushed it open. 'Don't say that. I'm glad you did, Elliot. It was wonderful. Please don't say you regret it.'

'I would be lying if I did,' he replied gruffly.

She was safe home and it was over. Deborah was awed by her own daring, filled with an exuberance that made her want to clap her hands with glee. 'I can't believe we did it,' she said. 'We really did it. We really did!' She felt buoyant, her delight fizzing, bubbling over, making her want to laugh so much that she had to stifle the sound with her hand.

Plucking Deborah's hand from her mouth, Elliot pressed his lips to the palm. Her presence had added spice to the whole venture, there was no denying it. Her daring roused him. Her excitement, too. He licked the raw, slightly swollen pad of her thumb where the rope had chafed. He felt the intake of her breath. She leaned into him. His exhilaration sharpened and focused into desire, like molten metal poured into the mould of a blade. He pulled her roughly into his arms and took possession of her mouth.

It was a kiss without finesse. A hard, dangerous and demanding kiss. For a moment Deborah did not respond, shocked by the rawness of his barely leashed passion. This was not the Elliot she had kissed before, but some other, more feral creature of the night. As she was, tonight. Just for tonight.

But his ardour, the very unstoppableness of it, unleashed her inhibitions. As Elliot pressed her against her own front door, feverishly seeking the soft flesh concealed beneath the constricting layers of her clothing, Deborah kissed him back. Her tongue clashed with his, her mouth opened to him and she returned his kiss with a fervour that cut them both free of thought and control. Where he led she followed. When he kissed her more deeply, his tongue penetrating, thrusting, she kissed him back, her tongue duelling with his, her lips clinging.

Never, ever, not even in her darkest fantasies, had Deborah been kissed like this. Never had she kissed like this. Not even Bella had kissed like this, for Bella was at heart a creature driven by colder, darker motives than plain passion. Deborah's kisses, like Elliot's, were pure passion in that moment, wild and fierce, abandoned kisses, transporting them both to a place which was all red velvet and raw silk.

His mouth plundered hers, but she did not feel conquered, incited instead to return pressure for pressure, by doing so asking for more, and still more. Nothing mattered, save that she have more. It was as if everything that had transpired this night had been arrowing to this moment, as if all she had experienced had by some process of alchemy transformed itself into this white-hot lust, must culminate in this rushing, tumbling, headlong flight to fulfilment.

She moaned in frustration as Elliot's seeking fingers found only layers of clothing and buttons. He fumbled for the latch and they tumbled together into the dark seclusion of the narrow hallway, still kissing.

The back of her legs encountered the hall table. The candlestick atop it fell over. He wrested her greatcoat to the floor, his own following. Her hat and his, too, her hair unfurling. She curled her fingers into the soft silk of his skin, on the nape of his neck above his neckcloth. Warm skin. He smelled of sweat and soap. Salty and tangy. Irreducibly male.

The rasp of his chin on the soft skin of her face reminded her of the stinging sensation of the rough rope chafing her legs. She was burning between her thighs, but it had nothing to do with the descent. She wanted him there. Touching her. Plunging into her. Shocking images, vivid in their clarity despite her lack of experience, filled Deborah's mind, making her moan. The solid ridge of his shaft was hard against her belly. Powerful. Fierce. Like the rest of him, incredibly, intensely male. Man. Elliot was all man. And such a man. She moaned again as he ground his hips against hers.

Elliot's breath came in harsh gasps. Under her coat, Deborah wore a shirt. No waistcoat. And no corsets. Oh God, no corsets. Her nipples thrust at him through the linen. He cupped one of her breasts, his thumb stroking the delightfully hard nub, relishing the way it made her quiver, made the blood pulse in his already aching groin. Her kisses were like molten silver, burning and searing. His knees bumped against the legs of some sort of table. He picked her up, placed her on to it, spreading her legs, one hand in the heavy fall of her hair, the other on her breast, cupping, stroking, moulding. He wanted to feel her flesh. Tugging the shirt from her breeches he nudged between her legs, wrapping them around his thighs, dipping his head to taste the hard peaks of her nipple.

Her heels dug into his buttocks; her fingers plucked ineffectually at the big silver buttons of his coat. The table shook. It was just the right height to allow him to slide into her, thrusting into the welcoming heat, the slick tightness of her that would envelop him. He was so hard, the release would be spectacular. He had known it would be like this. He had known it! He put his hands around the curve of her bottom to pull her closer. She was still trying to free his coat buttons. Impatiently, Elliot yanked them open.

The crushed canvas fell on to the floor. 'Damn!'

'What? What was that?' Deborah was hazily aware

of a pain in her back. She tried to sit up and whatever she was perched on rocked violently. She was sitting on a table!

'The painting,' Elliot muttered. 'I dropped it. I can't see a damn thing.'

She seemed to have lost a good many of her clothes. And the painting, which they had risked life and limb for, was on the floor somewhere. Deborah slithered back down to reality considerably more quickly than she had slithered down the rope not long before. The candle she'd left for her return was on the floor somewhere, too. It would be easier to fetch another from the parlour. 'Just a minute,' she muttered, stumbling down the hallway, feeling her way to the door, trying to tuck her shirt back into her breeches at the same time.

Lighting the candle from the still-smouldering embers of the parlour fire, she studiously avoided looking in the mirror above the mantel as she did so, having no wish to see her shame confirmed in her wanton reflection. Concentrating on trying to get her breathing back under control, she made her way back to the hallway. Elliot was as dishevelled as she. Clothes awry. Neckcloth untied. His lips looked frayed. Such kisses! Deborah held the candle aloft, well away from her own face, turning her gaze to the floor. 'Here it is.' The canvas had rolled under the table. She picked it up and handed it to him, embarrassed in the frail light, mortified by her behaviour in the dark. She had more or less ravaged the man. Savaged him more like, for she clearly remembered biting into him, her nails tearing at his skin. *Oh God!*

Elliot made no attempt to look at the painting. He wished to hell he'd let the bloody thing lie. Another minute of those kisses of hers and he wouldn't have given a damn. Looking at her now though, seeing the way she avoided his gaze, he knew the chances of him having another minute of her kisses were almost nil. Whatever had caused her to let go that iron control of hers was now firmly leashed.

And it was probably just as well. He, who prided himself on his finesse, had all but ravished her in the hallway, for God's sake! To say nothing of the fact that in their lust they had forgotten all about the extremely valuable painting they had stolen. A painting which was now looking rather the worse for wear. A wholly inappropriate desire to laugh took hold of him. He struggled, but could not stifle it. 'I'm sorry,' Elliot said helplessly, 'it's just—well, ludicrous. I assure you I didn't plan it. The last bit, I mean—at least not like that. Only you were so—and I was so—and there was the painting abandoned on the floor, after we went to such extremes to get it.'

To his surprise Deborah's face lightened. She did not smile back, but she looked as if she might. 'Is it always like this? After you have committed a crime, I mean? Is it always so—so intoxicating? Inflaming?' she asked, daring to meet his gaze now.

'I don't know, I've never had an accomplice before.'

'The painting—it's not damaged, is it?' Deborah asked anxiously.

Elliot unrolled the canvas and shook his head. 'See for yourself.' She came closer to inspect it. Her hair was perfectly straight, hanging well past her shoulders. If he looked, he would see the outline of her breasts under her shirt, for she had not put her coat back on. With a huge effort of restraint, he stopped himself.

'Such an ugly man,' Deborah said softly after a while of staring at the portrait. 'I would not like to have this on my wall. Is it valuable?'

'It's by Velázquez. I should hope so.'

'Will you sell it, then?'

Elliot began to roll the canvas back up, carefully this time. 'Yes,' he said tersely, 'I'll sell it.'

Deborah opened her mouth to ask what he did with the money, then thought better of it. Tiredness washed over her. Her shoulders began to ache. Anticlimax in every sense weighed like a heavy blanket, muffling her. 'It's late,' she said wearily.

'Yes.' Elliot hesitated. He was edgy with frustration. She had been so aroused, he was sure he could easily rekindle the flame between them, but something held him back. *Is it always like this?* 'It wasn't the house-breaking that made me turn to you like that,' he said, running his hand down the smooth cap of her hair, 'it was you. Ever since we met, I've wanted you. You must know that, Deborah.'

She jerked her head away. 'It will be light soon.'

'I see.' He didn't see at all. Rebuffed, puzzled by

the extreme swing in her mood, and too tired in the anticlimax to make sense of it, Elliot picked his hat up and, shrugging into his greatcoat, tucked the painting into a large inside pocket. 'Did it work?' he asked. 'Did it do as you hoped, banish the black clouds, make you feel alive?'

Deborah smiled tremulously. 'While it lasted. I shall keep a look out for reports of our heinous crime.'

'And paste them in a keepsake book?'

'Something like that.'

He kissed the fluttering pulse on her wrist, telling himself that her vulnerability was simply exhaustion. 'Goodnight, Deborah.'

She swallowed the lump in her throat. 'Goodbye, Elliot. Be safe.'

The door closed softly behind him. The parlour clock struck three. Only three. Wearily, Deborah picked up her man's coat and made her way up the creaky wooden stairs to her bed.

Outside, Elliot made his way home by a circuitous route through alleys and mews. She was like a chameleon, changing so quickly that he could not keep up with her. Her kisses. He groaned and the muscles in his stomach contracted. Such a delightful mixture of raw passion and innocence. Hot, burning kisses that even now made his blood surge and pound, yet they were neither knowing nor experienced. Deborah kissed with the savagery of a lion cub.

Elliot stood in the shadow of a stable building as the watch passed by, informing the empty street that all was well. It had frightened her, her passion; she had been far too eager to blame it on the extraordinary circumstances, as if by doing so she could distance herself from it. What kind of marriage had she had with that bastard of a fortune hunter?

He stepped out of the mews and made his way across Russell Square, letting himself in silently. A candle stood ready in the hall, reminding him of the clatter of the candlestick from the table at Deborah's house. The evening had been full of surprises. He should not have allowed her to come down that rope, but the sight of her dangling over him had been...

Mounting the stairs, he tried to put if from his mind. He was exhausted. Carefully stashing the painting, he willed himself to think of the chain of events he must set in train to dispose of it, but as he climbed into bed, the memory of Deborah—her mouth, her hands, her breasts, those long legs, that pert *derrière*—climbed in with him. He was hard. Persistently hard. Lying back against the cool sheets, Elliot surrendered to the inevitable.

Chapter Four

Deborah jerked awake, exhausted from lurid dreams in which she was always in the wrong place, with the wrong person, in the wrong attire, at the wrong time. Dreams in which she was endlessly chasing the shadow of the man who had made a shadow of her. Dreams in which no one could see her, no one would acknowledge her, in which she existed only to herself. When she spoke, the words were soundless. Time and again, she tumbled into the room where *he* was, only to have Jeremy look straight through her.

In her dreams, she was sick from her failures, sick from knowing that no matter how hard she tried, she would fail again. The familiar weight of that failure made the physical effort of rising from her bed a mammoth task. No amount of telling herself that it was just a dream, nor any reminder that it had no basis in reality, could shift that lumpen, leaden feeling, for the truth was that Deborah believed she *had* failed, and it *had* been her fault.

Long experience had shown her that hiding under the covers and willing fresh dreamless sleep had no effect whatsoever, save to nourish the headache which lurked just under the base of her skull. Slowly, with the care of a very old woman afraid of breaking brittle bones, Deborah climbed out of bed and went through her morning ablutions, blanking her mind against the lingering coils of her monochrome nightmares, forcibly filling her head with colourful images from her adventures last night.

She winced as she soothed a cooling lotion on the chafe marks at her knees and thighs, but as she folded away the male clothing she had worn, out of sight of the daily help, her mood slowly lifted. By the time she sat down to take coffee at her desk, she was smiling to herself. Bella Donna, that vengeful, voluptuous creature of the night, would not be confined to history after all. At last, after several barren months, she had her inspiration for the next story.

What would Elliot think if he knew he was her muse? Deborah paused in the act of sharpening her pen as a lurid image of herself atop the hall table, her legs entwined around him, flooded her body with heat. Closing her eyes, shuddering at the memory of his lips, his hands, the rough grate of his jaw on her skin, she was astounded at the speed and intensity of her arousal. Had the painting not fallen, had she not fetched a light and broken the mood, she would have given herself to him. As she recalled raking her nails on his skin, urgently pressing herself against the hard length of his manhood, she turned cold. What on earth had come over her?

It would be a salve, to persuade herself that she had become so caught up in Bella Donna's character as to have forgotten her own, but it would not be the truth. Bella Donna took her pleasures in a calculated way. Bella Donna used and discarded men as she used and discarded her various guises when she had no further use for them. Last night, Deborah had wanted, needed, desired with a purity of feeling which left no room for anything else. It frightened her. The intensity of her feelings, her lack of control, terrified her. She did not want any of it.

Ever since we met, I've wanted you, Elliot had said. But the circumstances in which they met were coloured each time by danger. It was surely that which made him want her, as it made her want him? Only the thrill of defying the rules, the edge which recklessness and daring gave to fear, could explain the strength of their mutual desire in its wake. Nothing else, surely, could explain why she had forgotten all the inhibitions her marriage had taught her and allowed an instinct she hadn't known she possessed to drive her.

No, last night, she had not been Bella Donna, but neither had she been Deborah. She could not reconcile that vivid, bold creature with the one sitting at her desk in her grey gown in her equally grey life. But then, wasn't that what she had wanted from last night's adventure? To shed her skin, to step out of the tedium of her day-today existence, to escape from herself for a few hours? She had certainly achieved it beyond her expectations.

Now, though, she must get back to reality, which might very well be grey by comparison, but at least it was safe. Never mind that it was unexciting, unadventurous and above all lonely. She was used to being lonely. Most of her married life she had been lonely. And lost. And hurt. She would do well to remember how quickly the bride with stardust in her eyes had become the hated wife.

Now she was no longer a victim of her own gullibility. She was not the source of every disappointment, the cause of every misfortune. She need not hide from her friends for fear they discover her unhappiness. She need not pretend to herself that she was anything other than miserable. Guilt and insecurity need no more drive her actions than that most cruel emotion of all, love. Her life might be bland, but it was her own. Safe from feeling, maybe, but it was also safe from pain. She intended always to be safe from now on. Whatever had come over her last night, the person she had been was not the real Deborah. The experience had been a release. Cathartic. An antidote, a dose of danger to counteract the malaise of boredom. That was all, and it was over now.

Resolutely, Deborah picked up her pen. *It was past midnight when Bella Donna made her way stealthily out into the night dressed in male attire, on a mission which would scandalise the* ton *and throw her into the orbit of the most dangerous and devastatingly attractive man in all of England,* she wrote.

* * *

'You look tired, Elliot.' Elizabeth Murray drew her brother a quizzical look.

The resemblance between the siblings was striking enough to make their relationship obvious. The same dark, deep-set eyes, the same black hair, the same clear, penetrating gaze which tended to make its object wonder what secrets they had inadvertently revealed. Though Lizzie's complexion was olive rather than tanned, and her features softer, she had some of her brother's intensity and all of his charm, a combination which her friends found fascinating, her husband alluring and her critics intimidating.

'Burning the candle at both ends?' she asked with a smile, stripping off her lavender-kid gloves and plonking herself without ceremony down on a comfortably shabby chair by the fire.

Elliot grinned. 'Lord, yes, you know me. Dancing 'til four in the morning, paying court to the latest heiress, whose hand I must win if I'm to pay off my gambling debts. Generally acting the gentleman of leisure.'

Lizzie chuckled. 'I am surprised I did not see you in the throng around Marianne Kilwinning. They say she is worth twenty thousand at least.'

Elliot snapped his fingers. 'A paltry sum. Why, I could drop that much and more in a single sitting at White's.'

Lizzie's smile faded. 'I heard that your friend Cunningham lost something near that the other night. I know it is considered the height of fashion, but I cannot

help thinking these *gentlemen* could find better things
to fritter their money away on.'

'You're not alone in thinking that.'

'Did you speak to Wellington, then?'

'He granted me an audience all right,' Elliot said
bitterly, 'but it was the usual story. Other more pressing commitments, a need to invest in the future, re-
sources overstretched, the same platitudes as ever.' He
sighed. 'Perhaps I'm being a little unfair. He told me in
confidence that he was considering taking up politics
again. Were he to be given a Cabinet post, he said he
would do all he could, but—oh, I don't know, Lizzie.
These men, the same men who have given their health
and their youth for their country, they can't wait for all
that. They need help now, to feed themselves and their
families, not ephemeral promises that help is coming
if only they will wait—we had enough of those when
we were at war.'

'Henry. I know,' Lizzie said gently, widening her
eyes to stop the tears which gathered there from falling as her brother's face took on a bleak look. She hated
to cry, and more importantly Elliot hated to have this
deepest of wounds touched.

'Henry and hundreds—thousands—of others who
were brothers, friends, husbands, fathers. It makes me
sick.'

'And Wellington will do nothing?'

'I'm sorry to say it, but at heart he's a traditionalist.
He is afraid, like Liverpool and the rest of the Tories,
that too many years abroad have radicalised our men.

He thinks that starving them will bring about deference. I think it will have quite the opposite effect and, more importantly, it's bloody unjust. I'm sorry, I shouldn't swear and I didn't mean to bore you.'

'Don't be so *damned* stupid. You neither bore me nor shock me, and you know it. I have no truck with this modern notion that we women have no minds of our own,' Lizzie said tersely.

She was rewarded with a crack of laughter. 'Not something anyone could ever accuse you of,' Elliot replied.

His sister grinned. 'That's what Lady Murray says.'

'Alex's mother is in town? I thought she never left that great big barn of a castle of theirs. Won't she be *afeart that the haggis will go to ground and the bagpipes will stop breeding without her,*' Elliot asked in an appalling attempt to mimic Lady Murray's soft Scottish burr.

'Very amusing,' Lizzie said drily.

'So what momentous event has driven her to visit Sassenach territory, then?' To his astonishment, his sister blushed. 'Lizzie?'

'I'm pregnant,' she said with her usual disregard for polite euphemisms. 'The news that's driven her south is the forthcoming arrival of a potential grandson and heir, if you must know.'

'Elizabeth!' Elliot hauled his sister from her chair and enveloped her in a bear hug. 'That's wonderful news.'

'You're squashing me, Elliot.'

He let her go immediately. 'Did I hurt you? God, I'm sorry, I—'

'Please! Please, please, please don't start telling me to rest, and put my feet up, and wrapping me in shawls and feeding me hot milk,' Lizzie said with a shudder.

'Alex?'

'Poor love, he's over the moon, but when I first told him he started treating me as if I was made of porcelain. Lord, I thought he was going to have me swaddled and coddled to death,' Lizzie said frankly. 'You can have no idea what it took for me to persuade him we could still—' She broke off, colouring a fiery red. 'Well. Anyway. Alex is fine now, but his mother is a different kettle of fish. Or should I say cauldron of porridge? She wants me to go to Scotland. She says that the fey wife in the village has always delivered the Murray heirs.'

'You surely don't intend to go?'

Lizzie's shrug was exactly like her brother's. 'Alex would never say so, but I know it's what he'd prefer. I'm already beginning to show, too. I have no wish to parade about the town with a swollen belly and I've certainly no desire at all to have myself laced into corsets to cover it up, so maybe it's for the best. It's not really a ruin, Alex's castle. Besides, you can't blame him, wanting the bairn to be born in his homeland.'

'Bairn!'

Lizzie laughed. 'Give me a few months up there and I'll be speaking like a native.' She picked up her gloves and began to draw them on. 'I must go, I promised Alex I wouldn't leave him with his mother for too long.' She stood on tiptoe to kiss Elliot's cheek. 'You do look tired. What have you been up to, I wonder? I know you've not been gallivanting, for I've lost count of the number of young ladies who've enquired after my handsome, charming, eligible and most elusive brother. And don't tell me it's because you lack invitations, because I know that's nonsense. What you need is…'

'Lizzie, for the last time, I don't want a wife.'

'I was about to say that what you need is gainful employment,' his sister said, in an offended tone. 'The Marchmont estates aren't enough to keep you occupied, they never were. You need an outlet for all that energy of yours now that you don't have your battalions to order around; you need something to stop you from brooding on incompetence and injustice. I'm not underestimating what you've been through, but it's past, Elliot, and you can't undo it. It's time to move on, put your experience to some use rather than use it to beat yourself up. There, that is frank talking indeed, but if I am to go to Scotland with a clear conscience, I don't have time to tread lightly.'

'Not that you ever do.'

Lizzie chuckled. 'Any more than you do. You don't lack opinions and certainly don't lack a cause. Why don't you go into politics yourself?'

'What?'

'I don't know why you look so surprised,' Lizzie said drily. 'What is the point in you berating the likes of Wellington and all the rest.'

'I hadn't thought.'

'Then think. And when you've concluded that I'm right, think about taking a wife, too.' She tapped his cheek lightly. 'A woman with a bit of gumption, who can force her way past that barricade of charm you arm yourself with. You see how well I know you, brother dear? You don't let people in very easily, do you? I expect the army is responsible for that stiff upper lip and all that—it makes sense in war, but we're at peace now, thank the Lord.' Lizzie nodded decisively. 'Yes. What you need is a woman of character, someone who can stand up to you, not some malleable little thing who would bore you to death before the wedding trip was over, no matter how pretty she was. I shall have to redouble my efforts before I go north, but I am quite set on it, so don't despair,' she said with a bright smile.

'I shall try my very best not to,' Elliot replied, as he opened the door for her.

'I wish you would be serious. I know I've spoken out of turn, but you're clearly not happy. I will fret about you down here all alone when I am up in Scotland.'

'You've got more than enough to worry about. I'm not unhappy, just not quite sure what to do with myself now that I don't have the army. I feel as if I've lost my purpose.'

'Politics will give you that. Will you at least think about what I said?'

'We'll see. Did you come in your carriage?'

Lizzie nodded, deciding against pushing him any further. She was on the step outside when she remembered the package. 'My book!' she declared.

Elliot retrieved the brown-paper parcel from the marble table which sat under the hall mirror. 'What is it?'

'Nothing. It's just a novel. Give me it.'

Intrigued by her cagey look, Elliot held on to the parcel. 'What kind of a novel?'

'I'm not…it's just that—well, Alex doesn't approve.'

'Good Lord, Lizzie, don't tell me you've been browsing in one of those bookseller's back rooms in Covent Garden.'

He meant it as a joke, but, to Elliot's astonishment, Lizzie's face crimsoned. 'And what if I did? Oh, don't look so shocked, it's not *that* kind of book. It's a novel. The latest Bella Donna novel, if you must know.' Seeing her brother's blank look, she sighed. 'The whole *ton* is agog at her exploits, I can't believe you've not heard of her. Bella Donna is the most shocking literary creation, she's a sort of voluptuous sorceress. The stories are quite Gothic, extremely racy and wholly entertaining. I personally see no reason why they should be kept under the counter, nor why I, a married woman, should not read them,' she said darkly. 'If Bella Donna were a man—well, it would be a different story, if you'll forgive the pun. It is the fact that she is a woman who treats—intimacy—exactly like a man that is so shocking. She is quite ruthless, you know, incredibly powerful. I think it would amuse you, I shall send it round once I am done with it if you like.'

'Why not,' Elliot said, surrendering the package, 'it sounds amusing.'

Lizzie chuckled. 'Yes, and now I can tell Alex that

you lent it to *me* if he discovers it. I really must go.
You'll come to dinner then, tomorrow? Oh, did I forget
to ask you? Never mind, I won't take no for an answer,'
she said, turning her back and tripping lightly down the
steps to her waiting carriage. 'I promised Alex I'd persuade you to join us. Lord Armstrong will be there—
the diplomat. You can talk politics with him.'

Wriggling her fingers at him over her shoulder,
Lizzie climbed into her barouche without looking back
or giving Elliot a chance to refuse her invitation.

He returned to the parlour, deep in thought. Incor-
rigible as she was, his sister was all too often right.
He could not continue in this mode for much longer.
Housebreaking, even if it was for a cause, was hardly
a lifelong occupation. And he did need an occupation,
though he had always known, as Lizzie herself said,
that he was not cut out to play the country gentleman.
Perhaps politics was the answer? It was certainly worth
considering. Lizzie's ideas usually were. She did not
know him as well as she thought, but she knew him
better than anyone else.

And a wife—was she right about that, too? Picking
up the *Morning Post,* which his man had left, carefully
ironed, on his desk, Elliot pondered this question half-
heartedly. He hadn't ever seriously considered a wife.
As a soldier with an increasingly dangerous sideline in
espionage, it would have been irresponsible to marry.
Not that that was the reason he hadn't. Such a precarious and transient life hardly lent itself to fidelity, but
Lizzie was right, curse her, that was just an excuse.

The fact was, he didn't let people in, he was wary of allowing anyone to see past whatever form of veneer he showed them. War made you like that. War taught you how fragile life was. It taught you how easy it was to be crushed by that fragility, too—he'd seen it too many times, written too many letters to grieving widows, listened to the last heartbreaking words of too many of their husbands. Pain like that, he could do without. It could not possibly be worth it.

He sighed. Blast Lizzie for putting such thoughts in his head. If she only knew that he'd been living like a monk since returning to England. What's more, until he'd met Deborah Napier, he had been relatively content to do so. Last night had been so—so bloody amazing! Just thinking about it—oh God, just thinking about it. If only he had not dropped the painting. If only he had not allowed Deborah to go in search of a candle, she would not have found her inhibitions.

'Dammit, what is wrong with me,' Elliot exclaimed, 'England must be full of attractive, available, experienced women looking for nothing more than a little light flirtation and a few indulgent hours in bed.' Except that wasn't what he wanted, not any more. He wanted Deborah. He didn't just want to bed her either, he wanted to understand her. He wanted to know what went on in her head and what had gone on in her past. He wanted to know why it took breaking and entering to release her passion. And he wanted her to release it again.

What was it Lizzie said he needed? *A woman with a bit of gumption, who can force her way past that bar-*

ricade of charm you arm yourself with. A woman of
character. Deborah was certainly that. Lizzie would
definitely approve. Not that he was in any way seeking her approval. Politics, perhaps he would consider.
Marriage—no. But the train of his thoughts disturbed
him. Elliot shook out the newspaper, seeking distrac-
tion. He found it in the middle pages.

*Last night, the Notorious Housebreaker commonly
known as the Peacock struck again, this time at the
abode of a most Distinguished Member of Parliament
who resides in Grosvenor Square. The Villainous Thief
has stolen a most valuable painting, the subject of which
being a Very Important Personage. Said painting, executed by a Spanish Master, was torn asunder from
its frame in the Most Honourable Gentleman's Study.
Once again, the Peacock had the effrontery to leave his
Calling Card behind, along with the Rope by which he
made his escape. Any Member of the Public who saw
anything or anyone suspicious is urged to contact the
Magistrates at Bow Street.*

The portrait of the Very Important Person was currently wrapped in oilskin and safely tucked under the
floorboards in Elliot's bedchamber. A certain Spanish
official, when approached by way of the intricate web
of contacts which Elliot had been careful to maintain
from his days in the covert service of the British Government, would most certainly pay a substantial sum
for it. Tomorrow, he would set about making the first
of those contacts. Today though, he had another alluring, beguiling and altogether intriguing contact to see.

Folding the newspaper into a neat square which would fit into his coat pocket, Elliot loped up the stairs three at a time, calling for his man to fetch his hat and gloves and his groom to have his curricle brought round.

Looking over from her writing desk at the clock, Deborah was astonished to discover that it was well past two. The stack of paper before her bore testament to her labours, the neat lines gradually deteriorating to an unruly scrawl as her pen struggled to keep up with her fevered imagination. She had forgotten what it was like, to be so inspired. It made her realise how much of a chore her books had become. The wisps of this story clung to her like plucking fingers, willing her to pick up her pen once more lest she lose the thread, but she knew that she had reached her limit for today.

Her wrist ached. Her head felt as if it were stuffed with cork. Wiping her ink-stained hands on the equally ink-stained linen smock she wore to protect her gown, Deborah thrust the manuscript into the desk and closed the lid.

Returning from the kitchen, where she had made herself a much-needed pot of tea, she froze on the threshold of the parlour.

Elliot was immaculately turned out, not a crease in his olive-green coat of superfine nor his biscuit-coloured pantaloons. The gloss on his tasselled Hessians showed not a speck of dirt. In contrast, Deborah was horribly conscious of her hair pinned up anyhow under its cap, her work smock, her grubby fingers. *Why did he always have to see her looking at her worst?* And why did he always have to be so much more attractive, every time she saw him? Taller. More muscular—those pantaloons fitted like a second skin. More everything! And why did he have to smile like that? And why, when she was quite resolved to forget all about him, was she so absurdly pleased to see him?

She clutched the tea tray to her chest. 'How on earth did you get in?' The shock of seeing him, as if he had just walked out of Bella's story, combined with the traitorous shiver of simple pleasure which had been her first reaction, made her sound aggressive, but better that, than let him see the effect he had on her.

'It would be a poor Peacock indeed who could not break into a house with such flimsy defences,' Elliot said with a grin, relieving her of the tea tray and giving her no option but to follow him into her own parlour.

'I did not think to see you again.' Deborah sat down on the edge of a chair by the fire. She longed to pour her tea, but was afraid her hands would shake.

Elliot raised a brow. 'Surely you must have known I would call?'

'We said goodbye last night.'

'*You* said goodbye.'

Deborah gazed at him helplessly. He waited for her to say something, but she began measuring leaves from the little wooden caddy. Water splashed as she poured it from the kettle into the pewter teapot. 'I brought only one cup.'

'I hate tea,' Elliot said, sitting himself opposite her.

She poured her drink, took a sip and then a deep breath. 'Why are you here?'

Her antagonism didn't fool him. She was as nervous as a cat, but she hadn't been able wholly to disguise the fact that she was pleased to see him. Elliot handed her the newspaper. 'I thought you might like to see this.'

Deborah scanned the report, her face lightening to a shadow of a smile as she read. 'I woke this morning persuaded that I had imagined the whole episode. I can't quite believe it happened even now, despite seeing it reported in print.'

'Fortunately, there is no indication that anyone knows I had an accomplice, but all the same, you must have a care not to let slip, even inadvertently, anything which might betray you.'

'I won't,' Deborah said, thinking guiltily of the account she had written just this morning of the episode, reassuring herself at the same time that she had changed sufficient details for it not to matter. 'There is nothing to fear, I am sure. You did not strike me as a worrier, Elliot.'

'I am not worried for myself, but for you. I care little for my own safety, but I would rather not have yours on my conscience.'

'You don't. It was I who persuaded you, if you recall.'

'I would never have allowed myself to be persuaded if I had not wanted you with me,' Elliot said with a wry smile. 'How does it feel, to be so vicariously notorious?'

'Vicarious,' Deborah replied pithily. 'I feel as if

it was someone else who clambered down that rope. Though I must confess, my conscience has been bothering me rather belatedly. That painting was very valuable.'

'And you're worried about what I'm going to do with the ill-gotten gains,' Elliot said. 'No, don't look like that, I can't blame you. I'm surprised you haven't asked before.'

'I am ashamed to admit that I most likely did not because I didn't want a reason not to go,' Deborah confessed. She put down her half-drunk cup of tea. 'Why do you do it, Elliot? I mean, I can understand, that it's partly what I wanted—the sheer thrill of it. I can understand, too, that you find civilian life rather boring compared to what you're used to, but—to say that you care little for your own life as you just did—I can't believe that you are hoping to be caught.'

'Of course not. I am bored though, that is a part of it. My sister thinks I need gainful employment and she's probably right,' Elliot said, grimacing.

'Gainful doesn't sound very like you. I didn't know you had a sister. Is she in town?'

'For the moment. Lizzie is married to a dour Scot, who has plans to whisk her away to the Highlands for the birth of their first child.' Elliot grinned, happy to be sidetracked. 'I foresee some epic battles between her and her mother-in-law and I know who I'd put my money on. Lizzie is short of neither opinions nor the will to enforce them.'

'I'd have liked to have a sister,' Deborah said with a

wistful smile. 'I don't have any family. My parents died when I was very young and my uncle, who became my guardian, was a bachelor, very set in his ways. When I came back to live with him after finishing school, he didn't know what to do with me. He didn't like Jeremy, he told me that he was only marrying me for my inheritance, but he didn't make much of an attempt to stop me either. "You must make your own bed, and don't come running to me if you don't like lying in it," he said. Not that I would have,' she concluded, with a twisted little smile.

Did she know how much she had given away with that last little sentence? Elliot wondered, touched by her pride, angry on her behalf at the need for it. 'Is he still alive?'

Deborah shook her head. 'He died five years ago. I rarely saw him once I was married. I often wish I had made more of an effort.' It was surprising how guilty she felt even now, and no amount of telling herself that Uncle Peter had made no effort to keep in touch either made any difference. She had been afraid to let him see her and had kept him at a distance as she kept everyone else. 'I don't know how we came on to this subject,' she said brusquely, 'you cannot possibly be interested in my rather pathetic life.'

'I'm interested in you, Deborah.'

She concentrated on tucking a stray lock of hair back behind her ear, dipping her head to cover the faint traces of colour in her cheeks. 'I can think of any number of topics more interesting.'

Elliot was much inclined to pursue the subject, but his instincts warned him it would be unwise. Teasing out secrets was second nature to him. Knowing when to stop lest he betray just how much he had garnered was a subtle art, but one which he knew he had mastered. Though it had to be said, he admitted wryly to himself, that Deborah was proving to be more of a challenge than any close-mouthed diplomat. 'Why did I invent the Peacock, then? Does that constitute a more interesting topic?'

Deborah nodded. 'Provided it does not also constitute an intrusion. I would like to know, for you puzzle me. Your victims are selected too carefully for them to be random. Do you have some sort of personal grudge against them?'

'What makes you say that?' Elliot asked sharply.

'I don't know.' Deborah frowned. 'I suppose I cannot believe you do it for personal gain and there are too many robberies for it to be simply the thrill of it which drives you. You'd have become bored by now if that was it.'

'You are very perceptive. It is to be hoped that none of the gentlemen at Bow Street has your wit.'

'None of the gentlemen at Bow Street has my inside information. Is it too personal? I will understand if you don't wish to say any more.'

Elliot drummed his fingers on the arm of the chair. His instincts were to confide in her, though common sense told him that by doing so he was taking an unwarrantable risk. Not of deliberate exposure, she would not do that, but an inadvertent comment, a remark let slip in the wrong company—how could he be sure she would not do that?

He just knew. She was as close as a clam and, of her own admission, she lived like a hermit. Besides, he wanted to tell her. He wanted her to know. 'You were right about my victims,' he said. 'They are very carefully selected. All of them were at some point responsible for the supply chain—or lack of it—to the army. Medical supplies, orderlies and doctors, boots, basic rations, horses. Most of all horses. They kept us short of all of those things, because after all, what does an army need to fight except guns? Even if you can't get the guns to the battlefield. Even if you can't get the men wounded by those guns misfiring back to a field hospital. What do they care? They don't,' he said flatly. 'I know they don't because all my letters and protests and reports fell on deaf ears at the time, and now—well, now it is done and everyone wants to forget all about it, so there is even less point in letters and reports and protests.'

'So you take what will hurt them instead.'

'Yes, that's exactly what I do.'

'Did you lose many men because of such shortages?'

'Yes.'

'Friends, too? Forgive me, but it seems to me such a very personal thing you are doing, there must have been someone…'

'There was. My best friend.' Elliot gripped the arms of his chair so tightly that his knuckles showed white.

'Henry,' Deborah said gently. 'I'm so sorry.'

Elliot nodded curtly.

'I truly am sorry, I didn't mean to upset you; you don't need to say any more.'

'I want to,' Elliot said, surprising both of them. 'I want to tell you.' He swallowed repeatedly, cleared his throat. 'We joined up together, Henry and I, I told you that already. We worked our way through the ranks together, though he was much too ill-disciplined to keep his stripes for long. He made it to captain once, but it only lasted about six months. He was a first-class soldier. We always looked out for each other. When I needed an extra pair of hands, I always turned to Henry. He was quick with his fists, but he knew the importance of keeping other things close, which was important in my—my alternative line of business.'

He paused. Across from him, Deborah was gazing at him intently. Would she be shocked? He doubted it, somehow. More likely excited, as she was by the Peacock. That decided him. 'The thing is, I wasn't just a fighting man. There's a reason why the Peacock is so able.' He grinned. 'Actually, it's ironic that the very skills I learned in order to steal secrets are the same ones I use to steal their property now. Most of which, I hasten to add, was stolen in the first place.'

Deborah stared at him in utter astonishment. 'You mean—what you're saying is that you—you *stole?* At our Government's behest? But why? What did you— oh! My God, you were a spy?'

He should have known how she would react. Her eyes were sparkling. Elliot laughed. 'Yes, I was.'

'Good grief! No wonder civilian life bores you. You must tell me—I wish you will tell me—I don't know—anything, all of it—no, I don't expect you can tell me *all* of it. Goodness, what secrets you must know.' Deborah chuckled. 'How horrified the likes of Jacob would be if they knew. You are quite right, Elliot, it is irony past price. *Can* you tell me more? Were you a master of subterfuge?'

Danger, even if it was vicarious, certainly brought her to life. 'I'm afraid it was rather more mundane than that. If anything, I was a master of patience.' He told her a few choice stories because he liked to see her laugh, because he found her laughter infectious, and he told her a few more because returning to the subject in hand was too painful, but he underestimated her.

'He must have been more like a brother than a friend. Henry, I mean,' Deborah said suddenly, interrupting him in the middle of a story. 'What happened?'

'He was wounded in the Pyrenees during the siege on San Sebastian. He took a bullet in the leg, above the knee. It smashed the bone—he'd have lost his leg, but it shouldn't have been fatal. Only they couldn't reach him because there were no carts and no mules.'

'Oh God.' Deborah covered her mouth, her eyes wide with horror.

Elliot's knuckles were white. 'For more than a week, he lay in agony in the blistering sun with his wound festering. He died of a fever a few days after they finally got him to the field hospital. I was with him, at the end, though he hardly recognised me. He died for want of a mule. A mule!' He thumped his fist down hard on the chair. 'But what do those bastards in the War Office with their lists and their budgets know of that? What does it matter, when a man with one leg would have been no bloody use to them anyway? What do they know of the suffering, the agonies that Henry and thousands like him went through, and what do they care now for the survivors?'

'But you care,' Deborah said, shaken by the cold rage. 'You care enough to steal from them, to make reparations for them, is that it?'

'The money goes to a charity which helps the survivors.' Now that he had opened the floodgates his bitter anger, so long pent-up, demanded expression. 'Someone has to help them,' Elliot said furiously. 'While they fought for their country, their country learned how to do very well without them. Now that the Government no longer needs them to surrender their lives, their limbs and their hearts on the battlefield, it has decided it has no need to reward them with employment, back pay, pensions. It is not just the men, it is their widows and children who suffer.'

'I didn't realise,' Deborah said falteringly.

'Few people do. All they see is a beggar. Just another beggar. Proud men, reduced to holding out a cup for alms! Can you imagine what that does to them? No wonder so many cannot face their families. And they are portrayed as deserters, drunkards, criminals.'

The scar which bisected his eyebrow stood out white against his tan. The other one, which followed the hairline of his forehead, seemed to pulse. How many other, invisible scars did he bear? His suffering made hers seem so trite in comparison. The grooves at the side of his mouth were etched deep. His eyes were fierce, hard. Deborah trembled at the sorrow and pain they hid, such depths, which made shallows of her own suffering. 'I just didn't know,' she said simply. 'I am quite ashamed.' The truth was so awful, it made her conscience seem like a paltry consideration. 'I wish now that we had taken more from that house in Grosvenor Square.'

Her vehemence drew a bark of laughter from Elliot. 'Believe me, over the last two years, the Peacock has taken a great deal more.'

'So it is a war of attrition that the Peacock is waging, is that it? And of vengeance?'

Deborah's perception made Elliot deeply uncomfortable. He was not accustomed to thinking about his motivations, never mind discussing them. 'What do you know of vengeance?' he asked roughly.

Enough to recognise it. Deborah hesitated, surprised at the strength of her urge to confide, but the very idea of comparing their causes appalled her. Besides, his voice held an undertone of aggression that warned her to tread lightly. He obviously thought he had said too much already. She could easily empathise with that. 'The painting that we stole,' she said, seeking to lighten the subject, 'you knew about it because of your spying, didn't you?'

'You've no idea how much ransacking and looting

goes on in the higher echelons in wartime. That paint-ing was a bribe.'

To Deborah's relief, some of the grimness left his mouth. She asked him to explain; when he did, she encouraged him to tell her of other bribes, relieved to see the grooves around his mouth relaxing, the sadness leaving his eyes. The battered armchair in which he sat, she had rescued from a lumber room at Kinsail Manor. His legs, in their tight-knit pantaloons, stretched out in front of him. If she reached, she could touch her toe to his Hessian boots.

'I've said too much,' Elliot said, interrupting himself in the middle of a story, realising abruptly how much he had revealed, how little he had talked to anyone of his old life before. It had been too easy to talk to Deborah. He wasn't sure what he thought of that, accustomed as he was to keep his own counsel. His instincts were to retreat. 'I must go,' he said, getting to his feet.

How did he close his expression off like that? Ignor-ing the flicker of disappointment, Deborah rose, too. 'You have certainly said enough to make me realise how shockingly ignorant I am. I shall not look on those poor souls with their begging bowls in the same way again.'

Outside, it was grown dark. Elliot lit a spill from the fire and began to light the candles on the mantel. 'I'd like to call on you again,' he said.

Deborah bit her lip. It would have been so much eas-ier, had he not chosen to confide in her, if he had not given her so many reasons to wish to know more about him. To like him. In another world, in another life, Elliot was the kind of man she would have…

But there was absolutely no point whatsoever in thinking like that. Slowly, she shook her head. The pang of loss was physical, a pain in her stomach. 'I live a very secluded life.'

'I'm not suggesting we attend Almack's together. We could go for a drive.'

Why did he have to make it so difficult? 'I can't, Elliot. I am perfectly content with my own company.'

'So content that you need to break into houses and climb down ropes to make you feel alive?'

Deborah flinched. 'I thought you understood. That was an escape from reality, merely.'

'I don't understand you.' Elliot cast the spill into the fire. 'One minute, you are hanging on my every word, the next, you imply that you never want to see me again.'

'I'm sorry. I didn't think that you would expect—I never considered us continuing our acquaintance after last night. I should not have encouraged you to confide in me, but I was so caught up in what you said and—I should not have,' Deborah said wretchedly. 'I'm sorry, Elliot.'

'And what about last night? You are sorry about that, too, I suppose? Dammit, I was not imagining it, the strength of attraction between us. Why are you hell bent on ignoring it?' Frustrated and confused, Elliot pulled her roughly towards him. 'You can't deny it! I can feel your heart beating. I can see it in your eyes that you want to kiss me just as much as I want to kiss you.'

'No. Elliot, please…'

He was so sure, so certain that if he could just kiss her, it would rekindle the flame that had flared between them last night, but he had never in his life used persuasion on a woman in that way, and would not do so now. Elliot threw himself away from her. 'I apologise,' he said curtly. 'I have obviously completely misjudged the situation.'

'No,' Deborah whispered, 'it is I who did so. Last night, I gave you to think that I would—when I could not. Cannot. You have nothing to apologise for.'

It went against the grain to leave her like this but she left him no option. 'Your servant, Lady Kinsail.' Elliot sketched a bow.

'Goodbye, Elliot.' He was gone before she had finished saying the words, the front door slamming behind him. Deborah could not resist peering out into the gloom through the window, but he did not look back.

Alone in the parlour, she squared her shoulders. It had cost her dear, not to kiss him. It had cost her even dearer, that look on his face when she behaved so contrarily, but it was for the best. Elliot was not Jeremy, but it made no difference. Never, with Jeremy, had she come close to feeling what Elliot made her feel, but that just made things worse. She did not want to feel anything.

'It's over,' she said to herself, pulling the curtains across the window. It would have been easier, knowing Elliot less, but it was too late for that now. Knowing him better simply made her more certain she was right. But staring into the flames of the fire, Deborah couldn't help wishing that things were different.

Chapter Five

As he walked home from Hans Town, Elliot was angry. He was hurt, too—at least his pride was hurt, that was all, he told himself. He was not used to rejection. He did not understand why Deborah had rejected him, but nor could he ignore the fact that she had and quite unequivocally. He would not see her again. It didn't matter a damn that she was the only woman who interested him, it was over. There were plenty more women in England.

As he changed into evening clothes, a melancholy seized him. It was not just his pride that was hurt. He had confided in her. He'd taken his sister's advice and actually let someone cross the threshold of his feelings. She'd understood him, too—a little too much for comfort, actually—but she had seemed so sympathetic. The more he replayed their conversation in his mind, the more inexplicable he found her behaviour.

Dinner at Lizzie's was a trial. Though he liked Alex, found the dour Mrs Murray amusing and under normal circumstances would have enjoyed baiting that wily old dog Lord Armstrong, Elliot was morose enough for his sister to take him aside and ask him if he was sickening for something. He left the party early.

Impatient with himself as he tossed and turned in a vain effort to sleep, determined not to succumb to the temptation to call on Deborah again in the morning, Elliot decided to pay an overdue visit to his estates in Hampshire. Lizzie was right, he needed an occupation; since he could not, for the moment, contemplate planning another outing for the Peacock, he would interest himself in the running of his lands.

'Well now.' Mr Freyworth, second of the sons for which the publishing house was named, laced his hands together and sat back in his seat. The spectacles which he used for close reading dangled on a chain around his neck. Across from him his client sat, her face as expressionless as ever, and once more Montague Freyworth found himself wondering how such a cold—nay, icy— female could possibly be the authoress of such shocking books. He looked down at the close-written pages before him and tapped one scrawny finger on the topmost. 'Well now,' he said again, 'this is certainly most— I think it would be fair for me to say that it is warmer than your last novel. In fact,' he said with an attempt at humour which did not sit with his sparse, crow-like form, 'I almost expected the paper to burst into flames while I was reading it.'

Deborah smiled tightly. Though her acquaintance with the publisher spanned the four years of Bella's existence, it could not be said that they were any closer than they had been that first day, when she had sat, sick with nerves, in this very seat in this very room, waiting upon his verdict. 'You said you thought that the last book was rather—flat, I believe was your word,' she said carefully.

The publisher nodded. 'Flat. Yes, you are quite correct. Lacking a certain *frisson*. Flat was, I believe, the very word I used.'

'I trust you do not wish to apply it to this story?'

Montague Freyworth's thin mouth stretched into the semblance of a smile. 'Indeed, no. *Indeed*, no. The housebreaking incident is most vividly described.'

He picked up a paper knife, then put it down again. His fingers began to drum on her manuscript which lay on his blotting pad. It was a habit which had often made Deborah grit her teeth, for though she did not mind ink stains or crossings out, she hated to have her original draft, which she thought of as her creation, her child, so roughly manhandled. With difficulty, she resisted the urge to swat her publisher's hand away. 'So you like it? The robbery, I mean.'

'First rate. I must say, Lady Kinsail, absolutely first rate. One could almost believe that you had been there yourself.'

Deborah produced a tinkling laugh that she was relieved to hear sounded almost natural. 'A compliment indeed.' Discomfited, she decided to overlook Mr Freyworth's overt use of her name. It was one of the many unwritten rules which governed their relationship, the pretence of ignorance on his part. Just as she was happy not to acknowledge that the respectable house of Frey-worth & Sons made a handsome return on the lurid volumes they printed for her under another publish-er's name.

'As I said, it was most enthralling.' Montague Frey-worth resumed fiddling with his paper knife. 'The aftermath, now—the scene between Bella Donna and the housebreaker—I think that—'

'What I tried to convey was that for once, Bella was quite carried away by the illicit excitement—the more acute sense of danger. The impulsive way she behaved, it was an outlet for her pent-up feelings.'

Mr Freyworth held up a hand. 'You have no need to explain, madam, I quite understood it. What I was going to say was that I was also rather—forgive me, but this scene too had about it an authenticity which elevates your writing to a new plane.'

'Oh! Oh, I see.' Deborah gazed in confusion down at her gloves.

Across from her, Montague Freyworth was astonished to note a blush staining her pale cheeks. Not such a cold marble statue after all, the Widow Kinsail. Well, well. Mrs Freyworth would gobble up that little snippet. It was she who, unbeknownst to the authoress herself, was responsible for the critical reading of every one of Bella Donna's lurid tales—tales which her husband found not just disturbing, but whose appeal he found incomprehensible. 'What I wanted to say,' Montague

said, 'was that I feel the book would benefit from—
er—more of such scenes.'

'More?' A hysterical laugh, quickly stifled, escaped
from Deborah. 'I thought you were going to ask me to
cut it.'

'No, no.' Montague shook his head vehemently, re-
calling his wife's admonition. 'It is felt—I feel—that
is—frankly, my lady—I mean, madam—' He broke
off, drumming his grubby fingers on the blotting pad,
trying desperately to think of a way of rephrasing Mrs
Freyworth's words. *The crime is all very well and
good, but what really excites the reader is the aftermath. What I'm saying, Montague, is that the insertion
is more interesting than the removal.'* He had to con-
cede that his wife had a singular ability to express herself both graphically and succinctly. She was every bit
as direct in the sanctity of their bedroom, a fact which
was almost entirely responsible for their astonishingly
satisfying marital relationship, but there were times—
many times—when Montague wished that she would
confine her remarks to that chamber.

He sighed heavily and inadvertently caught his
client's gaze. He never had been able to decide, in all
these years, what colour her eyes were. Was she laughing at him? He narrowed his own uncomplicated blue
orbs, but could not be quite sure whether the tilt of her
mouth was humour or impatience or simply a tic. She
had a way of tilting her chin at him, lifting one brow—
there, just like that—that made him feel rather more like
an insect she wished to stamp on than he liked. Mon-

tague put down his paper knife once more and picked up the manuscript, tying the ribbon which bound it. Handing it back, he saw that it was rather dog-eared and saw, too, from the look of distaste on the Widow Kinsail's face, that she had noticed and didn't like it. The tiny glow of his having irked her gave him the momentum he needed.

'The story needs another felony. And afterwards—well, suffice it to say that you can let that imagination of yours loose on your pen,' he said with something approaching a wink. 'Set the pages aflame, Lady Kinsail, and I am sure that we will run to three, maybe four editions.'

Deborah hesitated, torn between triumph and horror. 'I had not planned…'

'Nonsense! You've done exceeding well with the robbery of that statuette—how hard can it be to dream up another such?' Mr Freyworth got to his feet in an effort to cut short any protestation. 'Think of the returns, madam. Three, four editions I say, and that will be just the start. The interest will generate a demand for the earlier books, too, I am sure of it.'

He was actually rubbing his hands together, Deborah noticed, trying not to laugh, for Mr Freyworth's tall, scrawny frame, the hollowed cheeks, the thin, fluffy covering of black hair through which his skull showed like an egg, combined with the dusty black clothes he wore, made him look like one of the neglected Tower ravens. She held out her hand, tucking her manuscript under the other arm. 'I will attempt to do what you say, sir.'

'I am sure you will not disappoint, madam. I look forward to seeing the results. And if you could perhaps manage to complete the revisions in—say two or three weeks?—then we shall, if we put our minds to it, be able to rush through the first edition in time for Christmas.'

'I hardly think that Bella Donna's exploits will be the most popular of yuletide gifts,' Deborah said with a dry smile.

Montague Freyworth patted her shoulder. 'Now then, my lady, you must allow me to know my business rather better than you. You would be surprised by the number of people who will purchase your little story if it is nicely bound and discreetly marketed. I will not say that you will see it on every drawing-room table, but I will make an informed guess that you will find it in most boudoir cabinets. Good day to you now, madam. And happy writing.'

Rather dazed, Deborah made her way out on to Piccadilly. If what Mr Freyworth said was true, the profits from her pen could free her from the necessity of relying upon her widow's portion. Free her from the last tangible remnants which bound her to Jeremy. Just thinking about the possibility made her realise how much she still resented those ties, despite the knowledge that she was more than deserving of the income which was, after all, originally sourced from her very own inheritance.

Wandering down the busy street, oblivious to the

swarms of traffic heading to the park, for it was the beginning of the Season and approaching the hour for parading, Deborah surrendered herself to the dream of independence. True independence. And all it would take, if Mr Freyworth were to be believed—and why should such an astute businessman lie?—was one more robbery and its aftermath. Surely she could do it?

Three days later, Deborah scrunched up another piece of paper ruined by crossings out and ink blots, with a hole in the middle where she'd pressed her pen too hard in sheer exasperation. She couldn't do it. She just couldn't do it! Throwing the paper ball into the empty hearth with an accuracy born of far too much practice, she pushed back her chair and began to pace the room. Back and forwards she went, between the window and the far wall, a route taken so often that the carpet was beginning to show signs of wear. The familiar litany dogged every step.

Authenticity is the key.

Authenticity will bring you a third edition. A fourth.

Authenticity will bring you independence.

Independence will bring you freedom.

You will be free. Free of the past. Free of Jeremy. Free.

Authenticity will bring freedom.

Elliot is the key to authenticity.

Elliot.

You need Elliot.

You can't do it without Elliot.

He'll most likely be planning another robbery around about now in any case.

And it's for a good cause. The money you give now to every beggarly soldier is a drop in the ocean compared to what his ill-gotten gains can do. You'd be helping save those men and saving yourself.

You need Elliot.

Elliot is the key.

You need Elliot.

You need to see Elliot.

And here, as ever, her mind skittered to a halt. It wasn't that she *needed* to see him, it was that she needed his help. She hadn't missed him. She hadn't been disappointed every time the post brought no word, every time a knock on the door failed to produce him either in person or in the form of a messenger in the three weeks since she had forced him to say goodbye. He'd done what she wanted, he'd taken her at her word. He'd kept away.

So of course she was not looking for an excuse to get in touch with him. Absolutely not! Elliot Marchmont was an extremely attractive and intriguing man, but what she imagined him doing to her in the dark, in the secret of the night, it meant nothing. She knew perfectly well that there was a world of difference between fantasy and reality. She didn't want him. Not really. Not at all!

But she needed him. And unless she did something about it, she would have to pay her annual visit to Kinsail Manor next winter. Oh God no, she just couldn't bear it. Which meant...

With a decisive nod, Deborah resumed her seat and picked up a fresh pen. But having dashed off Elliot's name at the start of her note, she was struck by indecision. Chewing absent-mindedly on the tip of her quill—a disgusting habit she'd never been able to break herself of—she stared blankly at the watercolour landscape which hung on the wall over her desk. It was not just the unequivocal way she had ended their acquaintance, she was horribly conscious of the fact that she would be exploiting his most noble cause to her own ends. She could not, in all conscience, do so without some sort of explanation. Besides, without some sort of explanation, she doubted very much indeed that Elliot would agree.

In fact, the more she pondered it, the more she wondered if Elliot would not—quite justifiably—refuse her request to speak to him. The most likely outcome of her asking him to call on her would be spending the next few days waiting in vain for him to do so, because why would he call when she'd been so determined never to see him again?

Perhaps, then, she should suggest that *she* would call on *him?* It was unconventional, improper even, though she doubted he would be any more bothered by this than she was. But what if he refused her entry to his house? A melodramatic vision of herself pleading on the doorstep with Elliot standing aloof, barring the way, failed to make Deborah smile, for it felt quite possible.

She dropped the pen as her confidence oozed slowly

away. It was a familiar feeling. So many times, in Jeremy's absence, she had rallied herself to try again, or latterly to tell him that she was done with the pretence that was their marriage, that she would not stay, that a separation would make them both less miserable. Every time, every single time, she'd failed, and every defeat crushed her a little further, like a mallet pushing a peg into the ground. Catching sight of her distorted reflection in the window pane, a curled, slumped figure, Deborah sat up straight in her chair. 'Freedom,' she said aloud to rally herself. 'Think of it, Deb, freedom.'

No point in writing. She must leave nothing to chance. She would call on Elliot now. And if he was not at home, she would call again. And if he would not see her, she would refuse to go away until he did. And when he did, she would tell him. Not all, but enough to persuade him, enough to persuade herself, too, of the worthiness of her cause, even if it was a pale shadow of his.

Thus fortified, she ran lightly up the stairs to her bedchamber. Her sad little collection of gowns looked like the washed-out palette an artist would use to paint a November sea, but that could not be helped. Quickly changing into a walking dress and tidying her hair before she could change her mind, Deborah pulled on a pair of boots, tied her bonnet, fastened her pelisse and buttoned her gloves.

Elliot had returned to town in an even more morose mood than the one in which he had departed. Though he had tried to interest himself in the business of his estates, the factor whom Lizzie had trained was extremely efficient and Elliot had been unable to persuade himself that his presence was in any way necessary to the good heart of his land.

Ennui made him irritable and the feeling of unfinished business gnawed at him. No matter how hard he had tried, Deborah kept creeping into his mind and occupying his dreams. Her contradictions fascinated him and his fascination annoyed him. She was intriguing and beguiling, but she was also seriously emotionally repressed and apparently determined to remain so. She was wild and reckless one moment, totally lacking in confidence another. Her kisses were like no kisses he had ever shared, but they were not the kisses of an experienced woman. How could a wanton be an innocent? How could someone so incredibly attractive think herself, as she so patently did, so very ordinary? She was tough and she was fragile. The shadows cast by her past were enormous, but she refused to acknowledge them. She aroused his compassion and his passion. She encouraged his confidences, but would confide nothing willingly in return. It was pointless thinking about her and pointless trying to stop.

In the endless free hours his retreat from town had granted him, Elliot turned all of this over and over in his mind to absolutely no avail. Attempting to divert himself with the question of his future was equally frustrating. He needed to give his life form, but he had no idea what form he wished it to take; the only form which really interested him was Deborah's. There was only one thing for it, Elliot decided, and that was to go back to London and resurrect the Peacock, even if his appeal was, frankly, diminished.

Deborah arrived upon his doorstep the very day he returned. His heart gave a most unexpected little skip at the sight of her standing in his hallway. Telling himself that he could hardly send her about her business without at least granting her a hearing, even if that is what she looked as if she expected him to do, Elliot ushered her into the parlour.

She was out of sorts, nervous, jumping when he closed the door firmly on his over-interested batman, who also served as major-domo. Her eyes were over-bright, her hat askew, as if she had been tugging at the ribbons while she waited. 'Lady Kinsail. This is an unexpected surprise,' Elliot said with a very small bow.

'Deborah. It's Deborah,' she said, flinching at the irony in his tone.

'Won't you sit down?'

'Thank you.' She sat gingerly on the striped sofa. It was a pleasant room. Like Elliot, it was elegant without being ostentatious. Looking up at him through her lashes, she realised she'd forgotten again how tall he was. And the fierce look of him. And the way she liked the fierce look of him. His mouth. The top lip thinner. The grooves at the sides. She'd forgotten how he made her feel. Fluttery and soft and hot. Female.

Afraid that she would lose heart, she launched into speech. 'I know I shouldn't have called unannounced on you like this, but I wanted to see you and I was worried that—I thought if I wrote to you, you might ignore me. I could understand why, after the last time. I was rude, and I was most certain that I—that we should not—there are things—reasons—but that's no excuse. Except I thought it was for the best, and as it turns out— in short, I had to see you.'

Elliot tried hard not to smile at this convoluted speech, tried to hold on to his hurt, tried not to be interested, and failed in every attempt. 'I have been away, visiting my home in the country. If you had called yesterday, you would not have found me.'

'Oh.' The little tug upwards at the corner of his mouth, was it a smile? Deborah tentatively tried one of her own. 'Are you well?' she asked, though it was perfectly obvious that he was. 'You look well,' she added inanely. 'The country air obviously agrees with you.'

'You think so? I confess, I was rather bored.'

'Oh.' Deborah looked down at her hands. She seemed to have pulled off her gloves. There was a bluish tinge on the skin between her thumb and index finger which no amount of scrubbing could remove. 'Your home, I don't think you've mentioned where it is?'

'Hampshire.'

'You have family there? I mean I know that your father passed away and your sister is in town, but you must have other family. Most people do. Except me. But I am not most people.' She was wittering, but as long as she did so, she would be able to postpone having to broach the subject she had come to discuss.

'I have some cousins, but no other close family. It was just me and my factor, who is far too efficient for his own good.'

'You should count yourself lucky, a good factor is worth his weight in gold. I don't know how many times I told Jeremy that that man of his acted as though he was being asked to pay for repairs out of his own pocket. No wonder that we lost every decent tenant we had and the lands went to rack and ruin, but Jeremy didn't seem to care. "I'll be dead before I'll be bankrupt," he used to say, and—' Deborah caught herself up short, colouring deeply. 'Well anyway, you should count yourself lucky.'

'And your husband? Was he right?'

'What? Oh, you mean was he dead before he went bankrupt?' She shook her head. 'You'd think so, to hear his cousin talk, but it was not quite that bad. Most of the land was entailed and could not be sold, and the mortgages were not really—but that is not what I came here to discuss.'

Elliot sat down beside her on the sofa, touched by that heartfelt little speech. Her profligate husband had obviously succeeded in emptying the coffers suffi- ciently to leave his widow in severely straitened cir- cumstances, and, knowing the current Lord Kinsail's miserly tendencies, it was unlikely that he'd made any attempt to alleviate them. 'I'm glad now I took that blue diamond,' he said impulsively. 'If I'd have known, I'd have taken the family jewels as well and given them to you.'

He said it to make her smile, but Deborah's expression was not amused. 'I want nothing from the Kinsails and I don't want your pity, Elliot.'

Her haughty look was back. She was as prickly as a damned thistle. 'I wish you would tell me what it is you do want from me,' he said, exasperated as much by himself as her abrupt change of mood, 'because I haven't a clue.'

'I need the Peacock,' Deborah blurted out. 'I need to commit another felony.'

The starkness of this statement startled him into laughter and a combination of nerves, and the infectious quality of that rumbling sound which was like a rough caress, made Deborah laugh, too. 'It's not funny.'

'Yes, it is. *I need to commit another felony.* You made it sound as if you'd been prescribed a purgative.'

'Elliot, I am deadly serious.'

His smile faded. 'Categorically, no.'

'Why not?'

'Once was risky. To court such danger a second time would be foolish beyond belief.'

'You have done so countless times.'

'My life is my own to risk.'

'As is mine.'

Elliot launched himself to his feet. 'I don't need an accomplice,' he said through gritted teeth, furious with himself for having hoped that she had called simply because she wanted to see him. Furious at himself for having hoped anything at all when he had quite decided that he would think of her no longer. 'I should have had my man turn you away. I cannot believe you have had the nerve to ask me this after you made it so perfectly clear that you wanted nothing more to do with me.'

'You're angry with me.'

'I'm mad as bloody fire! The last time I saw you, you told me that you were perfectly content with your own company—this, despite the fact that you have admitted several times that you're lonely. You encouraged me into telling you things I've never talked about—and yet you are like a clam. And that night—you kissed me as if you were starved of kisses. If I hadn't dropped that portrait you'd have done a damn sight more than kiss me, but the next day you turn the cold shoulder on me. And now you swan in after almost three weeks of silence and demand—of course I'm angry with you, what did you expect?'

'I shouldn't have asked,' Deborah said miserably.

'No, you should not have.' Elliot kicked at a smouldering log in the grate. Ash floated up from it, marring the polished perfection of his Hessians. He hated losing his temper. He hated that white, pinched look on Deborah's face, and hated himself for having caused it even though she deserved it. He hated himself even more for caring. He dug his hands deep into his pockets and leaned his shoulders against the mantel, warring with the urge to agree with her outrageous request simply because he wanted to.

Deborah twisted her gloves round and round, pulling the worn leather completely out of shape. Seconds stretched and still Elliot said nothing, his expression withdrawn, the lines around his mouth deep grooves.

His anger sapped her will, for it was wholly justified. She was a fool to have come. 'You are quite right, I shouldn't have asked. I beg your pardon, I will go now.'

He watched her get to her feet. He dug his hands deeper into his pockets as she pulled on her gloves. Her hands were shaking. She was biting her lip, unable quite to look him in the eye and he felt like an utter bastard, even though he was right. *He was absolutely right, dammit!*

Deborah got to the door. She was leaving. She was walking away without a fight, even though she had a cause worth fighting for. She was walking away, just as she always did. She hesitated with her hand on the brass door handle. She hadn't even tried to explain. She owed it to herself to at least do that much.

She let go of the latch and turned around. 'You're right,' she said shakily, 'I shouldn't have asked to come with you, but I did none the less because I have a very good reason for doing so. It's not as good a reason as yours. I could lie to you, I could say that it's just because I want to help you fight your battle, but I wouldn't presume, even though I can empathise, and more importantly I *won't* lie to you. If you will do me the courtesy of listening—which is more than I deserve, I know that—then I will explain. If my behaviour has already put me beyond the pale, I'll understand.'

It felt like a victory, simply having had the courage to stand her ground. She was breathing fast, as if she'd been galloping over the Downs, as if she'd been running, and the exhilaration of it was the same, too. She remained where she was, hovering at the door, for the moment not caring what Elliot said, just happy to have spoken up for herself. She was almost surprised when he crossed the room to where she was standing. His nearness made her heart beat even faster. His expression was still grim, but at least he was looking at her and not beyond her.

Their eyes met; for a startling moment all Deborah could think about was kissing him. For a second, an infinitesimal second, she gazed at him, imagining that kiss, dark and hot and velvet. He would thrust his tongue into her mouth, pull her tight against him. It would not be a gentle kiss, no sweetness nor restraint. She would clutch at him, pressing herself shamelessly into the hardness of his chest, his thighs, wanting to be crushed into oblivion. She would kiss him fervently, longingly, as if she would drain him of his strength in order to bolster her own.

Her skin heated. Her breath quickened. She saw it in his eyes, a recognition of the direction her thoughts had taken, and drew herself back, looking away, plucking at her gloves once more. 'Will you allow me to explain, Elliot?'

It had cost her dear, to turn around like that. It had cost him dear to let her go. He was still not sure that he would have, was irked at his relief in not having to, but already his curiosity had begun to subdue his anger. Already, whatever it was about her that plucked a chord in him had overcome his resolution. 'I will listen, but

I make no promises,' Elliot said gruffly, leading her back to the sofa.

Deborah chewed on her lower lip, her thoughts turned inwards. Then she nodded, the way Elliot had noticed she often did when she had come to a decision, and he struggled to contain his smile. She straightened her shoulders, tucking a non-existent strand of hair behind her ear, another endearing habit he'd noticed. She had the look of one preparing for battle. He eased himself back on the sofa a little, because the proximity of his knee to her was distracting. His anger was forgotten. Once more, he was simply intrigued. 'Go on,' he said gently.

'Yes. Yes, I will.' Deborah nodded again. 'You must be aware by now that my circumstances are somewhat straitened.' She spoke quietly, looking not at him, but at her hands. 'My jointure is—well, according to Lord Kinsail it is more than adequate, which perhaps explains his reluctance to pay it regularly.'

'Surely the terms of your husband's will, your marriage settlement...'

'Are not the point, Elliot. The point is that I would prefer not to be beholden in any way to my husband's estate.' Glancing up at him, she realised that her words were very much open to misinterpretation. 'Goodness, don't look like that. I'm not about to suggest that you cut me in on your profits,' she said with a horrified little laugh. 'No, I meant that I—what I am trying to say is that I have found an alternative way to earn my bread. I have taken up writing.'

Whatever he had been expecting, it was not this. Elliot sat bolt upright. 'You write—what, exactly?'

'Books.'

'You never fail to surprise me. What sort of books?'

'Novels. You will not have read any of them, they are not—they are written for—they're not your kind of thing.'

'What kind of thing are they, then?'

'Just stories.'

'For children?'

'Good God, no,' Deborah replied, looking appalled. 'They are sort of adventure stories. Revenge allegories. For adults.'

She was blushing. He tried to snag her gaze, but Deborah remained fascinated by her hands. 'Revenge? I remember now, you told me you recognised vengeance—was that what you meant, that you write about it? Do you not think that is a rather strange topic to choose?'

'It doesn't matter what they are about, save that they are books, that they sell well and that my publisher says that this next one will sell even better. Enough for me to be able to dispense with my jointure.'

'Why would you do that, when it is your legal entitlement?'

'I don't want it. I don't want anything from the Kinsails. That is the point of my writing, to be free.'

'That is an odd choice of word for financial independence.'

Deborah shrugged.

'I still don't understand what this has to do with me.'

'In my latest story, my heroine carries out a robbery and...'

'Wait a minute. You're not telling me that you've put what we did into a book?' Elliot said slowly.

'I know, I should have told you, but...' Deborah twisted her gloves into a tight knot. 'I've changed the details obviously, you need have no fear that there is anything which will betray us. She—my heroine—acts quite alone, and though she does escape by a rope, it is not a portrait, but a statuette she takes.' Her voice faded into a whisper. Put like that, it seemed heinous not to have told him. 'I assure you Elliot, no one would realise—save you, of course, and you are not likely to read it.'

'On the contrary, I shall make a point of doing so.'

'*No!* Good God, no! It's not your sort of thing at all.'

There was no doubt about it now, Deborah was blushing furiously. 'What on earth have you written that you're so embarrassed about?' Elliot asked.

'Nothing! I'm not embarrassed.' Aware that the blush on her cheeks gave lie to her words, she tried to cool them with the backs of her hands. 'I have never told anyone about my work. No one save my publisher knows, and even he pretends to be in ignorance of my real identity.' She risked a look at Elliot, a smile that was almost impish. 'He knows my name full well of course, but he pretends not to. He calls me *madam,*' she said in a fair imitation of Mr Freyworth, 'and only when he is annoyed with me, or very anxious to persuade me of something, does he resort to *my lady.*' Her smile faded. 'He resorted to *my lady* when he read my latest story. He thought my description of the theft had great authenticity. In fact, he liked it so much that he insisted I include another. He told me that such a book would run into several editions. Several, only think of it. I can't tell you how much that would mean to me, Elliot. I tried, I really did try to make something up, but I could not.'

Silence, but this time she had no difficulty in reading the look on his face. He was aghast. 'You don't think it's a good idea,' Deborah said, nodding her head matter of factly, ignoring her sinking heart. 'And you're right. It's not. I should have seen—only I was so very eager to do as he asked because of the sales...'

'You've come here to ask me to take you with the Peacock so you can put it in a book.'

Deborah cringed. 'Yes, yes, I know, when you put it like that...'

'Having already written our first little outing into that same book so successfully that your publisher wants another?'

'Yes.'

'But your imagination has failed you, so you want me—I beg your pardon, the Peacock—to fill in the gaps. Have I that right?'

Deborah nodded mutely.

'And the reason you need to write books in the first place is because you won't take what you're legally entitled to from your dead husband's estate?'

'I won't take it because I don't feel entitled to it.'

'Why not?'

She shouldn't have said that—Elliot was far too perceptive. Deborah stared, wide-eyed, fighting the urge to flee. He wasn't angry any more. He wasn't looking at her in that hard way, though his mouth was still grim. She looked down at her gloves. They were quite ruined.

'Deborah?'

There was a hint of impatience in his voice now. 'I wasn't a very good wife,' she said.

He had to strain to catch her words, and when he did, he almost wished he hadn't, for it was impossible not to be touched by such an admission. Elliot disentangled Deborah's gloves from her fingers. Her hands were icy. He clasped them between his own to warm them. 'From the little you've told me,' he said carefully, 'he wasn't a very good husband.'

'We shouldn't have married. He was only interested in my money, I told you that.'

'It is your money which provides you with your jointure, Deborah.'

'It's not mine, not any more. I don't want it. I don't deserve it. You don't understand.'

'I'm trying to.'

'You can't, Elliot. I can't talk about this. I'm sorry,' she said wretchedly, snatching her hands free of his and scrubbing at her eyes. 'Thank you for your time. It's too much, I understand that, but I appreciate your having listened.' Once again, she made for the door.

'What will you do?'

'Make something up.' Deborah smiled bravely. 'I'm

a writer, it's what we do—invent things. I should go now.' She held out her hand.

Elliot took it, but did not let it go. He felt like a complete heel in the face of such spirit. After all, was she really asking so much? What if he chose one of the safer jobs, one of the ones he'd actually put to the bottom of his list because it would be so boring? Whatever went on between her and her husband, she had obviously suffered. Who could blame her for wishing to sever the ties with his family? Who would not honour her for wishing to be independent? If he managed the risk, would it be so wrong to take her, knowing that by doing so he was helping her fulfil a most worthwhile ambition? She had already proved herself reliable, capable. Wouldn't it be wrong *not* to take her?

'Elliot?'

'Does it really matter so much to you?'

'It's not just about the money. It's freedom, a chance to forget the past. To try to forget the past, at any rate. But it's my past, not yours. I should not have...'

'I'll take you.'

'Elliot!' Deborah's smile faded almost immediately. 'No, I can't let you. You're just feeling guilty because I've been so pathetic.'

'It's because you've not been pathetic and it's nothing to do with guilt.'

'I can't let you.'

'I want to.'

'No. You said yourself it would be too risky. What if I did something stupid?'

'You won't. I won't let you,' Elliot said, exasperated by her protestations, for now that he had decided, he had set his heart on it.

'I might, though. What if I cried out, or dropped something, or—?'

'For God's sake, Deborah, I'll take you! I want to take you!' Elliot exclaimed.

Annoyed to discover how much he wanted to, he pulled her towards him. She stumbled and his arms automatically went around her. She smelled of lavender. Her eyes were melting brown. Close up, they were rimmed with gold. A pulse beat wildly at the base of her throat. Her lips were the most seductive pink. He wanted to kiss her. The way she looked at him, she was expecting him to kiss her. Was this why he had agreed to do as she wished, for more of her kisses? No. *No!* There were other reasons. Plenty of reasons, though he couldn't remember them right at this moment, when the softness of her breasts pressed his chest, when he could feel her breath on his mouth.

'I want you.' She had not moved away. She'd made no attempt to free herself. 'I want you to come with me, I mean,' he said raggedly. 'If it means so much to you.'

'Yes.' Deborah's heart beat wildly. She wanted him to kiss her. She was so sure he would kiss her. She touched the scar which sliced his brow. He was so very male, yet it did not frighten her, merely heightened her own sense of being female. Jeremy had never—but Elliot was not Jeremy. 'If you're sure. I won't let you down.'

'I know you won't.' He kissed her then, but it was the

merest touch of his lips before he drew back. 'I don't want there to be any more misunderstandings between us,' he said. 'I did not agree to help you in return for your kisses.' A wicked smile teased the corners of his mouth. 'I do want your kisses, make no mistake about that, but only when you are ready to give them to me.'

Deborah shivered. She wanted to, but she was afraid. But she wanted to, despite the fact that she knew herself lacking in some essential ingredient which made other women desirable. Reluctantly, she stepped clear of Elliot's embrace. 'I understand,' she said tightly.

'Good,' Elliot replied, wondering if *he* did. Until he had met Deborah, he had considered himself rather well versed in the ways of women. Where other men declared roundly that they wished their wives or lovers would simply say what they wanted, Elliot relished feminine subtleties and nuances, the complexities and layers in women's language which made them so very different from his own sex. But Deborah was not so easily read. Had she wanted him to kiss her or not? Did she want him? He had no idea.

'Will you send me a note with the arrangements, as you did last time?' she asked, interrupting this rather frustrating chain of thought.

Elliot nodded. 'In a week or so. I've nothing planned yet, it takes time.'

'I could help you. I could help you with your reconnaissance, and your—whatever it is you do in your planning.'

'To put in your book?' he asked quizzically.

She hadn't been thinking of her book. 'Yes.' Deborah bit her lip. 'No. I mean I would like to with your permission, but that's not why I suggested it. I'd like to help. And I'd like to—to be with you. Because I want to.'

She said it so defiantly, tilted her chin at him in that way she had, that Elliot couldn't help laughing. 'Then I would like that, too,' he said.

'What is it you gentlemen say? We have a deal?'

'We have a deal,' Elliot replied, though he kissed the fingers she held out, rather than shaking them.

Watching from his doorstep as her cab rumbled over the cobbled streets in the direction of Hans Town, he realised that the fog of ennui which had accompanied him like a sodden pack of kit, all the way from London to Hampshire and back again, had now departed along with the bitter taste of rejection. There was no need, yet, to solve the thorny question of the future. Deborah had given him plenty of other things to think about.

She had been most coy with regards to her writing. He wished she could bring herself to confide in him, but he could not see the harm in failing to wait for her to do so. He poured himself a glass of Madeira and took a sip, rolling the wine around his mouth, enjoying the rich, fruity taste of it. It brought back an image, of a night at the royal palace in Lisbon, a ball, a dusky beauty, the scent of bougainvillea. So long ago, he felt as if the memory belonged to another person entirely.

Elliot took another sip of wine. So many times since the war had ended, he had wished himself back in those days, but right now, the present was much more interesting. The past was fading, dimming in comparison to the promise of the next few days. He finished his wine. His hand hovered over the decanter, but he decided against another. He had some digging to do and this kind of digging required a clear head.

Chapter Six

It was too dangerous for them both to reconnoitre, he told her when she suggested it. Though the job was a simple one, Elliot was thorough and Deborah was studious. They were poring over his sketches of the house and grounds together, papers and notes scattered over the polished table in his small dining room, when Lizzie came upon them.

They did not hear her at first; she had waved aside the servant's offer to announce her. Standing in the doorway, she watched them, the flaxen-haired stranger and her brother, looking younger and more carefree than she'd seen him for years. They were seated side by side. Elliot's arm lay on the table, almost but not quite brushing that of his companion. She was reading something, a frown making question marks of her fair brows, so deep in concentration that she didn't notice the way Elliot was looking at her. Lizzie's own brows shot up. She must have made a sound, for Elliot looked around, quickly gathered the scattered papers together and got to his feet.

'Lizzie. I wasn't expecting you.'

'Obviously not,' his sister said archly. 'Am I interrupting?'

'You know perfectly well that you are, else you would have allowed my man to show you into the parlour. Deborah, this is my sister, Mrs Alex Murray. Lizzie, this is Lady Kinsail, the Dowager Lady Kinsail.'

'How do you do?' Lizzie dropped a polite curtsy. *Widow,* she was thinking. *Kinsail. There was a scandal there. I must ask Alex. Not young. Twenty-six, seven? Not beautiful, but memorable.* 'I had no idea you and my brother were acquainted. He goes so little into society, I'm surprised that your paths have crossed.'

'How do you do? I would have known you for Elliot's—Mr Marchmont's sister without an introduction. You are very like.' Deborah eyed Lizzie's carriage dress enviously. Cherry red, with a deep border of black beading, a short velvet jacket with the tightly fitted sleeves finished with the same pattern of beadwork, it was very elegant. And its owner was very perceptive, she thought, tilting her chin under that lady's scrutiny. 'Elliot and I met through my late husband's cousin,' she said. 'Lord Kinsail—the current Lord Kinsail, that is—was of some assistance in a matter concerning the army.' She threw a mischievous look over her shoulder at Elliot, who was ushering them into the parlour, and regretted it instantly when it was intercepted by Lizzie, who was obviously just as sharp as her brother.

'I see.'

'I doubt it,' Elliot said drily. 'I suppose you'll want tea? I'll just go and see to it.'

'Lovely,' Lizzie said, sinking into her favourite sofa and patting the cushion beside her, giving Deborah no option but to sit at her side. 'I don't know if Elliot's told you, but I'm expecting and it's doing horrible things to me. My ankles swell. Do you have children, Lady Kinsail?'

'No. No I was not—we were not—no.'

'I'm sorry. I didn't mean to upset you.'

'It doesn't matter. And it's Deborah, please.'

'Lord, I hope I'm not going to turn into one of those bores who can talk of nothing but babies.' Lizzie cast aside her bonnet with the carelessness of one who had several more. 'I wasn't the least bit interested in them until I started increasing; now I find that little else interests me. It's as well I'm going to Scotland next month, else my reputation for wit will be quite spoiled. What was it that you and my brother were so anxious to hide from me?'

Deborah smiled. 'Your wits have not wandered very far yet. Why don't you ask Elliot?'

'Because he'll tell me to mind my own business, only he won't do it as politely as you. How long have you known him?'

'Not long.'

'He's kept you very quiet.'

'Perhaps because there's nothing to tell.'

Lizzie chuckled. 'Oh, have it your own way. I would

not have brooked any interference in my courtship either.'

'Mrs Murray…'

'Lizzie.'

'We are not—there is nothing of that nature between us. We are merely engaged upon a business venture.'

'Do you really think that? No, for you are blushing. This, let me tell you, is excellent news, for now I will be able to hide myself in the wilds of Scotland without worrying about my brother.'

'You must not be thinking…'

'Oh, don't worry, I shan't say anything,' Lizzie said airily, confining the list of eligibles she had drawn up in her head to the virtual flames. 'Besides, I would not dream of playing the matchmaker for Elliot,' she added, with a fine disregard for the truth.

'I doubt your brother needs anyone's help in attracting female company,' Deborah said.

'Now who is digging? There has been no one since he returned to England, so far as I am aware. Does that answer your question?'

'What question is that?' Elliot asked, kicking a small table into position in front of his sister and placing the tea tray upon it.'

'Deborah was asking me about Scotland,' Lizzie said.

He looked sceptical, but chose not to pursue the matter. Over tea, he watched with interest as Lizzie kept up a polite stream of chatter and gossip. Either Deborah was unaware of the lures being cast, or she was too careful to rise to them, for she expressed nothing other than polite interest in the names Lizzie dropped and claimed not a single one of her impressive list as acquaintances. His sister was baffled and Elliot was amused to see her so, even more amused when Deborah declined the invitation to call.

'I would not dream of intruding, when you will be so busy with your preparations,' she said politely but firmly, equally politely and firmly taking her leave alone.

'Don't hate her,' Elliot said, showing Deborah out. 'She does not mean to be interfering.'

Deborah chuckled. 'She does, but since she does it only because she cares for you, I could not possibly be offended. I liked her.'

'I thought you would,' Elliot said with satisfaction, though he knew Deborah well enough now not to press Lizzie's invitation further. 'Until tomorrow night, then? If you are sure?'

'You know I am.' Deborah's eyes gleamed with excitement. 'Until tomorrow, Elliot.'

She surprised him, standing on tiptoe to kiss his cheek. It was over before he could react and she was gone, tripping lightly down the steps in her faded gown and practical shawl, before he could stop her. Elliot watched her walking across the square. He could tell from the angle of her bonnet that she had her chin up—that haughty, touch-me-not look she used to repel strangers. Her walk was not seductive, but it was very feminine. Those long legs of hers covered the distance quickly.

'I like her.' Lizzie joined him on the step. She had put on her bonnet and was drawing on her gloves while signalling to her coachman, who had been walking the horses round the square. 'She's very unusual.'

'Yes.'

'Sad, too. There was gossip about the husband, you know.'

'What?'

'I wish I could remember. Do you want me to find out?'

'She'll tell me if she wants me to know.'

Lizzie raised her brows. 'That's not like you.'

'No.'

His sister threw him a look, but said nothing more.

Alone again, Elliot leafed through the plans he and Deborah had been studying. This last week had flown by. They had spent hours in each other's company, plotting and scheming. She was more relaxed with him now, but he was under no illusions. Any edging over the line from the general to the personal made her tense. She had a caustic wit, a sharp mind, an eye for detail, a head for numbers—he knew all those things about her. She'd written stories as a child. She'd told him some of them one rainy afternoon, mocking her younger self. He had the sense not to ask her outright what had changed her so dramatically, but she had seen the question in his eyes, clamming up straight away, refusing to recount any more.

Elliot began methodically to tear up the plans and feed them into the fire. They had served their purpose. Deborah's handwriting was surprisingly bad, an almost illegible scrawl. 'As if your pen cannot keep up with your thoughts,' Elliot had teased her when he'd first seen it and she'd laughed at that, telling him that was exactly it. 'I am amazed that Mr Freyworth can read it sometimes,' she'd said. A rare slip, which Elliot had pounced upon, secreted and used. It had not exactly been taxing, tracing her publisher from that snippet. More difficult was identifying her *nom de plume,* but he had his sources. He always had his sources.

'Though I wish to hell I didn't have to use them,' he exclaimed, casting the last of the paper into the flames. 'Why does she have to be so secretive?'

Why could she not trust him? Why would she not, just once, admit that she wanted to kiss him? Because he knew she did. Attraction crackled like lightning between them all the time, driving him mad with frustration, but he would not surrender to it until she did, he would not! A man had his pride. Though he was tempted, on occasion, to consign his to the flames with the plans.

The simple fact is that he wanted her more than he'd ever wanted any woman. It was because she was so stubborn, he told himself, that's all it was. Elliot used the poker to tamp down the fire. That wasn't all, he knew that, but it was all he was prepared to admit. He had more important matters to focus on right now. Like a housebreaking.

And after that? Elliot placed a fire screen over the hearth. He would think about after that when it happened.

It was twelve miles or more to Richmond. In the dark, travelling across country when they could, in an effort to avoid being noticed, Deborah focused all her attention on simply enjoying the ride. It was the one thing which made her visits to Kinsail Manor tolerable, having the run of the stables, the one privilege she was granted, and one of the things she missed most in London. Tonight, the freedom of her attire and the illicitness of their purpose added a delightful *frisson* to the shivering awareness of the man who rode beside her. Cloaked by the dark, she could admit to herself that Elliot's very presence was arousing. Her blood fizzed and sang in her veins. Her heart beat in time to the thunder of her horse's hooves. She felt truly alive.

Beside her, Elliot felt his mood swing between exhilaration and trepidation. He was as certain as it was possible to be that there were no flaws in their plan. A straightforward break-in, an old-fashioned safe, servants' quarters located in a remote attic, a proprietor forced to retire from Government service because even with the aid of his ear trumpet he could hear nothing quieter than a bellow. Such a simple, failsafe task, that under other circumstances he would have scorned it for the lack of challenge.

As they made their way around the perimeter of a field hedged with hawthorn, Deborah's horse snickered as a rodent of some sort ran across their path. She held it effortlessly back from bolting and Elliot managed to restrain himself just in time from laying his hand on her bridle. She was a consummate horsewoman. When he'd thrown her into the saddle tonight, he'd seen that tinge of anticipation in her face, sensed that edginess in her which was so familiar to him.

His response had been a stab of nerves. Normally, he did not consider failure. Tonight it worried him, the risks he was taking, the safety of the woman by his side, who never gave it a thought. The field gave way to a narrow lane. Soft and muddy from the recent rains, it muffled the sound of their hooves. 'Five minutes and we'll be at the main gate,' Elliot said softly. 'You remember all?'

He caught the flash of Deborah's smile in the gloom. Quietly, but succinctly, she recited the plan. Just before they reached the gatehouse, they came to a halt and dismounted, tethering the horses in the shelter of a line of poplars. 'I don't suppose there's any point in my suggesting you wait here?' he said.

Deborah shrugged out of her greatcoat. Her heart was beginning to beat more erratically. Her excitement had the jagged edge of fear. She'd forgotten that from the first time, but she shook her head at Elliot as she threw her coat over her horse. 'I think you know the answer to that question.'

He caught her hand. Like him, she'd taken off her gloves. Her fingers fluttered in his. 'Deborah, you must promise me, if we are discovered...'

'I am to run as fast as I can without waiting for you,' she said. 'I've already promised. What's wrong—surely the infallible Peacock is not nervous? You said yourself that this was a simple job.'

'I know what I said. But if any harm came to you…' His hands tightened on hers.

'It won't.' Without thinking, she stood on her tiptoes in her topboots and kissed him on the cheek. His skin was cool. He tasted of fresh air and sweat. Alerted by the sharp intake of his breath, she realised her lips had lingered a fraction of a second too long, her body had strayed just a fraction of an inch too close. Awareness flashed, brief as a shooting star. She stepped away. The crack of a branch snapping under her boot made her start, and her start made her realise that fear had the edge. She took a deep breath. Focus. She tucked her hair behind her ear. Focus.

Elliot consulted his pocketwatch. Deborah crammed her hat down over her hair. His expression was remote, closed, intimidating. Intent. Her fear ebbed. 'If things go to plan, we should be back here in under an hour,' he said.

'They will,' Deborah replied, gathering up her courage like petticoats around her. 'Stop worrying.'

He hadn't counted on the dog. How had he missed its existence? Though he'd hardly call the thing a dog. To Elliot's eyes it looked like a rug with paws. In fact, were it not for the high-pitched yapping nose which emitted from somewhere under the heavy fringe of fur, it would have been impossible to tell which end of the creature was which. It came at them from its bed in front of the fire, which had long since died, in the library which also contained the safe. Elliot cursed and made a lunge for it, then cursed again as a pair of extremely sharp incisors sank into the fleshy pad of his thumb. It was Deborah who managed to catch the incensed canine, smothering its yelps with her hat, hugging the wriggling body tight against her, muttering soothing clucking noises that, to Elliot's astonishment, had some sort of mesmerising effect.

One minute, two minutes, three. He counted tensely as they waited, all three of them, behind the window curtains. On five, they moved. His heart was hammering. He dropped a pick. The soft tinkle of thin wire on the boards made Deborah glance towards the door through which they had come. She was struggling with the dog. The lock gave way with a soft click. Though he never hurried, he hurried now, raking through the contents, finding the neat little box of lacquered wood. A quick check inside, then it was tucked into his pocket and they were back out in the long hallway. By the light of the lamp which burned there, he caught a glimpse of Deborah's face. She was biting down on a laugh. Down the stairs, through the baize door, into the kitchens they fled, the dog loosed from her hat now, making energetic attempts to free itself, whimpering and yelping.

'I can't hold it much longer,' Deborah said as they reached the basement window. 'I'm sorry, Elliot, it's more ferret than canine.' She was shaking with muf-

fled laughter now. 'What are we going to do, kidnap
it? I doubt anyone in their right mind would pay a ran-
som for this thing.'

'We'll take it with us part of the way, then release
it. It will find its own way back, don't worry.' Elliot
climbed out of the window, jumped the three feet to the
ground, then held up his hands. The dog, astonished into
temporary silence, flopped into them and then bit him
again. He cursed under his breath. Two long legs—he
tried not to look at those long legs—and Deborah arrived beside him. 'Run,' he said, taking her hand.

They ran at full tilt. At some point before they
reached the gate, the dog escaped and fled in the opposite direction, back towards the house, making enough
noise to raise the dead. Deborah was flagging, but Elliot pulled her on remorselessly, throwing her into the
saddle almost before she had her greatcoat around her.
She was off before he had gathered up his own reins,
down the path at speed, careless of ruts and rabbit holes.

They were halfway back to town, travelling along
the river, before he felt it was safe enough to slow down.
Great clouds of steam rose from the flanks of the horses.
He could see Deborah's breath. His own chest was heav-
ing. Elliot reined in beside a small boathouse. 'We'll let
the horses rest here awhile.'

Deborah dismounted fluidly. 'You'd have thought the
hounds of hell were after us,' she said, laughing between
trying to catch her breath. Her hat was gone. Her hair
rippled like moonlight on the dark wool of her greatcoat.

'I wouldn't call that damned creature a hound, but it was definitely hellish,' Elliot replied, looking ruefully at his bitten thumb.

'So the Peacock is not so infallible after all.'

Her voice was teasing. She was smiling, quite transformed from her daytime self. Elliot felt as Pygmalion must have done, seeing Galatea come to life. 'Flawed,' he said, clutching theatrically at his chest. 'Alack, my feet of clay have been discovered.'

'I think we both have feet of clay.' Deborah looked ruefully down at her mud-clogged boots. A soft breeze fluttered through the willow which wept into the deceptively still waters of the Thames, making her shiver, for she had once again thrown her coat over her horse.

'We can wait in here while the horses cool down.'

Elliot pushed open the door of the boathouse. Inside, it smelled of oiled rope, dried sailcloth and damp wood. He lit the lantern which he always carried with him. The flame cast a soft glow around the narrow building. Through the slats in the wooden floor, they could hear the water shushing against the stilts. The boat, some sort of decorative barge, took up most of the available space. He stepped into it and held out his hand to help her.

Deborah climbed over the wooden edge, sitting down next to him on the cushioned seat built into the stern and it was there, suddenly and indisputably, between them. Awareness. The air resonated with it. Awareness of the kisses they had been avoiding, the desire they had been ignoring. Everything seemed sharpened by it. The smell of the boathouse, the sound of the water, her breathing, her heartbeat, her pulses. Her skin prickled with longing. She had to make a physical effort to keep herself from creeping towards Elliot, close enough to touch. 'May I see our spoils?' Even her voice sounded strange.

The box he placed on his knee was small, like a cigar box, only ornately lacquered, inlaid with gold. 'Japanese,' Elliot said. Deborah's breeches were stretched tight across her legs. Her knee was inches away from his. He concentrated on the box, fiddling with his most delicate pick at the lock, trying not to think about the way her presence intoxicated him. He hadn't planned this, had conscientiously avoided even thinking about afterwards, but now here it was, and it was the same— more—than that first time. Was he imagining that she felt it too, simply because it was what he wanted?

The box opened. Deborah's hair brushed his shoulder as she leaned over to get a closer look and their eyes clashed. Their breath hitched. There was no mistaking it, though they both instantly dropped their gazes to the box. Desire, clear and sharp.

'Are they what we were expecting?' Deborah asked. 'Miniature carvings, you said. Ivory set with precious stones. Unusual, you said.'

'So I was told.'

'By your sources,' she agreed with a quick smile. 'May I see?'

The box was inlaid with velvet. Elliot removed the covering layer of cloth. There were ten figures, set in two rows of five. Deborah picked one out, frowning, turning it over in her hand. A diamond caught the light. Only then did Elliot realise what they had stolen. Deborah's eyes widened as she examined the detailed, highly skilled carving. A woman. Naked. Astride a naked man. 'Good grief,' she exclaimed.

'I was told they were idols,' Elliot said, fascinated by the way her fingers caressed the ivory, tracing the outlines of the figures, trying desperately not to think of those same fingers touching him so intimately.

'I think this one has been broken at some point. See, the woman is not quite fixed.' She pulled gently, and the ivory carvings separated. 'Oh!' The male figure lay on his back in the palm of her hand, quite undamaged and extremely true to nature. She traced the exaggerated length of manhood which had joined the couple with her fingertip and shivered. The expression on the figure's face was not lascivious, but rather ecstatic. The woman, too, now she looked at it.

She picked it up from where it had fallen on the cushion between them and slotted the two back together again. The movement was sleek. She hadn't meant to look at Elliot, but she couldn't stop herself; when she did, her belly clenched at the way his eyes blazed down at her. 'Are they all like this?'

'Variations on a theme,' Elliot said in a voice that sounded strangled.

'Let me see.'

He handed her the box. She ran her fingers over the carvings, an orgy of copulating couples, all created with the same attention to detail as the first. She selected first one, then another, turning them over in her palm, detaching them and then sliding each together, obviously fascinated. Though some of the positions portrayed, in Elliot's opinion, did not merit the challenge of their execution, none was new to him. In fact, the set was actually relatively tame compared to some he had seen.

Deborah, however, seemed to find almost every variation novel. Her face was rapt. He wished she would look at him like that. He wanted her to touch *him*, not some ivory carving. He wanted to slide inside her, certain that they would fit together even more perfectly than the little Japanese idols.

Slotting a female back into position beneath her lover, Deborah shivered again. None of Bella Donna's couplings had the sensual quality portrayed here. Bella's pleasure was to dominate, subjugate, control. But these figures looked as if they were in a state of bliss. 'Do you think—are they all possible?' she asked doubtfully.

Elliot hesitated, taken aback by the innocence of her question. 'Certainly they're all possible. Whether they are all worth the effort is another question.' Deborah stared at him wide-eyed. She seemed more intrigued than shocked. Did she have any idea what an invitation her interest was? 'The set was obviously made as a marriage gift,' Elliot explained.

'I wish someone had given *me* such a gift,' Deborah said. 'Have *you* tried—oh God, don't answer that, I can't believe…'

'Yes, I have. All of them.' Elliot took the ivory from her and put it back in the box, making no attempt to hide the wicked curve to his smile. 'And before you ask, no, I didn't particularly enjoy them all.'

'Oh.'

Elliot pulled her closer. 'But I'd be willing to try them again,' he whispered into her ear, 'just to satisfy your curiosity, you understand. If you wanted me to.' He nibbled on the lobe of her ear, then kissed his way down the column of her neck to the collar of her shirt.

Deborah's heart was racing, a mixture of excitement and fear. *Could she?* She had broken into a house in the middle of the night. She had assisted in a safebreaking and, what's more, she'd managed to shut that damned dog up. She was in an unlocked boathouse in the middle of nowhere with a man she had been fantasising about since first he fell out of the night and landed on top of her. *Could she?*

'Deborah?'

She laughed and threw her arms around his neck. 'Just kiss me, Elliot.'

He pulled her to him and did just that. His lips were like a feather abrading her skin. He pulled her closer and she sighed, letting the tip of her tongue touch his, drinking in the heat, the scent, the reassuringly solid maleness of him. He sank backwards on to the cushioned bench, taking her with him. She lay over him now, her breasts crushed to his chest, the hard length of his erection pressed into the soft flesh of her belly. So hard. So different. Everything about him was so different.

His kiss deepened. She pressed herself into the unyielding strength of his body and kissed him back, relishing the tightening of his hands on her waist, the way his lips clung to hers, his tongue plundered her mouth, relishing the way he was so very male, the way he made her feel so very female. Their kisses were lush, like ripe fruit. Then deeper kisses, edged with desperation.

Elliot pulled her astride him. 'I want to see you,' he said raggedly, running his hand down her arms, tugging at her coat. 'Curves. Skin. So lovely. I want to see.'

Her coat was cast overboard. Elliot's followed. Then his waistcoat. His eyes were hungry on her as he pulled her shirt free of her breeches, his fingers dealing efficiently with the buttons, pulling it over her head, his eyes blazing as he looked, drinking in her naked flesh. The way he looked was unbelievably rousing. His eyes feasted on her, gloried in her, as if he could never have enough of her. It was incredibly empowering, overcoming any trace of embarrassment.

'So much better than dreams,' he said, flattening his palm over her breasts, down the curve of her waist. 'So much better than in your hallway in the dark.' His mouth curved into a sensual smile that made all her muscles clench. 'So very, very lovely.'

He fastened his mouth to her nipple and sucked deep. Jolting heat, like a streak of light connected straight to the fire in her belly, to the tension knotting there, and lower. Elliot growled as she writhed, holding her still, his lips suckling, licking, teasing more and more heat from first one nipple, then the other, until she was in a frenzy of need and want.

Deborah tugged ineffectively at his shirt. Impatiently, he pulled it over his head and cast it aside. She touched him, warm skin, rough hair on his chest arrowing down to the dip of his stomach. His muscles flexed as he breathed, his breathing became shallower, faster, as she touched him, as he touched her, his eyes fierce on hers.

'I want you.'

She did not doubt him. Could not. And she wanted him, too, painfully, achingly, in a quite alien, wholly adult way she could not have imagined. 'Yes,' she said. 'Yes.'

He pulled her to him with a ruthless kiss, rolling her under him, blazing a trail of kisses down to her breasts, then more kisses, licking, rousing kisses, nipping, plucking kisses, until she was so hot she could not bear it, and more kisses, until they were no longer enough.

When he unbuttoned the fall of her breeches, slipping his hand inside, stroking down her belly, she cried out. Down he stroked, to the soft flesh at the top of her thigh, over the curls at the apex, then the other thigh. She moaned again and dug her nails into his back, arching up for him. She was tense, tight, knotted, but she could feel the knot fraying under his insistent caresses, his mouth, his fingers, the scent of him and the weight of him. He shifted slightly, lifted his head from her breast, muffling her instinctive cry of protest with his mouth, a deep plunging kiss, shadowed by the stroking, slipping, sliding plunge of his fingers into the damp, hot flesh of her sex.

The knot inside her tightened. It was not the first time, for she had of necessity learned how to take solitary pleasure, but it had never been like this. This was not just a release. This was no panacea. This was different. Wildly different. A slow climb, the pleasure in the climb itself, so pleasurable that she did not want to reach her destination. Not yet. She clenched and tried to hold on. Not yet. But Elliot's tongue plundered her mouth as his fingers thrust, and stroked and slid. She was slipping.

'Let go,' he said, his voice guttural in her ear, his touch purposeful, stroking harder, faster, until she thought she would die of anticipation, until she could hold on no more and let go, muffling her cries in his shoulder, shaking with the force of her climax, clinging, panting, shocked beyond measure.

Elliot held her fast, a surge of blood making the ache between his legs almost unbearable. Abandonment. Ecstasy. Just exactly as he had imagined, only more. He kissed her hair. She clung to him, burrowing against him, her cheek pressed into his chest. Then her lips on his skin. Then she slipped her hand into the tight space between them and touched him through his breeches. A tentative touch, but enough to make the blood surge. She fumbled with the buttons which fastened his breeches. He yanked them free, wriggled clear of them, kneeling on the floor of the barge beside her to do so.

Deborah pushed herself upright. Elliot was much bigger than what she had seen of Jeremy. And so hard. Jeremy had never been so—he had always had to—but

Elliot's erection seemed to have a life of its own, jutting up, thick and curved. She wanted to touch him, but she was afraid to. When she'd touched Jeremy…

She didn't want to remember. Desperately, Deborah tried to push back the memories, but they were gaining strength now and her courage was wilting as surely as Jeremy's manhood. This was different. Elliot was different, she told herself, but still she couldn't make her hand move towards him. The very fact that she wanted to touch him so much made failure too terrifying to contemplate. Her confidence, the fizz of her climax, the wild excitement of the night fled, leaving her utterly deflated. Deborah edged away, huddling into the corner of the barge. 'I'm sorry. I'm sorry, I just can't.'

The suddenness of her retreat left Elliot stunned. 'Can't?' he repeated, trying to make sense of the word, trying to understand how the flagrant goddess with her pale hair tumbling over full breasts, the nipples rosy, pink as her sex, could be so quickly transformed into this timid creature. 'Did I hurt you? Have I frightened you? I didn't mean…'

'No, it's me. I shouldn't have—I thought I could, but I can't. I'm so sorry, Elliot.'

He was aching with need. She was so hot. So wet. So ready for him. What had he done to deserve that tight white face, the obvious fear in those big eyes? Realising that he was still blatantly hard and pointlessly naked, Elliot scrabbled for his clothes, quickly pulling on his shirt and breeches, handing Deborah hers before sitting down to pull on his boots.

Beside him, Deborah was shaking, struggling into her waistcoat. 'Here, let me,' Elliot said, fastening the buttons. A tear plopped on to his hand. 'Can't you tell me?'

She shook her head.

'I thought you wanted to.'

'I can't.' Deborah sniffed, wiping her eyes on the sleeve of her shirt.

'Will you tell me why?'

'I can't.' Deborah drew a shaky breath. 'I thought I could—but I shouldn't have. I shouldn't have—I should have stopped you, but you made me feel—and then I thought—but I shouldn't have. We should go, before the horses take a chill.' She pushed him aside to drag on her boots, stumbling out of the boat.

'Damn and blast the horses to hell!' Elliot exclaimed, catching her by the shoulders. 'What the hell went on in that marriage of yours to do this to you? Look at you, you're shaking.'

'You're angry. You're right to be angry. It's my fault. I'm sorry.' It had always been her fault. What a fool she was to think that this time would be any different. Another tear slipped down her cheek. Deborah blinked frantically. A storm of emotions was gathering in her breast that she didn't want Elliot to see. She didn't want them to overwhelm her, not like this, so she did the only thing she knew how. She blanked out everything. She pictured herself as a stone, hard and glittering and untouchable. It was difficult, much more difficult than she remembered, but she'd had years and years of practice. 'We should go.'

'Is that it? You're not even going to explain?'

'I can't. I'm sorry.' Deborah forced open the boat-house door.

'Dammit, stop saying you're sorry.' Elliot stormed out after her. She already had her greatcoat on and was untying her horse. Her face was set. Elliot watched her, fighting a desire to shake the truth out of her, or kiss the truth out of her, or just kiss her. What was going on in that mind of hers? 'Deborah…'

'I just want to go home. Please don't ask me to explain because I can't. It was a mistake. Please, Elliot, just let me go home.'

He had no option but to mount his horse and follow her. They rode in silence all the way back to London. By the time he bid her goodnight, her stony face and determined silence had provoked his temper and roused his pride. He bid her a curt goodbye.

Chapter Seven

Deborah took up her pen early the next morning because she didn't want to think about last night, and because she couldn't stop thinking about last night. She had to finish her book. She eyed the blank page with a weary eye, having dragged herself from her bed, exhausted by dreams of running and falling, falling and running. She had to finish it. Her book meant freedom and freedom meant—she would think about that later.

She worked frantically after that, driven by the vision of liberty. She wrote, laughing as she recalled the dog, transformed in her story to a sleeker, more vicious version of itself. She wrote on the next day, too, and when tiredness made her head ache, her wrist throb, her fingers too numb to keep the quill upright, still she carried on, until she came to what Mr Freyworth called the aftermath and her pen skittered to a halt.

She could not believe it had been her, that abandoned creature in the boathouse. The soaring, falling-apart feeling of her climax still had the power to make her shiver with delight. Bella's climaxes were gloating, triumphal, a powerful metaphor for victory, but that's all they were. Bella might be technically proficient, but she took her pleasure rather clinically. For the first time in their shared history, Deborah felt she had the upper hand.

Elliot would smile at that piece of convoluted logic. Guilt and longing made her close her eyes. For just a moment, Deborah allowed herself the indulgence of conjuring him. The taste of him. The feel of him. The scent of him. The sheer, undeniable maleness of him. The way he looked at her, touched her. For a while, in the boathouse, she had been happy in her own skin, glad to be Deborah, because Elliot desired her. And then she had spoilt it. Most likely ruined it.

How could she have expected anything else, with seven years' worth of failure stacked up against her? But she had. She had believed it would be different, until she allowed Jeremy back into her head. Jeremy had shaped her far too well and, until she broke the mould he had made for her, it would never be different, she realised with a sickening flash of insight. He was dead, but he haunted her still.

Until now, the idea of being emotionally frozen had been an attractive one. Without feelings she could not be hurt. Why was she being so contrary? she wondered, chewing on the end of her quill, because, despite the fact that she knew it would have been disastrous, she couldn't help wishing that she had made love to Elliot.

Made love! What the devil did she know about that!

Nothing—nor was she ever likely to. But she knew enough now to imagine, didn't she? And if she could imagine, then Bella could experience, couldn't she? Deborah took up her pen with renewed determination.

Less than a week later, she delivered the revised manuscript to Mr Freyworth's office and staggered home, numb with tiredness. She went straight to bed, but sleep would not come. She had hoped that allowing Bella to spread her emotional wings would be cathartic. Instead, it seemed to have effected some sort of internal rebellion. The past, which had been kept at bay for two long years, was escaping through the gate which her writing had unwittingly opened. Memories crowded her mind, a host of stalking animals, vying miserably for her attention.

Deborah paced the floor of her darkened bedchamber, the curtains drawn against the afternoon light, her hair in tangled hanks where she had repeatedly twisted it around her fingers. This should be the first day of her freedom, yet Jeremy's ghost was gathering strength, his taunts pounding out a horribly familiar rhythm in her head.

She had misled him. She had ruined him. She was cold. She was so repulsive that she unmanned him. She was not even a woman, but a barren piece of marble. No wonder he took to the tables in search of comfort. No wonder his friends shunned him. He should never have married her. He had never loved her. He despised her. She had ruined his life. He should never have married her. Never have married her. Never.

Deborah threw herself on to the bed and buried her head under the pillow, screwing her eyes tight shut, but Jeremy wouldn't leave her alone. 'It wasn't my fault,' she said aloud, swallowing a sob, but her voice lacked conviction. She curled up into a ball, wrapping her arms tight around her chest, willing the voice to leave her be. She tried to blank her mind. She tried to rock herself to sleep, buried deep under the blankets, but unconsciousness retreated even further. Scenes, long-forgotten scenes, replayed themselves. Snippets of their life together flickered through her mind's eye like the pages of a hellish scrapbook.

Handsome Jeremy sweeping her off her feet. His kisses were chaste. The perfect gentleman, she'd thought him.

Their wedding night. Jeremy's concern for her innocence. He loved her too much to hurt her, he told her. He loved her too much to subject her to base desire, he said.

And there she was, younger and infinitely naïve, plucking up the courage to take the initiative after too many chaste nights, innocently pressing herself against her husband's body. Were she an artist, she could still capture that instinctive flash of revulsion on his face after all this time.

The messy, unsatisfactory fumbles which followed, eventually carrying her over the threshold from maiden to wife, merged and morphed one into the other, none memorable, all unforgettable. Ignorant and embarrassed, still enough in love to deny her disappointment, Deborah watched herself turn again and again from the look of shame on her husband's face as he touched himself.

An angry scene when her uncle refused to advance her inheritance. A furious one later, when Uncle Peter would not be persuaded. Jeremy's wit, which she had loved, turned cruelly upon her. The pain, still raw, of that moment of revelation from which there was no turning back. Not Deborah, but her inheritance. Not love, but money.

Coldness then, months and years of it. Their marriage a stark, barren country neither wished to inhabit. Jeremy never kissed her. He never touched her, save for during those shameful couplings, always in the dark, her on all fours, her husband fumbling first with himself, then her. The undisguised revulsion on his face when she turned around to look at him. After that, she was glad of the dark.

And then the last time. Deborah curled her knees up to her chest, trying to make herself as small as possible. The last time. She closed her eyes, leaning back against the headboard, forcing herself to remember. It came back to her in stark detail, as if it were a play which had been waiting for the curtain to go up.

Jeremy threw himself from the bed, still clad in his shirt, his utter lack of arousal painfully obvious even in the dim light of the bedchamber. Bruised and aching, her flesh cringing at the very notion of trying again, Deborah sat up, forcing herself to smile, a pastiche of allure. She'd wanted him once. If she could want him again, she could make it right.

She'd studied the books she'd discovered hidden behind a rare complete set of the Encyclopédie. *Fascinated and ashamed, she had perused them, learning from the luridly explicit illustrations just how limited her experience was. Telling herself it was worth the mortification to save her marriage, she touched her breasts, mimicking the drawings. Jeremy's face took on a greenish tint before it became an angry red.*

The shock of his fist sent her flying back on to the pillows. Blood stained her fingers when she touched her cheek. 'You hit me.' The words came from far away. This wasn't happening to her. 'What have I done to make you hate me so, Jeremy?'

'You married me.'

'I loved you.'

He gave her a hard look. 'Five years we've been married and you still don't have a clue, do you? You never loved me. Poor little orphan Debbie, you were just desperate for a bit of attention,' Jeremy sneered. 'God, you made it so easy. You more or less pulled the wool over your own eyes.'

'That's not true,' Deborah argued, though what he said had an ominous ring to it. 'I did love you. I thought you loved me.'

'All I ever loved about you was your money.'

'And you've had that, you've had all of it now, even if you did have to wait for my majority. Jeremy...' Deborah plucked at the sheet, willing herself to speak, know-

*ing that if she did not, she never would. 'In all the time
we have been married, things have not been—we have
not been—I've been wondering if this failure of ours
was the reason we have not been blessed with a child.'*

*'Failure!' Jeremy cursed bitterly. 'If there has been
any failing, it has not been for want of trying on my
part. Do you think I enjoy poking away at that soft
flesh of yours?'*

*Deborah shrank at the viciousness of his look, but
five long years of pointed barbs and cutting accusa-
tions, five years of blaming herself for failing to arouse
him, five years of guilt and frustration, watching her
romantic dreams fade, seeing herself transformed into
this empty shell—all of this coupled with her new-found
knowledge for the first time made her angry rather than
ashamed. 'I know perfectly well that you don't, you've
made it quite clear from the first. I disgust you, I always have and I want to know why. What is so wrong
with me?'*

*For the tiniest of moments, when she saw that bleak
look on his face, she felt sorry for him. Then his laughter cut through her pity, bitter and sharp. 'I find you
physically repulsive, my dear wife, because that is what
you are. Look at you, playing the harlot in the vain
hope that it will make me want you. The extent of your
naïvety astounds me. Can you not see what is obvious
to half the* ton? *You could never please me, no matter
how many tricks you learned. My tastes are quite beyond your ken, my dear wife. I've never wanted you.
Your only attraction for me was your money and I have*

*done with that.' Jeremy pulled on his breeches and gath-
ered up the rest of his clothes. 'I have done with you. I
am quite sick of you and the pretence of our marriage.'*

*'You wish us to separate?' A flicker of hope sprung
in Deborah's breast, for it was what she had sadly concluded was the only solution if tonight failed. And tonight had failed spectacularly.*

*Jeremy laughed again. 'No, that form of satisfaction
I will also spare you. I won't give the tabbies any more
ammunition. Having the protection of a wife, even one
such as you, is still something. Since it is quite obvious
that my efforts to overcome my distaste for your flesh
are never going to result in an heir—another thing
you have denied me—then I see no reason to make any
more attempts. I am going back to London now. You
can remain here at Kinsail Manor. To be honest, if I
never see you again it will be too soon. I wish you joy
of your isolation.'*

Deborah opened her eyes and found she was rocking
herself on the bed, her lashes wet with tears. Her face
burned, the kind of burning that comes from cold skin
on snow. It was so painful to watch, that little ghost of a
person who had been too foolish, too alone, too insecure
to stand up for herself. Was she born to be a victim?

But she had struck back, for Bella Donna had been
conceived that night, the only child of their barren
union. Her birth, several months later, was a small, secret act of revenge to heat the icy wastes of their marriage bed. But Bella Donna was a panacea, not a cure.
When Jeremy died, she'd thought that was the solution.

Deborah forced herself to uncurl, getting stiffly to her feet. Her heart was thudding, her body clammy with sweat. Her head ached. She hadn't seen Jeremy again. He had died in his sleep not long after, thanks to a lethal mixture of brandy and laudanum. They told her he'd looked peaceful and she had clung to that, just as she had clung to the certainty that the overdose had been accidental. Whatever his problems, Jeremy would never have shamed the Kinsail name with any hint of suicide. Besides, if he'd meant to kill himself, she was pretty certain he'd have chosen a gun or a riding accident. If there was an explanation for the many contradictions in her husband's behaviour, not least his determination to keep her officially tied to him, he had taken it to his grave.

Night had fallen. With shaking fingers, Deborah eventually managed to strike a light from the tinderbox for her candle. This life she had formed for herself since, it was not really a sanctuary but a cell, and of her own making. A prison, the bars she had erected to protect herself serving only to emphasise her loneliness. She could see that now. Elliot had made her see that and, thanks to Elliot, she was ready to make the first step towards confronting it, too.

Today, she had finished her story. If Mr Freyworth was right, it would give her freedom. The thought kindled warmth in her toes. Perhaps tomorrow she would write to some of her old friends. She was ready now to breach the gap she had allowed her marriage to wedge between them.

And Elliot? Deborah plumped up her pillows and clambered back into bed. *Oh, Elliot.* How she wished she had known him when she was whole. How much she wished she was not broken, but she was. She could patch herself up, and she could try to find some form of contentment, but she could never be anything other than alone. Perhaps the distance of time would make the past fade, but some things would never heal. Her one foray into love had damaged her and the scars were permanent.

The way Elliot had made her feel was beyond anything and far too much. It frightened her, but the idea of losing him from her life for ever frightened her more. She didn't want to retreat back into the gloom in which she existed before she knew him, but tempting, terrifyingly tempting as it was to continue down the path they had taken together in the boathouse, she knew it would be wrong.

She would fail him and then he would have every cause to despise her. She had to find a new path. Surely there must be some way to forge a friendship which was not so intimate? If she could manage to incorporate repaying him for what he had done for her, too, that would be even better. Happily deluding herself by focusing on this knotty problem, Deborah fell asleep.

'You've made up your mind, then? Elizabeth will be pleased.' Alexander Murray swallowed the remnants of his sherry and put the glass back down carefully on the table at his side. His appearance was as reticent as his temper. Neither tall nor short, fat nor thin, his hair was what his doting wife liked to call strawberry blonde and most others would—rather more accurately—describe as ginger. His pale complexion had an unfortunate tendency to freckle in the sun. Alexander was not the kind of man who stood out in a crowd and nor would he wish to.

Despite which, he had a business acumen second to none. In the City, he was known as The Oracle. In the rather more recondite world of Government financing, to which he lent his considerable expertise in considerable secrecy, he was revered. His position as one of the fast-growing Empire's unofficial bankers made Alexander's rather large ears privy to a wealth of information, most of it unwelcome, a very little of it useful, and some of it downright distasteful to his Scots sensibilities. 'I see the Peacock has been up to his tricks again,' he said.

Across from him, Elliot managed to disguise his surprise at the sudden change of subject with a relaxed smile. 'Yes, you have to almost admire the devil. He's clearly smart.'

'More than that. I would say he was driven.'

Elliot raised an enquiring brow. 'Why do you say that?'

'The press concentrate on the crime, of course, but it seems to me that there is a pattern forming in terms of the victims.'

'Really? Do elaborate.'

Alexander beetled his rust-coloured brows. 'They

all are, or were, involved in some way with the armed forces. It strikes me that this Peacock fellow might be a military man with an axe to grind.'

'I see.' Elliot was not one of those fooled by his brother-in-law's unassuming ways but he had, it seemed, underestimated him none the less. 'Have you shared this interesting theory with anyone?'

'Of course not. I have no desire to play the blood-hound,' Alexander said contemptuously.

'Then why are you telling me?'

'You're an ex-soldier, I thought you might have an opinion. Come on, man, don't look so surprised. Your views on how the men were treated are well known. I would imagine you might even be sympathetic to the Peacock's cause.'

'I heartily approve of his choice of victims, if that's what you mean. A more deserving bunch of miscreants I cannot imagine.'

'Aye, but my point is, would a regular soldier know that?' Alex steepled his fingers. 'I mean, some of the things taken—that diamond of Kinsail's, for example,' he said airily, 'you'd need insider information to know it even existed.'

'Insider information which you are obviously privy to,' Elliot said drily. 'I saw no report of a diamond in the newspaper.'

Alexander smiled ruefully. 'No, Kinsail kept that to himself, but it was the Peacock all the same. How would such a fellow come by that kind of information, do you think? If you ask me, this Peacock was involved in espionage.'

Elliot shrugged.

'You worked as a spy for the Government during the war, did you not?'

'What the deuce are you trying to imply?' Elliot asked impatiently.

'Lizzie would break her wee heart if anything happened to you,' Alexander said, his face becoming grim. 'I love that lassie. What she sees in me I don't know, but whatever it is, I'm eternally grateful. I won't have her upset, you understand me?'

'You have no cause to worry.'

'Aye, but I do worry, Elliot,' Alexander said with a sigh. 'I need your word.'

'I've said, you've no cause to worry.'

The basilisk look made Alexander swallow the words of protest he had been about to utter. It was easy to see what it was that had made the man such a fine soldier. 'I'm relieved to hear it. She's fretting about you, you know.'

'She has no reason to. Have you set a date for going north yet? Lizzie tells me that she's set on having that bairn of yours born in the ancestral home.'

'Did she?' Alexander's face softened. 'She's a wee darling, that sister of yours. I'm a lucky man.'

Discovering somewhat to his surprise that he agreed, for domesticity had never appealed to him, Elliot got to his feet to show his brother-in-law to the door. He was restless after his guest left. These last few days, he'd managed to occupy himself with disposing of the ivory figurines, paying overdue calls on friends, attending conscientiously to the little business his efficient bailiff sent his way. Avoiding thinking, in other words, he now admitted to himself as he prowled aimlessly from one room to another. Avoiding thinking, because he didn't know what to think, a state of mind to which he was wholly unaccustomed.

Elliot threw himself into the most uncomfortable chair in his book room and stared at a speck of dust on his Hessians. He still couldn't quite believe what had happened. To be so close. She had been reaching out to touch him. Just thinking about it made him sweat, and he'd thought about it a lot. What the hell had gone wrong? She had been so—and he had been so—*oh God!*

He got to his feet and flicked, unseeing, through the account book which lay open on his desk. It would have been mind-blowing. He drummed his fingers on the desk. He couldn't doubt that she'd wanted him there in the boathouse, he couldn't doubt the passion which flushed her cheeks, her breasts.

Her breasts. Elliot groaned. Dammit! *What the hell had happened in that marriage of hers?* It went against the grain, but he wished he'd asked Lizzie to sniff out the scandal. Ha! As if he'd have listened! The packet of books his source had delivered three days ago remained unopened in the drawer of his nightstand. Deborah's books. Which, despite the odds, he still hoped she'd trust him enough to tell him about herself.

Elliot picked up his letter opener and began methodically to slice through the topmost sheet of paper on the blotting pad. Why was he being so persistent? Why was giving up so impossible to contemplate? Despite the time they had spent together, in many ways Deborah was still an enigma and he was always a man who liked a challenge. Was that it? And if he succeeded in getting her to tell him her story, what then?

He slid the letter opener back into its holder. He didn't know. And he didn't need to think about it, because he hadn't succeeded yet. No point in worrying about the step after the next one, he told himself, blithely ignoring the fact that planning subsequent steps right to an end point had been his lifetime's *modus operandi*. He would give her time to finish that book of hers. She would realise she owed him an explanation. Sooner or later it would dawn on her that if she didn't, he would accuse her of using him merely to get her Peacock story.

Had she? Had she thought to pay him with sex, and then been unable to go through with it? For an appalling moment, Elliot considered this, dismissing it with immense relief. She wasn't capable of such guile. She would come round, he had only to be patient. Until then, what he needed was to do something practical with his time.

Relieved to be spared any further navel-contemplating, Elliot decided to pay a visit to Jackson's Salon in the hope that he would find someone on whom to expend some excess energy.

* * *

He returned two hours later, considerably refreshed, to find Deborah had called. 'I beg your pardon, I know you were not expecting me, but I finished the changes to my book in record time and I had to talk to you.' She smiled nervously.

'I hope you haven't been waiting too long,' Elliot said, ushering her into the parlour, surreptitiously checking his neckcloth, which he had retied without the benefit of a mirror, wondering if his hair was in a similar state of disarray.

'I wasn't sure if you would receive me after—after the last time.' Deborah stood in front of the empty grate. 'I wouldn't blame you if you didn't want to. Only I didn't want you to think—I was worried that you might think that I had—had pursued our acquaintance simply so that I could break into houses with you,' she said in a rush. 'I mean that was the point at first, but I hadn't thought—I didn't mean it to end as it did. And I hoped that despite the fact that I could not—and that I was so stupid—in short, I have come to see if there is a way that we can put that behind us and make a fresh start. If you want to. Though I'll understand if you don't and—and—well, that is all.'

Clearly, she was not ready to explain further. The cost of what she had already said was clear in the way she was clutching at her reticule as if it would save her from drowning. If it had been anyone else, he'd have given up the ghost a long time ago. But there was no one quite like Deborah. Was he prepared to wait? Stupid question. He had no intentions of failing, not now. Elliot disentangled Deborah's reticule from her fingers and took her hands between his. 'I'm happy to make a fresh start, but I won't promise you anything other than that. You must know how much I want you—it was perfectly obvious,' he said with a teasing smile. 'And no matter what convoluted logic is going on in that clever mind of yours, I know that you want me, too.'

'Elliot, I can't...'

His mouth smothered her protests. His lips were gentle, soft, and persuasive. He tugged her closer, so that their interlaced hands were pressed against his chest, and she made no attempt to resist. Warmth and light flooded her.

Elliot released her just as the warmth turned to heat. 'You see,' he said, kissing the tip of her nose, 'you can.'

She could think of nothing to say. Risking a glance at him through her lashes, she caught his smile and couldn't help returning it. She had missed him. She only just caught the words before they betrayed her.

'You look different,' he said.

'A new dress. Do you like it?' The walking dress had been an impulse purchase from Madame LeClerc's in Bond Street, which had cost her a ridiculous amount of her savings. The round gown of primrose-jaconet muslin was simple enough, but the three rows of French work around the hem made it much more fashionable and elegant than anything she had ever worn. The matching spencer was mint green with full puffed sleeves trimmed with satin, and the same satin lined her leghorn bonnet. She was absurdly pleased that Elliot had noticed. She had bought it for herself, because she wished to have some colour in her wardrobe, but she had worn it for him.

He took her hand and bowed over it. 'New gloves, too. You look quite charming.'

Deborah blushed. 'Thank you.'

'I've been sparring. I suspect I look as if I've been dragged through a hedge.'

'A little windswept.' She had missed him. She liked him this way, slightly dishevelled, smelling of clean sweat. Deborah reached up to straighten his neckcloth, then pushed back a lock of black silky hair from his brow, realising too late what she was doing and so deciding to pretend that she hadn't. 'Are you any good— as a boxer, I mean?' She allowed herself a moment to imagine him, stripped to the waist, his torso glistening. She liked that he was so tall. And so solid. Muscle-packed described him perfectly. Everything about him was so very masculine and so very Elliot. And so very, very not Jeremy. 'Have you got—is it science?

Elliot laughed. 'I'm good enough, but I'm too tall. I spar simply to exercise. In the army, I spent my time breaking up mills rather than taking part in them. When it came to the fancy, Henry was your man.' His smile faded as he realised what he'd said. He never mentioned Henry in casual conversation. He ushered Deborah into a chair and sat down opposite her.

'Actually,' she said, 'I'm pleased you mentioned Henry. I've been thinking about him.'

'And?' Elliot stretched his legs out in front of him, crossing them at the ankles. He wondered what on earth was coming next. Judging by the way Deborah was making a play of untying her bonnet strings, they were getting to the crux of her visit.

'I'm embarrassed at how little I know of the war,' she said, having carefully placed her hat on the floor at her feet. 'The suffering that went on in the battle-fields, the suffering that goes on still, right under our noses. The sheer extent of it all, what your men and their families endured and surrendered so that we could have peace—it's overwhelming. So many men must have gone through what Henry did. Their families and friends and comrades must be struggling with their losses, too.'

Deborah paused, waiting for Elliot to comment, risking a glance at him, but his face was impassive. 'You've made me realise I've been walking about with my eyes closed—well, me and practically everyone else. The press make such a fuss about the begging and the pilfering, the tavern brawls and the picking of pockets which have increased so dramatically since Waterloo. And housebreaking.' She risked a small smile. 'The reports about the Peacock's activities—they are interested only in the fact that the law has been broken. No one thinks to question why.'

'Except my brother-in-law,' Elliot said drily. 'He was here this morning, subtly warning me off. He's put two and two together and near as dammit made four.'

Deborah's eyes widened. 'What will he do?'

'Oh, there's no need to fear, I gave him short shift and he's no idea of your involvement. Alex won't inform—the last thing he wants is to see me brought to justice, for that would upset Lizzie, and not upsetting Lizzie is all he really cares about.'

'All the same, Elliot, it is surely becoming far too risky for you to continue as the Peacock.'

He shrugged. 'It's more a case of running out of victims, to be honest. I've almost exhausted the list of those who can be held directly accountable. I could always turn Robin Hood, I suppose.' Elliot grinned. 'Steal from the rich to give to the deserving poor. That would certainly give me an occupation for life.'

'If you did that, I suspect your brother-in-law would turn Sheriff of Nottingham,' Deborah said with a chuckle.

She began to twist her gloves between her fingers. 'It's not enough though, is it? However much the Peacock can steal, there have been more than three hundred thousand men demobilised—you see, I do listen. No matter how successful you are, the need will always be too great. Three hundred thousand men, Elliot—it's such an incredible number. And what about the thousands and thousands who did not come home, the thousands more who are too maimed to look for work? Against such a mountainous problem, housebreaking, no matter how successful, can only scratch the surface of need.'

'You put it depressingly well.'

'I'm not trying to make what you've done sound pal-

try,' Deborah said earnestly. 'What you've done is—
is—I can't tell you how much I admire you. You have
made me realise how inward-looking I have allowed my
own life to become. You've made me think and you've
made me want to help. I don't care that you've broken
the law to further your aims, the law deserves to be
broken, if doing so helps just a little.'

Elliot's mouth curled into a smile once more. 'Thank
you,' he said. 'I shall employ you to speak on my behalf
at my trial, should it come to that.'

'I sincerely hope it shall not,' Deborah replied curtly.

'Then we are at one on that,' he said, regretting the
flippant tone immediately as she began to retreat behind
her haughty look. 'I'm sorry, I didn't mean to upset you.'

Deborah studied him for a moment, her lips pursed.
Obviously deciding he passed muster, she gave one of
her serious little nods that always, rather perversely,
made Elliot want to laugh. He refrained and instead
gave her an encouraging look. 'You have a plan for
raising funds without breaking and entering. Go on, I
promise you I'm interested.'

'Very well, then. Pamphlets and preaching are how
philanthropists who aren't housebreakers raise money,
but pamphlets are such dull things and preachers are
generally more worthy than interesting. It is no wonder that they raise more hackles than funds,' Deborah
said caustically. 'I think what we need is a story. A real
story about a real man, something dramatic, not a dull
old piece of polemic. If we could tell people what this
man was really like—funny, brave and flawed—if we

could show, in the language of a novel, what happened to him, how he suffered and died—how could they *not* listen? If we could do that, no one would be able to ignore his legacy.'

Deborah spoke quickly in the rush to make him understand, to share her enthusiasm for her idea, leaning forwards in her seat, her gaze fixed on his. 'I'm talking about Henry's story, Elliot. Henry's bravery, Henry's sacrifices, Henry's life cut tragically short—that's a story that needs to be told, don't you think? I'm a writer, I can tell it, but I need your help. What do you say?' She sat back and tucked a non-existent strand of hair behind her ear, gazing at him expectantly.

'I'm not sure what to say,' Elliot answered, somewhat dazed. 'What exactly are you asking of me?'

'Tell me about Henry. Show me where all the money the Peacock earns goes. Help me to understand what else needs to be done. Help me to reach those who won't or don't listen now. Such a story could make a huge difference, in the right hands. Your hands, for instance.'

'What would I do with it?'

'I don't know,' Deborah said candidly. 'I was hoping that you'd have some ideas.' She grinned. 'I'd rule out becoming a Member of Parliament, though. Frankly, the more I think about it, the less I can see you joining political forces with the likes of Wellington.'

'There we are in complete agreement.' Elliot got to his feet and disentangled Deborah's new gloves from her restlessly twisting fingers, putting them out of reach on the window seat along with her bonnet, which he retrieved from the floor. 'My sister and her husband have been making a concerted effort to introduce me to the many members of the Establishment in their acquaintance, but I'm sorry to say that the more I see of the lot of them, the more I am certain that I don't want to join their club.'

'Despite the fact that there would be a delicious irony in knowing that they had taken a Government spy-turned-housebreaker for one of their own, I think you're right,' Deborah said. 'Elliot, I don't pretend to have a fully formed battle plan, but I do believe that I have the kernel of a very powerful weapon. I want so desperately to help and I believe that doing so will give me a purpose that I lack.'

Deborah fished for her gloves, found her lap empty and began to lace her fingers together instead. 'You see, I am being honest. I cannot pretend to be wholly altruistic.' She had had no intention of saying anything of the ghosts which she had set loose these last few days, so it had taken her unawares, this sudden temptation to speak. But where to begin? And how much could she say, before Elliot began first to pity, then to despise her? She couldn't do it. He was the only person in her life who had no connection with her past and she wanted to keep it that way. 'I have been at a loss, since Jeremy died,' she said awkwardly instead.

'You told me once that you didn't know who you were.'

'Did I?' Deborah grimaced. 'Well, at least I know now who I *don't* want to be. I've had enough of being

Jeremy's widow. And enough of being—of writing the stories I write. It's time for a change.'

'For both of us, you mean?' Elliot said wryly.

Deciding it was wiser not to rise to this bait, Deborah shrugged.

Elliot got to his feet, gazing sightlessly out of the window. 'It's a new approach, there's no doubt about it,' he said. 'Do you really think you can write something which will sell?'

'I have done before. This will certainly be different. I don't know, but I'm willing to try.'

Elliot held up his hands in mock surrender. 'Then so, too, am I,' he said, laughing. 'If only they would allow women into politics, I'd put you forwards. You have most expertly manoeuvred me into a corner.'

'Yes, but is it one from which you wish to escape?'

She was offering him a get-out, but Elliot had already decided not to accept it. Deborah's eyes had a sparkle to them today; there was a vibrancy about her that he hadn't seen in the cold light of day before. It roused him, just as it had when they had broken into houses together. He was touched, too, not so much by what she proposed as by the thoughtfulness and understanding which had led to it. Whether something productive would come of their collaboration he had no idea, but the opportunity it offered to postpone thinking about the future made Elliot more than happy to agree. That, and the rather more enticing opportunity her proposition presented. 'You realise,' he said musingly, 'that we'd be forced into each other's company for significant amounts of time if we're to do this properly?'

Deborah studied her hands. 'I am prepared to suffer for our cause, if you are,' she said lightly.

Suppressing a smile, Elliot tugged on the bell by the fireplace. He was glad he had resisted opening that parcel of books. Relieved he had resisted the temptation to dig into the scandal which Lizzie had hinted surrounded Jeremy's death. Here was the opportunity to persuade Deborah to trust him enough to confide in him herself. 'Champagne,' he ordered the astonished underling who answered the summons. 'Unconventional, I know, in the middle of the day,' he said to Deborah, in response to her raised eyebrow, 'but that seems to me a perfect reason to drink it, for you are the most unconventional female I have ever met.'

Relieving his servant of the tray when he returned a few minutes later, Elliot closed the door firmly behind him. 'Stand up, I have a toast to make.' He handed Deborah a glass full of bubbles. 'To a unique partnership and a most unique woman,' he said, smiling. 'Let us drink to our success. To us.'

His smile was half-mocking, wholly sensual. Their eyes met and locked. A shock of awareness made Deborah's skin prickle. 'To us,' she said. As she touched her glass to Elliot's, she imagined their lips meeting. She sipped and the champagne bubbles tickled her tongue. The fierce force of his gaze made her look up again. The message in those dark eyes reflected her thoughts. Mesmerised, Deborah stepped into his arms.

The touch of his lips on hers made her head spin. Save for that first time in the park, she had never kissed him in daylight before—not properly. It felt different. His mouth was warm on hers, his hands cradled her face, making her feel precious. Their lips clung, then parted. It was the sweetness of it which dazed her. The perfection of it. The completeness, for it was a beginning and an end in itself. She touched Elliot's cheek, rough with the day's growth of stubble. His thumbs stroked the line of her jaw. Their eyes met in a smile which was different, too. Like the kiss, a beginning and an end in itself.

Deborah disengaged herself and Elliot let her go. She lifted her glass again. 'And to Henry,' she said.

'To Henry,' Elliot replied gruffly.

Chapter Eight

They spent the next hour laughing over foolish plans and drinking the champagne. 'I think the bubbles have gone to my head,' Deborah told Elliot as she struggled with her bonnet strings, 'for this ribbon simply refuses to co-operate.'

'Here, let me.'

'Certainly not. Gentlemen don't tie lady's ribbons.'

'No, more often than not they untie them.' Elliot untangled the crushed satin from Deborah's fingers. It hadn't occurred to him that half a bottle of champagne would go to her head, but he was amused and charmed by the effect.

'Have you untied many ribbons?' Deborah asked, grasping Elliot's wrist and quite ruining the bow he had been about to finish.

'A gentleman never discusses such things.'

'You are a spy and a housebreaker, which should pre-clude you from being a gentleman.' Deborah thought this over, frowning. 'But it doesn't. How strange. So, have you known lots and lots of beautiful women?'

'Lots.'

'And drunk champagne with them, in the middle of the afternoon?'

An image of himself, sprawled naked on a bed with satin sheets, popped into Elliot's head. Rose satin. He'd hated those sheets. He couldn't for the life of him remember who they belonged to, though.

'You have!' Deborah exclaimed indignantly.

Despite the champagne, her gaze was remarkably clear-sighted. She would know if he lied. 'I have,' Elliot confessed with a wicked smile, 'but I've never done it with all my clothes on.' He straightened Deborah's bonnet. 'You, madam, have the honour of that first,' he said, planting a kiss on the tip of her nose. 'Though if you were willing, I would of course be more than happy to oblige you by divesting us both of clothes and calling for another bottle.'

'Oh! That was…'

'Outrageous? Shocking? Scandalous?'

'Delightful, is what I was going to say, actually,' Deborah said, turning up her nose, 'but since you obviously didn't mean it, I shan't oblige you now.'

For a startled moment, Elliot was quite speechless. It was her eyes that gave her away, positively dancing with mirth. 'You are a minx, did you know that?'

The low, husky note of his laughter whispered over her skin, making her acutely aware of his masculinity, making her intensely aware of her own femininity.

Deborah's smile wobbled as heat washed over her. Her heart began to beat erratically. Her mouth was dry. She wanted him to kiss her again. She wanted him. The intensity of her wanting made her reach for him. 'Elliot.'

His laughter faded as he caught the hand she held out to him. She saw it in his eyes, the reflection of her desires, and it was the strength of it which brought her to her senses. Too much. 'I think I should go home now.'

Elliot hesitated. His fingers twined with hers. Then he nodded. 'Perhaps you should.' He rang the bell, asked his servant to call a hack, then retrieved her gloves from the window seat and helped her button them. 'I'll call for you tomorrow.'

'Yes.'

'Deborah.' He tilted her chin up, so she could not avoid looking at him. 'Whether we are fully clothed or naked as nature intended, you are the only woman I want to drink champagne with in the middle of the day. Or the middle of the night, for that matter. I promise.'

'Oh.'

'Exactly,' Elliot said, relieved to see that she was smiling again. Quite enchanted, he kissed her. Then he straightened her bonnet again. He would have kissed her again, had not his servant interrupted them with the information that her transport was waiting.

'I thought we'd start at the dispensary in Spitalfields,' Elliot said, extending a hand to help Deborah into his curricle. He picked up the reins and set the horses off at a smart trot. Traffic was light at this time of day, after the rush of morning deliveries, before the modish hour for shopping. 'How is your head today?'

'Much clearer, thank you,' Deborah replied primly, keeping her eyes fixed firmly ahead.

'Don't be embarrassed, you have no need to be.'

'I got hiccups in the hackney on the way home. I am eight and twenty, far beyond the age for hiccups. It was mortifying.'

'I thought you were quite charming, in your cups.'

'I was not in my cups!' Deborah exclaimed indignantly. 'A little half-sprung perhaps, but hardly jug-bitten,' she said, sliding him a mischievous smile.

Elliot gave a shout of laughter. 'How the devil came you to be so familiar with such terms?'

Deborah chuckled. 'I have my sources,' she said, tapping the side of her nose.

'Touché, madame.' She was dressed in one of her older gowns today, of a rather washed-out blue, with a serviceable grey pelisse and plain bonnet. It was practical and wholly appropriate, given their destination, but Elliot was much relieved that her mood was not as sombre as her apparel. This caustic, skittish mix of humour of hers appealed to his own. It pleased him to see that the bluish shadows below her eyes were fading. Just having her at his side pleased him. It wasn't just the nearness of her, her skirts brushing his buckskins, her shoulder brushing his as they turned a corner, it was more than that. It was her, whatever it was that made her Deborah. He liked it.

As they made their way from the town houses and

neatly kept squares of the west to the bustle of Clerken-
well, she began to ply him with questions, scribbling
notes in the book she extracted from a pocket in her
gown with a little silver pencil. Past Moorfields, where
Signor Lunardi's balloon had taken off, the impressive
frontage of the Bethlem Hospital distracted her temporarily, but then she returned to her questions. Those, too,
were in her little notebook, Elliot was amused to see, as
she ticked one off. 'You are nothing if not thorough,' he
said. 'A Bow Street Runner would be impressed with
your preparation.'

'I want to make as good a job of this as I can. Are
you laughing at me?'

'No, truly. I'm impressed.'

'I know how much it matters,' Deborah said.

'To both of us,' Elliot replied. They were past the
coaching inns of Bishopsgate, approaching Spitalfields now. Though the curricle was smart rather than
fashionable, his horses well matched but hardly prime
'uns, they were attracting much interest none the less.
'This place used to be the heart of silk manufacturing,
but most of the work is done in the countryside now.
Cheaper labour, more room for the new machines. You
wouldn't believe it, to look at the rundown state of the
place, but it was thriving not so long ago.'

It was like another world to Deborah. Scantily clad,
filthy children stared out from faces so gaunt their eyes
were made huge. The gutters streamed with effluvia
on which dogs, cats and rats almost as big as the cats
feasted. Raucous cries came from the open door of a gin

house. There were few horses on the road, but a good
many hand carts, the men bowed over them as dirty
and badly clad as the children. The stench, which had
been creeping up on them since Bishopsgate, was eye-
watering. The air tasted thick and ripe. In contrast, the
streets, the buildings, the people, seemed to be sepia-
washed, almost colourless, as if dipped in depression.
Appalled, and no little intimidated, Deborah put away
her notebook and shuffled a little closer to Elliot.

They skirted round the worst of the rookery. 'The
few weavers who are left have moved out of there,' he
said as they bypassed Dorset Street. 'A good many of
our men have ended up in places like this—in one of
the rat-infested lodging houses if they're lucky, sleeping rough if they're not. It's slightly better here, around
Christ Church—at least some of the water is clean.
Cholera and typhus are rife, though.' He pulled up in
front of a large house in significantly better repair than
the rest. 'This belonged to one of the richer silk mer-
chants.'

As Elliot bartered with a bold child over the price
for the safekeeping of his curricle and pair, Deborah
surveyed the building. It was a pleasing but simple edifice of red brick with four windows on either side of the
door, nine on the floor above that, and a set of dormers
build into the low-pitched roof. The shallow flight of
steps were semi-circular, leading up to a plain black-
painted door framed by two Doric columns topped with
a swan-necked pediment into which was set the insti-
tution's motto. *'Nil desperandum,'* she read. She eyed

the gleaming windows, the shining brass door fittings
and the pristine white steps—such a stark contrast to
the streets through which they had just driven. 'It's certainly a shining example of cleanliness, but what is it?'

Elliot rapped on the door. 'It was an army hospital
during the last years of the wars. After Waterloo they
closed it down, despite the fact that many of the men
were still in dire need of medical services—it can take
months for the wounds from an amputation to heal properly, sometimes longer if it is aggravated by pressure
sores. The men brought any number of recurrent fevers
back from Spain and Portugal, too, and some—war is
a harsh thing, Deborah. Some men are wounded in the
mind. Those poor bastards ended up in Bethlem and
places like it.'

The door was opened by a middle-aged man dressed
in plain black livery. Despite the wooden peg which
formed the lower half of his left leg, his carriage was
upright. Seeing Elliot, he stood smartly to attention and
saluted. 'Major Marchmont, sir.'

'Good to see you, Sergeant Lyle. This is—'

'Mrs Napier,' Deborah said hurriedly. 'How do you
do?'

'Mrs Napier is interested in what you do here, Lyle.
I'm just going to show her around, if that's all right?'

'Perfectly, sir. Anything I can do to help, you just
give me a shout, I'll be right here. And I'll keep an eye
on that gig of yours, too,' the old soldier said, with a
meaningful look at the boy holding the reins.

'Lyle was twenty years in the army. He served under

me in Spain. He knew Henry, too, you might want to talk to him at some point,' Elliot said, ushering Deborah towards a heavy green baize door at the back of the hallway.

A volley of noise hit them as he pushed the door open and Deborah stopped on the threshold, staring around her in astonishment. They were in a large room which looked as if it ran the full length of the house. With windows on the three sides which did not adjoin the back of the house, it was bright with the late-morning sunlight and alive with industry.

'Despite what the press will have us believe, what most men want is to work,' Elliot said, raising his voice to compensate for the cacophony of sound. 'For those who have lost limbs, finding work is nigh on impossible simply because they have no access to artificial limbs and bath chairs are quite beyond the means of those who need them most.'

'So you established a workshop to provide what was needed,' Deborah said, looking around her in awe. 'And who better to make such things than those who require them in the first place,' she added, noticing what she had not seen when she first entered the room, that every single one of the workers was an amputee. 'May I take a closer look?'

'Of course you can, but I'll let Captain Symington here do the explaining, since he's the one in charge. How are you, George?'

Captain Symington grinned and punched Elliot on

the shoulder. 'I wondered why we hadn't seen your ugly face for a while,' he said, looking at Deborah.

'This is Mrs Napier. She is interested in the work you do,' Elliot said repressively.

'How do you do, ma'am,' Captain Symington said, making his bow.

'Captain Symington, it is a pleasure.' Deborah said, hesitating to extend her hand, for the captain's right sleeve was empty, but he noticed her unease and extended his left quite naturally.

'Why don't you leave me to show Mrs Napier round?' the captain said to Elliot. 'It's not often we get such charming company, and it's certainly the first time it's come courtesy of you. Go on, leave us to it, that's an order. You don't outrank me here, you know.'

'Deborah?'

'I'll be fine, Elliot.'

He left them reluctantly, for he suspected George's motives, though he could not very well say so without leaving himself open to questions he had no wish to be asked. The charmer was already leaning on Deborah's arm. He could not hear what he was saying, but he was leaning damned close to say it. And Deborah was smiling up at him, laughing, dammit! He had a good mind to warn her.

Elliot sighed and unclenched his fists. What possible harm could come to her in a factory full of men? Several things jumped immediately into his mind. His fists clenched again. He unclenched them again. George would take care of any importunities and, if George importuned, he would take care of George! Dammit, he was making something out of nothing. George was a charmer, but he was a gentleman and played by a gentleman's rules. He would know that Deborah was not— Deborah was—Deborah was not…

Elliot sighed again. Across the room, Deborah had slipped free of George's embrace to inspect one of the new chairs with wheels. Satisfied—or telling himself that he should be—Elliot went in search of Sergeant Lyle.

'It is really most ingenious,' Captain Symington said. 'Try it for yourself.'

Deborah sat gingerly into the movable chair. It was surprisingly comfortable, with a padded leather seat and a rest for her feet, though she had some dificultly arranging her skirts in its narrow confines.

'You see, these two large wheels can be manipulated with a bit of practice, and the little castor on the back gives you balance so that you can propel yourself around without any help.'

Deborah tried to do as he said, but her hands made no impression on the wooden wheels at all. Captain Symington took hold of the little handles set into the back of the chair. 'How long have you known Elliot?' he asked.

Deborah clutched at the arms of the chair as it began to move. It was a most unnerving experience. 'A little while,' she replied.

'And how came you to meet?'

'We had business in common,' she said, just as she had answered Lizzie.

'What does your husband do, Mrs Napier?'

'He is dead, Captain Symington.'

'Ah.'

'I cannot see your face, Captain Symington, but I suspect the quality of that ah.'

He pushed the chair back to the work bench and held out his hand to help her up from it. 'You are quite right, Mrs Napier, I am very curious,' he said with a disarming smile. 'I've not seen Elliot with a female, save that terrifying sister of his, since we came back to England.' Captain Symington frowned. 'He's a good man, you know. I don't know anyone I respect more. This place—it was his idea, by and large, and though the money comes from his mysterious benefactors, the grit and determination to get it off the ground were all Elliot's. He feels guilty for coming through it all unharmed. I've told him all of us feel guilty who've survived, but you know Elliot, he has to take the brunt of it. Did he tell you about…?'

'Henry. Yes, yes, he did.'

'I was there when they brought him into the field hospital—I lost my arm in the same battle. I thought at one point that Elliot was going to go up into the mountains himself, which would have been madness, for not even he could have carried Henry back without help. He was mad with rage. Then when Henry died, he almost stopped speaking. Went about like the walking dead himself.'

'I'm going to write about Henry. That's why I'm here.'

'What do you mean?'

She told him, as they wandered around the workshop, breaking off to admire the workmanship of artificial limbs and the surprising variety of devices which the men had invented to give those like themselves some independence. 'Do you think it will work?' she asked, when they had completed the tour of the school room which took up the second floor.

George Symington shook his head. 'I've no idea, but it's certainly an original notion. May I ask why you're doing this?'

'I want to help.'

'Yes, but it can't just be that. It's a big commitment you're making, if you don't mind my saying so—you must have a more personal reason.'

She had relaxed in his company this last hour, but under the keen scrutiny of his handsome face Deborah drew back. 'It's a cause worthy of significant commitment. I don't need another reason,' she said.

Under that haughty look, Captain Symington flushed, taken aback at the transformation. 'I'll take you back to Elliot,' he said. 'In fact, here he is.' With relief, he saw the major waiting at the foot of the stairs. His farewells were formal, his bow reserved.

'What did you say to George?' Elliot asked, amused and relieved by his friend's obvious retreat.

'I have no idea,' Deborah answered blithely. 'I expect he is just worn out with all my questions.' She tapped her silver pencil on her notebook. 'I still have plenty more—may we visit the dispensary?'

'It's not pleasant.'

'I don't expect it to be, but how can I tell others what I have not seen for myself?'

'Isn't that what writers do, use their imagination?'

'I've done plenty of that, believe me,' Deborah said, thinking of Bella Donna, 'but there are some things best not left to the imagination.'

'Such as housebreaking?'

'And tending the sick.'

'If you're sure,' Elliot said.

'I'm sure,' Deborah replied, taking his arm.

The dispensary took up the second floor and the attics of the main house, with beds for the most serious cases. Though most of the patients were veterans and their families, it was fast becoming a much-needed part of the Spitalfields community. No one was turned away.

After an hour, Deborah was reeling with emotion and information. As they made their way back down the central staircase of the house, she leaned heavily on Elliot's arm. 'I'm sorry, I feel a little faint.'

She staggered, slipped on the marble step and would have fallen had Elliot not caught her. 'Have you eaten today?'

'I forgot. I was so excited about coming here.'

'And last night?'

'I went straight to my bed after I returned from your

house.' She clutched at the ornate wrought-iron banister. 'I'll be fine in a minute. Perhaps a glass of water.'

'You're not drinking the water here.' She was alarmingly pale. Elliot checked his pocket watch. After three and she had eaten nothing since yesterday. He cursed under his breath. 'Have you an ambition to join the patients upstairs?' he said, scooping her into his arms.

'Elliot, put me down, I'm perfectly capable of walking.'

'I know, you are eight and twenty, and more than old enough to do so without help, one would have thought,' he said, ignoring her protest, 'but since you don't seem capable of feeding yourself, I'm not going to trust you to walk. Stop fussing, put your arm around my neck and we'll get along much better. Lyle, is my curricle still intact?'

'It is, Major. Would you be needing a hand there with Mrs Napier?' the sergeant asked, grinning.

'I don't think so. Make your farewells, Deborah. And much as I'm enjoying your wriggling,' Elliot said, lowering his voice for her ears only, 'I'd prefer if you waited until we are alone.'

Blushing, Deborah cast him a fulminating glance. 'Goodbye, Sergeant Lyle. Thank you for your hospitality. I hope the next time I visit that you will spare me some of your time. I would very much like to hear about your experiences. I regret I am not at liberty to do so at present,' she said tightly.

'Major Marchmont knows best, I'm sure, madam,' Sergeant Lyle said, failing to stifle his laugh.

'That was mortifying,' Deborah said, pulling the rug from Elliot's hands to tuck it around her legs herself.

'Think how much more embarrassed you'd have been if you fainted.'

'I never faint.'

'You looked damned close to it there.' Elliot tossed sixpence to his makeshift groom and threw a handful of coppers at the ragged collection of his cohorts, earning himself a cheer. 'You don't look after yourself,' he said, urging the horses into a walk.

'I am perfectly capable—'

'Deborah.'

She folded her arms across her chest. 'What?' she said belligerently.

'Why don't you just sit back and let me look after you?'

'I don't need looking after.'

'You do. And I want to. So why not let me?'

All of a sudden, she felt like crying. Before she could stop it, a tear plopped on to her cheek. She scrubbed it away with her glove. 'I'm sorry. Perhaps I do need something to eat.' Another tear fell, and then another. She turned her face away, desperately trying to compose herself, hoping Elliot hadn't noticed. She cast him a surreptitious glance and her eyes clashed with his. He'd noticed. 'Sorry,' she said again.

He fumbled in his coat pocket and produced a large, pristine white handkerchief. 'Stop apologising, there's no need. It's my fault. The dispensary was too much for you. I shouldn't have taken you there.'

'I insisted that you did.' Deborah mopped her face. Elliot's mouth was set, his brows drawn. His scar showed white. She knew him well enough now to surmise that his anger was turned on himself and not her. Guilt made her confess what she would much rather have kept to herself. 'It wasn't the dispensary. It was just that no one ever offers to look after me. There, that's made me sound quite pathetic.'

'I wish you would not describe yourself so,' Elliot said harshly. 'You are very far from pathetic.'

'Sorry.'

'Stop saying sorry, too.'

'Sorry. I mean—sorry.' Deborah managed a weak smile. 'I promise I'll eat something as soon as I get home.'

'You're not going home yet. I'm taking you to dinner.'

'I'm not dressed for dinner.'

'It's early and I'm not proposing anywhere fashionable. There's an excellent coaching inn at Holborn, the Old Bell, where the food is very good. No, don't bother protesting,' Elliot added. 'Short of grabbing the reins, there is nothing you can do, so save your breath and let me concentrate on my driving. Much as it pains me to admit it, the volume and variety of traffic on London's roads rather tests my handling of the ribbons to its limit. They'd never have me at the Four Horse Club.'

'I think you are being too modest; driving a curricle and pair is not exactly easy. Though I admit, I can't see you in a yellow-and-blue-striped waistcoat, let alone a spotted cravat.'

'God, no, no more can I. How do you know what they wear?'

'Jeremy was a member,' Deborah said shortly. 'Horses were his greatest passion. It was one of the few things we had in common.' She chewed her bottom lip. 'Actually, it might have been the only one.'

She lapsed into silence and the haunted look was back in her eyes and her complexion wan. Compassion and anger kept Elliot quiet, though his grip on the reins tightened enough to make his horses aware of it. Their steps got out of kilter and it took him a few moments to rectify the problem; when he next looked at Deborah, her eyes had drifted closed.

They remained so until he pulled in to courtyard of the Old Bell, when she blinked and looked about her in surprise. 'Are we here already?' She descended shakily, glad of Elliot's arm as his curricle was led efficiently off over the cobbles to the stables.

The inn was large, the original tavern having been much altered, with a two-storey extension built on to the original gable wall, and another, three-storey building at right angles to this, the whole joined on the first floor by a precarious set of galleries.

Elliot steered Deborah to the open door of the main building, where the landlord, in pristine white apron, was waiting for them. 'A private parlour, and the lady will wish to freshen up,' he said. 'Dinner as soon as you can bring it.'

'Certainly, sir. You have timed your visit well, if I may say so; you've just missed the Bristol mail. I have an excellent parlour at the back, away from the noise of the tap room.' The landlord snapped his fingers and ordered a maid to take madam upstairs, and to fetch a jug of hot water, then led Elliot through to a small parlour where a fire was already burning.

Fifteen minutes later, Deborah joined him. The table was already set with pewter plates, a jug of claret and a loaf of bread, still warm from the oven. 'I feel much better, but you're right, I am hungry.'

'There's a white soup, a haunch of venison which I thought you'd prefer to mutton stew, but I wasn't sure, so I ordered the carp in case you fancied fish. There's asparagus and peas, too, and some mushroom fritters. They don't run to much in the way of dessert, but there is a Stilton which the landlord assures me is fine, and—'

'Stop,' Deborah said, laughing, 'you are not feeding an army now. It sounds lovely, Elliot, much better than bread and mousetrap, which is all that I have in my own kitchen,' she added, touched by the care he had taken. 'My mouth is already watering.'

She sat down at the table and took a sip of the wine. The food was excellent and Elliot an attentive host, putting the most succulent morsels on her plate, distracting her with witty anecdotes of make-do meals he had eaten on the campaign trail, so that she partook of every dish and ate far more than she normally would have.

The wheel of Stilton with quince jelly, was served by their host along with a fine port, which Deborah declined. Outside, dusk had fallen. As the door closed behind the landlord, the sound of a horn could be heard, the answering clatter of clogs on wooden boards rushing to the courtyard as a stage coach pulled in.

'Thank you,' Deborah said with a contented sigh. 'That was quite delicious.' The maid who cleared the table had lit the candles. Their reflections flickered in the bevelled glass of the window beneath which the table was set. It was an intimate scene. Domestic.

She and Jeremy had never sat together thus, so comfortably together. The arrival of the port was the signal for Deborah to leave the table, even when they were alone. She propped her chin on her hands, drowsy with the heat and the food and the wine. 'At Kinsail Manor, the dining table seats twenty-four,' she said, half to herself. 'It is so old there are no leafs to be removed and Jeremy was so punctilious about etiquette, he insisted that we sat at opposite ends, even when we were alone. I'd forgotten that. I'd forgotten how fond of pomp and ceremony he was. There was an epergne, a hideous thing, some sort of heirloom, that sat in the middle of the table which made conversation absolutely impossible. I had it removed to a side table once, but Jeremy had it moved back. He couldn't bear anything to be changed in his precious Manor, which was strange, considering how happy he seemed to be to let the place go to rack and ruin. I wondered, after he died, if it was deliberate, you know? A sort of self-inflicted punishment. He let himself go to rack and ruin, too.'

Her eyes were unfocused, lost in the past, but for the first time since he had known her, she seemed contemplative rather than troubled by what she saw. Elliot sipped his port, watching the emotions flitting over her face, almost afraid to move lest he break the mood.

Deborah began to cut the quince jelly which lay untouched on her plate into little cubes, using her left hand to hold the knife, resting her cheek on the other. 'He was indifferent to what we ate, too, provided it was served on the appropriate service with appropriate aplomb. The kitchens at Kinsail Manor are about as far from the dining room as it is possible to be, so whatever we had, it was nearly always cold. I tried to persuade him to have a new kitchen built, but the expense was prohibitive, he said. I suggested we move the dining chamber closer to the kitchen.' She laughed. 'You'd think I'd suggested that I be allowed to cast a vote in an election. He was appalled.' She put her knife down, looking in surprise at the quivering mass of quince she had cut. Her mouth drooped. 'Poor Jeremy. The Manor, the title—they meant so much to him. I wonder how different things would have been, if he'd had an heir.'

She sat up, suddenly conscious of the intensity of Elliot's gaze. He had what she called his fierce look. 'I am become maudlin,' she said, finishing the last of her wine. 'I think it is time I went home.'

'You would have liked children?' Elliot stayed her hand when she would have risen from the table.

'One cannot always have what one would like,' Deborah said lightly, though the lump rose in her throat all the same. She pushed back her chair and busied herself with putting on her bonnet, collecting her gloves and shawl.

'Tomorrow, if you wish, I can take you back to Spitalfields to talk to Lyle.'

'There is no need, I am sure I can get a hackney to take me.'

'You don't need to prove your independence to me. And before you say it, you're not beholden either. Our cause is a joint one, I thought we agreed?'

She opened her mouth to protest, but then thought the better of it and laughed. 'I'm not sure I like your ability to read my mind.'

'I wish I could read it more often.'

His smile was no more than a shadow, a sensuous tilt of his lips, which made her toes curl, her skin flush. Her own was uncertain. She wished she really could read his mind. Did he want to kiss her?

She had her answer when his lips claimed hers. It was the softest of kisses. One of his kisses-for-no-other-purpose-than-kissing kisses. Gentle. Sweet. And over, before it could become more. Elliot straightened her shawl, tucked her hand into the crook of his arm and led her out into the bustling night.

Chapter Nine

'Well?' Deborah hovered in the open doorway. 'Did you read it, or should I go out again? Only if I walk around the square another time your neighbours will think I'm up to something.'

Elliot got up from the seat at her desk and untangled her gloves from her fingers. She was pale, there were circles under her eyes again, testament to the long nights she'd spent with her pen. 'You can stay. I've finished it.'

'Oh.' She sank down suddenly into her chair by the hearth, her knees turned to jelly. She felt sick. She pressed her hands together tight to stop them from shaking. 'And?' Her voice was no more than a whisper.

Elliot sat down opposite, stretching his legs out in front of him. He had been planning on teasing her, but he was no proof against that anxious white face. 'And, I think it's absolutely brilliant,' he said with a grin.

'You're not just saying that because you don't want to offend me?'

'Deborah, it's wonderful. Truly. It's funny and moving and it's angry and it's tragic.'

'And Henry?'

Elliot swallowed hard. 'It was difficult to read. You've captured him so well.'

Deborah got up and caught his hand against her cheek, kneeling at his feet. 'I'm so glad. I wanted so much to get him right.'

'Well, you did.' They stayed in silence for a few moments, Elliot's hand resting on her head. 'The guilt of the survivor—is that what you think I suffer from?'

His eyes were dark, the lines around them etched deep with his frown. Deborah smoothed the scar on his brow. 'Not just you,' she said carefully. 'Almost every man I spoke to felt it to a degree, but I think you suffer from it more because you came through unharmed. You have no scars to show, save these little ones.' She kissed her fingertips and pressed them to the other scar, just below his hairline. 'But it doesn't mean you don't have other scars, which no one can see.'

Except you. The words hung in the air between them, unsaid. These last few weeks had gone by so quickly, he hadn't noticed how far he had dropped his guard, had been aware only that in Deborah's company he could speak his mind without thinking, without worrying that she would be shocked, or wouldn't understand.

'I can change it if it makes you feel uncomfortable,' Deborah said, displaying her ability to read his mind yet again. 'It's not as if Henry's friend is an accurate portrait of you, and it's only a draft. I don't want to upset you.'

Elliot smiled at her. He was always smiling at her.

'No. It was—difficult, but it's too good to change. Actually it's more than good, moving without being mawkish. And the battle scenes, so real without being bloodthirsty. You have a great talent.'

Deborah blushed with pleasure. 'Thank you.' She got to her feet, and paced over to the window. Her eyes were bright when she turned back to him. 'I can't tell you how much it means to me that you like it. Are you *sure* you do?'

Elliot laughed. He seemed to be doing a lot of that lately, too. 'It's perfect, I assure you. I hadn't realised you'd be finished so soon.'

'Well, as I said, it's only a draft, but the sooner the better, surely? I know that there's no immediate worry about funding for the dispensary, for Captain Symington told me that he had several new benefactors to add to the list.'

Deborah arranged her pens in a line on the blotter, her brows drawn together in a deep frown. Though she wanted to tell him, confidences still came so hard to her.

'What is it?' Elliot asked.

'I've something I want to tell you.'

'And you're not sure how to say it.' He led her over to the seat beside the fire. 'You know me well enough by now, surely? Just say it.'

Deborah smiled faintly. 'It's important. To me, anyway.' She plucked at a loose thread on the arm of her chair with her left hand. It came away in her fingers, leaving a tiny hole in the worn damask.

'You've taken off your wedding ring.'

Deborah examined the dent in her finger. The skin was pale, softer than the rest. 'Yesterday. I shall return it to Jacob. It's an heirloom. The only thing I have left of Jeremy's. Jacob will be relieved to have it back, though I doubt his wife will be particularly eager to wear it,' she said drily.

'What made you do it?' Elliot asked, realising as he did so how much he'd disliked that ring.

Deborah began to worry at another loose thread. 'That's what I wanted to tell you. Writing Henry's story has been a very emotional experience for me. Cathartic, I suppose. When I finished the draft, I knew it was good. Much better than anything I've written before. All that emotion. It made me realise how much was missing from my books.' She gave him a strange little smile. 'I appreciate that you haven't asked about them, I know you must have been curious.'

Elliot thought of the brown-paper parcel of books, still neatly wrapped, still sitting on the table by his bedside. 'Curious enough to obtain some copies for myself.'

Deborah's jaw dropped. 'You *knew*? How did you— did you *spy* on me? Have you read them?'

Elliot grinned. 'I have my sources. Of course I didn't spy on you, I just made enquiries. I've had them for weeks, but I haven't read them, I promise. I was waiting for you to tell me.'

'Good grief, how very self-restrained of you.'

Elliot gave a crack of laughter. 'Deborah, our entire relationship has been an exercise of remarkable self-restraint as far as I'm concerned. You know that.'

'Yes,' she whispered. So many times, over these last weeks, a touch, a glance, a brush of lips to cheek, one of those kisses-for-kisses'-sake kisses could have led to more. She knew he wanted her. She knew, too, that he was waiting for some sort of signal from her. Time and again, her desire for him led her to the edge, but her fear of failure kept her teetering there. At times, just looking at him made the muscles in her belly clench and perspiration break out in the small of her back. The silence between them was becoming charged. Deborah returned to her excavation of the arm of the chair. 'I was telling you about my writing.'

Elliot blinked, dragging his mind away from the delightful visions of Deborah naked that it conjured up so easily. 'Yes. So you were. Go on.'

Deborah pulled out another thread. It was longer than the first. She began to twine it round her fingers. 'You know, we both have a secret other, you and I. You have the Peacock and I have—I have Bella Donna.'

'Bella Donna?'

'That's the name of my heroine. It's a joke, really—you know, Deadly Nightshade. Beautiful and toxic. According to Mr Freyworth, my publisher, she is notorious.'

'You are the author of the Bella Donna books?'

'You've heard of them?'

'I've read one. Lizzie lent it to me.'

'Your sister, Lizzie?' Deborah squeaked in horror.

Elliot laughed. 'She is a great admirer of yours—though her husband, apparently, is not.' He shook his

head in disbelief. 'I could not imagine you writing romances along the lines of Mrs Burney's, but I did not
think your books were the kind that women hid from
their husbands.'

'And husbands from their wives, if I am to believe
Mr Freyworth,' Deborah said drily. 'Which one did you
read? Did you like it?'

'*Hemlock.* I did like it. It was clever and funny,
though the humour was very dark.' Elliot uncrossed
his ankles and sat up, his expression quite bemused.
'The main thing I liked about it was that it was so subversive. Your Bella is voluptuous, but quite vicious—
she really does enjoy humiliating her victims. What on
earth made you think of such a female?'

Deborah had wound the thread so tight around her
fingers that it was painful. 'Bella Donna is everything
I am not, you see,' she said. 'No man can resist her and
she is determined to live her life in her own way, even
if she has to be cruel. She doesn't care who gets hurt as
long as she gets what she wants, but she's not a hard-
nosed harlot. She's like a diamond—she glitters and
she's infinitely desirable, but she's hard, no one can
hurt her. She's invincible.'

'And immensely popular, according to my sister.'

'Even more popular, thanks to the Peacock, if Mr
Freyworth is to be believed.'

Elliot grinned. 'I wonder what Lizzie would make
of that?'

'Elliot! You would not…'

'God, no, that would set the cat among the pigeons. Alex is already—but I told you that.'

'You're not planning another break-in, are you? Ever since you told me about your brother-in-law's suspicions, I've been worried. I couldn't bear you to be caught.'

'I still have several names on my list.' Elliot frowned. He hadn't actually thought much about the Peacock at all in the last few weeks. 'There is no real risk, Alex won't say anything. You worry too much.'

'Any *you* don't worry at all!' Deborah exclaimed. 'It's dangerous, Elliot.'

'This, coming from you, my two-time aider and abettor,' he teased. 'Wasn't it you who told me that the Peacock was infallible?'

'It's not a laughing matter.'

'I won't tell you anything, then you won't have sleepless nights.'

'Why should it bother me?' Deborah asked caustically. 'It's not my neck that will be stretched.'

'I'm hoping that it won't be mine, either.'

'Are you sure about that? You told me once that you didn't care.'

He had. And he didn't. Then. And now? 'We were talking about you, not me,' Elliot said, mentally shrugging aside the issue of whether or not he had changed. 'Bella Donna, not the Peacock. What made you think of her? When did you start writing?'

Deborah made a face. 'It was at a—a low point in my marriage. There was—I knew we could not—that Jeremy and I—I knew it was over, even though he would not consider a separation. I still don't understand why he wouldn't. The Kinsail name, I suppose.'

'What happened?'

Deborah wrapped her arms around herself. 'It doesn't matter.'

'It obviously does,' Elliot said grimly.

She shook her head. 'What matters is that it made me fight back—through Bella. She was my—my secret weapon. While Bella wreaked revenge, I could just about bear the mess I had made of my life.' Realising that her nails were digging into her skin through her gown, Deborah forced herself to uncross her arms. 'It's not a mess now,' she said awkwardly. 'That's why I'm telling you. To thank you. Bella helped me survive the last years of my marriage, but lately—working with you, writing Henry's story—I've realised how much I've been living through her, hiding behind her. She's not protecting me any more, she's holding me back, and you've helped me realise that. I've decided to kill her off.' She smiled wanly. 'I've promised Mr Freyworth another book in payment for publishing Henry's story. He won't be too pleased when he discovers that it is Bella's final curtain.'

'You know,' Elliot said, getting to his feet, 'you are the most surprising woman I have ever met.' He pulled her from her chair, bowing low over her hand. 'I hardly know what to say, save that I salute you and I thank you for finally confiding in me. It means a lot, truly.' He turned her hand over and kissed her palm. 'All those secrets. You make me feel like an open book.'

'With many blank pages,' Deborah said sarcastically. Relieved to have finally spoken, she was flattered and fluttered by his reaction. The intensity of his gaze made her acutely conscious of her body beneath her new gown. Her palm tingled where his lips had lingered.

Elliot grinned and pushed back her sleeve to kiss her wrist. 'There's something I'm not clear about though,' he said.

'What is that?' Deborah's pulse fluttered under his mouth. Her corsets were laced too tight.

'Bella is such a very experienced woman. Most inventive.' Elliot's smile was wicked. 'I'm wondering where you got your material, because I'm pretty certain that it was not based on first-hand experience.'

Deborah flushed. 'If you must know, I found some books hidden in the library at Kinsail Manor. With pictures. That was the extent of my research.'

Elliot chuckled. 'So resourceful. I should have known.'

'You're not shocked?'

'Did you think I would forbid you to darken my doorstep, condemn you for corrupting the morals of society? That would be a bit rich, coming from a housebreaker, don't you think? I'm not shocked, but I am very, very intrigued. What sort of things does Bella get up to in the other books?'

'Elliot! I can't possibly…'

'What about those ivory figures we stole? Anything like that?'

'You're enjoying this! I should have guessed you would!' Deborah wanted to bite back the smile which plucked at the corners of her mouth in answer to that sensual curl of his lips, but she could not. It was delightful to discover that he found Bella as exciting as she did.

'I am, I admit it.' Elliot tucked Deborah's hair behind her ear, letting his fingers trail down the soft skin of her neck. 'What a vivid imagination you must have. Do you have a favourite—situation?'

Goosebumps rippled where he touched her. There was that tug of awareness between them as she met his eyes, and became conscious of the weight of his hand on her hip. 'How can I? As you pointed out, my experience is rather limited.'

Elliot caught his breath. 'You do realise that is paramount to a challenge?'

'I realise *you* would see it that way,' Deborah said, tilting her chin. '*I* am such an innocent, I meant no such thing.'

'Liar. Have I told you that you're irresistible?'

'Thus your remarkable exercise in constraint?' She could feel the rumble of his laughter vibrating through his chest. The release of her confession was making her reckless. Deborah put her arms around Elliot's neck and nestled closer. 'I think you are confusing me with another.'

'Bella?' Elliot ran his hand up her side, from hip to waist to breast. 'How much of you is in her, I wonder?'

His hand settled on the curve of her breast. He was kissing the pulse at the base of her neck now. 'If I were Bella,' Deborah said, 'what would you do to me?'

'If you were Bella, it would be more a question of what you would do to me,' Elliot said, nuzzling her ear lobe. 'I should warn you, I'm not particularly keen on being tied and bound.'

'Good God, you mean you've actually…' Deborah bit her lip, but she was too fascinated to keep silent. 'Was it—I mean, did you—what did you—I didn't actually think that people—not in real life, I mean.'

Elliot ran his fingers down the sweet curve of her spine. 'You'd be surprised at what goes on behind the closed doors of the most respectable of houses.'

And what had not gone on, Deborah thought grimly. *Don't think about that.* She was Bella. Elliot thought she was Bella. For one last time, she *would* be Bella. 'The doors of this respectable house are closed right now,' she said, garnering her courage.

Elliot tensed. He had waited so long for this moment that he could not allow himself to believe it was happening. Yet she seemed so different today. He kissed her lightly, though even that was enough to send the blood rushing to his groin. 'Did you have any particular goings-on in mind?'

'I rather thought I would leave that up to you.'

'Are you sure?'

She was sure that she wanted him. She stroked the indent on her ring finger. *Don't think.* 'Yes,' she said, 'I am.'

He pulled her roughly to him and kissed her, a brief, savage kiss that left her in no doubt of his need, before scooping her up into his arms. Yanking open the parlour door, he carried her effortlessly up the stairs. When he set her on her feet in her bedchamber, she was breathless, her heart pounding.

Light filtered in through the window, showing up the spartan room, the simple bed with its plain cotton sheets, the polished boards bare save for the one rug beside the bed. Deborah plucked at her gown. When Bella needed to dispense with clothes, she did so miraculously, without the need for description. Should she take it off? Before the reality of the situation could intrude on her fantasy, Elliot pulled her close and she forgot all about such mundane things as undressing as he ran his hands up and down her spine.

'You taste of summer,' he murmured against her mouth. 'The freshness of a morning heady with the promise of heat.' He wanted to plunge into her and drink deep, but he made himself sip until the tip of her tongue touched his, drawing him in, and the heat went straight to his groin.

Elliot shrugged out of his coat, dropping it carelessly on to the floor. He turned Deborah around in his arms and began to unhook her gown, planting more kisses on the skin revealed by each button, turning her back to face him as he drew the long sleeves down over her arms, the bodice over her breasts, then the skirts over her hips. She was blushing, but she watched him intently, as he watched her.

He kissed her neck, her throat, her shoulders, the creases in each elbow, the pulse at each wrist. He kissed the soft mounds of her breasts above her corset. When he turned her round again to undo the laces, he kissed her shoulder blades, the knot of her spine. His waistcoat was hastily discarded before he faced her once more. He kissed her mouth again. He could never have enough of her mouth.

Elliot's kisses made her weak with wanting. The way he looked at her left her in no doubt that her wanting was returned. The way he looked at her made her want him all the more. It was strange. Exciting. She tugged Elliot's shirt free from his corduroys. He yanked it over his head and she inhaled sharply, seeing for the first time in the clear light of day what she had only touched in the dark of night. She touched him hesitantly, running her palms over the span of his shoulders, his chest, feeling the beat of his heart, the smoothness of his skin, the roughness of the smattering of hair which arrowed down to the fastening of his breeches. His nipples hardened, just like hers did. She hadn't known that. The muscles in his back flexed under her touch. She looked up, and met his fierce gaze, and smiled. Then he kissed her again and it was hotter, somehow. More, somehow.

Elliot scattered the pins from her hair over the floor, combing his fingers through the length of it. 'I've imagined this,' he said, kissing the valley between her breasts, 'your hair spread out on the pillow behind you.'

He untied the ribbons of her chemise and pulled it down over her arms, over her breasts. The cotton abraded her nipples, making her stomach clench, making her close her eyes as a shivering heat whispered over her. He lifted her on to the bed and removed her shoes. He untied her garters and removed her stockings. 'The problem with being tied and bound,' he said, cupping her breasts, 'is that it is rather restricting.' His thumbs caressed the hard tips of her nipples as he eased her on to her back. 'But you know, that isn't really a problem if you are content to let someone else provide the entertainment.'

Before she realised what he was doing, he had her first wrist bound, tied with her garter to the cast-iron post. She tried to snatch her other hand away, but he caught it. 'Trust me,' he said, smiling one of his wicked smiles, 'I'll make it worth your while.'

He did not bind her ankles, but left her stretched on the bed, laid open to his gaze. His eyes blazed with desire as he looked at her, stripping her of embarrassment, leaving her naked and hot. The remainder of his clothes were dropped unceremoniously on to the floor. His erection was as thick and hard as she remembered it. She would not be able to touch him if he kept her like this. *Was that good or bad?*

'I don't want you to do anything,' he said, as if he had read her thoughts. He kissed her briefly. 'You know, there were two rather glaring omissions from Bella's experiences in the book I read. Of course, I haven't read them all, but I doubt very much that they were remedied in any of them.'

He lay down on the bed beside her. Long legs, tightly

packed muscles, almost but not quite touching. She had never lain naked like this before. She tried to turn towards him, but her bonds frustrated her. 'What omissions?'

Elliot kissed her again, leaning over her so that his chest brushed against her breasts. 'Poor Bella. I can't help feel that her victories are something of an anticlimax,' he said, trailing his fingers over her breasts, her belly, back up to her breasts. 'She takes so little pleasure from them, you see.' He eased himself a little way down the bed to capture one of her nipples in his mouth.

Deborah shivered. 'You're wrong,' she said, fighting for control, 'in the last book, the one I have just finished…'

'Yes, but you wrote that after you met me,' Elliot said, looking smug.

He turned his attention to her other nipple, licking, sucking, teasing, so that Deborah moaned, arching up from the bed. She wanted to touch him. 'What was the other thing?'

Elliot leaned over her, covering her body with his. It felt so strange. Not frightening. Deeply exciting. Warm skin. Hard muscle. She could feel his erection, reassuringly, enticingly solid against her thigh. What would it be like to have him inside her? Her muscles clenched, making her shiver again.

'The other thing.' Elliot kissed his way down the valley between her breasts. 'The other thing is a kiss.'

His mouth was on her belly now.

'A kiss? Bella has—she has lots of kisses.'

Elliot looked up, his eyes gleaming. 'Not this kind of kiss.' In one fluid movement he slid between her legs, tilted her towards him and covered her sex with his mouth.

Deborah cried out in shock. Elliot kissed her again, then his tongue slid into the crease at the top of her thigh and he kissed her there, too. She whimpered. He kissed the crease at the top of her other thigh. She whimpered again. Then his tongue slid inside her and she cried out.

Elliot's heart began to hammer so hard that he struggled to breath. She was so damp, so hot, so wet. He licked further into her folds and over the swollen nub of her. He slid his finger inside her as he licked, slowly, slowly, feeling her tighten and swell, feeling the corresponding rush of blood to his already hard shaft.

He tried to regulate his breathing, but he couldn't concentrate on it. Deborah was flushed. Her face. Her breasts. Her lids were heavy, almost closed. He slid his fingers higher and licked her. Thrust again and licked. She shuddered. His shaft pulsed in response. He licked. He circled. He sucked. He licked again.

Deborah strained urgently at her ties. His tongue, his fingers, all seemed to collude, to centre, to tighten her deep inside, as if she were being wrung out. Thrust and lick and slide and tighten. Thrust and lick and slide and tighten. She bucked up underneath him and the world exploded, shattered, scattering glittering pieces of her high into the sky as she floated and burned beneath them. She could hear herself crying out far away, a feral, needy sound as she floated and reformed.

She opened her eyes to find him looking at her, the way he looked at her making her shiver again, making her stretch luxuriously under his gaze, flaunting her body sinuously, like Bella did.

Elliot caught his breath. Deborah lay beneath him, eyes heavy and dark, drugged with desire. Hair streaming over the pillow, so much better than he'd imagined. Her nipples were dark pink. The curls which covered her sex were dark blonde. He had never been so hard. He leaned over to untie her wrists and his erection brushed her belly. 'Are you sure? Because if not, you need to say so now.'

Deborah sat up, twining her arms and pressing her body sinuously against him, just as Bella did. Elliot's hands skimmed her back, her bottom, back up to her breasts and he kissed her. Ravaging kisses. He tasted different. Of her, she realised, and it excited her, this most intimate sharing. His erection strained against her belly. His hand cupped her breast and she felt herself gathering anew, her climax building again before it had even ebbed. 'I want you,' she said, knowing that this time she really meant it, even though she was fast realising she had no idea what it meant. 'I want you.'

Her hands fluttered over his skin, sending little jolting shocks with every touch, which connected up, setting a flaring path to the ache of his erection. Elliot was beginning to doubt his ability to retain any sort of control, with his shaft almost screaming its need. Her mouth was hot, her hands needy. She was so delightfully naked. Had it ever been so glorious before, this skin on skin? He couldn't remember. 'Touch me,' he said urgently, 'I want you to touch me.'

She wanted to, but she faltered, her lack of experience detracting from Bella's confidence. As if he read her thoughts, Elliot took her hand and placed it on his shaft. Solid muscle, sheathed in silk. So hard. So potent-looking. She traced the length of it cautiously. Elliot groaned. Deborah snatched her hand back. 'Sorry.'

'No. God, don't be sorry. You have no idea how long I've waited.' Elliot kissed her, wrapping her fingers around his girth, showing her how to stroke him, wondering how much of it he could take before he came. 'This is what you're doing to me,' he said, slipping his finger back inside her and thrusting. 'And this,' he said, sliding up, over, then back inside. 'This is what you do to me.'

She could feel him pulsing under her caress. She stroked him, slowly tracing the path of silken skin to the friction of the tip. Elliot's chest rose and fell sharply. His shaft thickened. The throbbing between her legs began to pulse, like the shaft in her hand. She stroked him again, astounded and enthralled at the way her touch made him respond, marvelling at the solidity of him, the heft of him. So different. So amazingly, delightfully different.

'Deborah, if you keep doing that I don't think I'm going to be able to wait.' Elliot eased her on to her back, his self-control straining as he anticipated the darkly pink folds between her legs closing around him. He could feel her dampness, her heat, could feel the tightening beneath his erection which told him he was only just clinging on.

He entered her slowly. She felt every inch of him as he eased his way in, clinging to him as she did so, shivering as she sheathed him. She could feel the tension in him, too, in his clenched shoulders, the sinews of his arms standing out. He was panting. Beads of sweat on his forehead. His chest heaved. She lay under him, not knowing what to do. Then he tilted her towards him, and she stopped thinking.

His first thrust was pure pleasure. He took that slowly, too, leading her. She learned quickly, thrusting with him the next, finding a rhythm with the next, roused in a whole other way by the clinging of their bodies, her softness giving way to his hardness, yet holding him, melding with him. This time her climax was sudden and violent, a snapping of wires that made her cry out as Elliot thrust high inside her, made her wrap her legs around his waist, dig her nails into his back, arching up against him to hold him higher inside her until with one last deep thrust he came, too, withdrawing at the last possible moment, the force of his release making him cry out.

Deborah opened her eyes reluctantly. She was lying on the same pillow as Elliot. They were all tangled up, too, arms and legs entwined, so she wasn't quite sure who was what. His heart beat against hers. She felt too heavy to move. She had never been held thus. She had never felt like this. Bella had never felt like this. Sated.

Elliot kissed her lingeringly and rolled on to his back. He smelled of sweat and sex. His hair was a wild tangle. She had never seen him look so good. He smiled at her, the curl of his mouth lazy, incredibly sensual. Just thinking about what he could do with that wonderful mouth made her shudder with delight. She couldn't resist running her fingers over the rough hair on his chest, down to the ripple of muscles on his stomach.

'I was right, wasn't I?' he said, catching her hand. 'Now Bella knows something she did not.' He began to work his way along her hand, kissing the tip of each finger.

'You need not look so smug. It is most ungentlemanly of you,' Deborah said, trying not to laugh.

Elliot pulled her on top of him and ran his fingers down her spine, cupping the curve of her bottom. 'You know perfectly well I am not a gentleman. Besides, I have every right to feel smug. There is no mistaking the look of a satisfied woman. You should be feeling rather smug yourself, you know.'

'Should I? Why is that?' Her breasts were pressed into his chest. Her hair trailed over them both. It was delicious, lying on top of him like this.

'Because you have, lying beneath you, one very, very satisfied man.'

Deborah beamed. 'Really?'

'Completely,' Elliot said, kissing her. 'At least,' he said a few moments later, 'I thought I was. Only I find that perhaps…' He moved suggestively underneath her.

'Elliot! So soon?' Deborah exclaimed.

He couldn't help laughing, she seemed so genuinely surprised. 'I do apologise, but you have only yourself to blame, you know. You are a diamond. Infinitely desirable. You said so yourself.'

Bella. Deborah. Bella. Even Elliot had confused her with her creation. Deborah smiled Bella's wicked smile. 'So it is my fault, is it?'

'Completely.'

'Then I suppose it is up to me to take remedial action.'

'I'd say we should make a joint effort.'

She shook her head. 'It occurs to me that there is something else missing from my—Bella's repertoire that we might try.'

'What is that?'

Deborah wriggled down Elliot's body, kissing his chest, his stomach. Her heart pounded at her own daring, but the sense of power, the illusion of Bella, and the headiness of sexual satisfaction gave her confidence. 'I'll show you,' she said, deliberately echoing Elliot's own words, and began to kiss the thick, hard length of his shaft.

'I am supposed to be dining with Alex at his club,' Elliot said sleepily some time later as they lay in the tangle of sheets.

Deborah opened her eyes, surprised to see, through the uncurtained window, that dusk had fallen. Where had the day gone? How could the hours have passed so quickly? What was she doing here, lying naked in bed, with Elliot?

With Elliot! She closed her eyes, then opened them again. He was still naked. She was still naked. *Oh God!*

He smiled at her lazily and kissed the tip of her nose. 'I find the idea of dinner with Alex incredibly unappealing. I want to stay here.' He tucked a long strand of her hair behind her ear. 'What do you say?'

'Say?' Panicked, Deborah pushed him away and sat up abruptly, clutching the sheet around her. She hadn't thought beyond—beyond—she hadn't thought! When Bella was done with a man, she simply donned her clothes and vanished into the night. Or she made *him* do so. When Bella was done with a man, there were no consequences, no repercussions, no discussions, no expectations. There was certainly no suggestion of spending the night together. Had Elliot not realised? Had she not made it clear?

Oh God, she hadn't thought to explain. She had been so—and he had been so—*why* hadn't she thought? 'Why would you want to stay?' she asked agitatedly.

Confused by the edge in her voice, Elliot, too, sat up. 'Well, for a start there is the matter of finding your favourite situation. I am not suggesting that we can exhaust the possibilities in one night, but—'

'Elliot, there can be no question of—of exhausting the possibilities. I'm not Bella. I mean, I *was* Bella when we—when we were…' Deborah clutched at the sheet. 'I told you, I'm going to kill Bella off.'

'Because you no longer need her. I understand that,

but I'm not sure I understand why you're being so...'
Elliot stopped, momentarily at a loss. 'Don't you want
me to spend the night?' he asked, realising as he did
that spending the night, the thing he never did, was precisely the thing he most wanted.

The very idea of Elliot in her bed, sleeping beside
her, waking up beside her, holding her through the
night, making love to her through the night, was ex-
quisite torture. Deborah stared at him, stricken, as the
last remnants of her fantasy dispersed. Elliot wanted
to spend the night with Bella, but Bella was well and
truly gone, and no matter how much Deborah wanted to
spend the night with Elliot, he would not want to spend
the night with her and...

'Deborah?'

If she didn't know him better, she would think him
offended. She didn't want to think about that. About
why he was offended. About what he wanted. She didn't
want to think about what she wanted either, because it
didn't matter. What mattered was making things clear,
which she should have done before, only she had been
so carried away with Bella and Elliot. Especially Elliot.
Oh hell! 'I thought you understood. This afternoon, it
was a—a last performance. Bella's last performance. I
thought you realised that, Elliot. When we were talking about the books. When you were talking about what
Bella liked, what Bella did not know, I thought you
knew that it was just—that it wasn't real.' She felt as
if her skin, her body, was metamorphosing with every
passing moment, from beautiful Bella to disgusting

Deb. Terrified that he witness her transformation, she pulled the sheet up to her neck.

Elliot ran his fingers through his hair, staring at her in consternation. The voluptuous creature who had been lying in his arms only moments before had been replaced by a haughty, icy female who looked like her maiden aunt. 'Are you telling me that you regret this? That you wish it had never happened?'

'I'm saying it won't happen again. I can't have an *affaire* with you. I think you should go.'

Though an *affaire* was what he would have proposed—given the chance—Deborah's out-of-hand rejection made Elliot wonder whether it was what he actually wanted. He hadn't thought beyond this moment, but now that it had happened and it had been all, more than he had dreamed, he was very far from the point where he wanted to make it finite. This realisation confused him. Deborah's dismissal of an offer he hadn't even had a chance to make hurt. Elliot got out of bed and began to pull on his clothes. 'It is customary to await an offer before turning it down,' he said curtly. 'I haven't asked you to be my mistress.'

'Oh. You mean you did understand after all—about Bella?'

Elliot stopped in the middle of buttoning his waistcoat. 'Are you seriously saying that this afternoon, you and I, it won't happen again?' Deborah looked like a trapped animal. He sat down on the bed again and tried to take her hand, but she shrank from him. 'What the hell is wrong?' he snapped, even more offended. 'What have I done to upset you?'

'Nothing! You haven't. I'm sorry. It's my fault.'

'*What* is your fault?'

'This. I shouldn't have—we shouldn't have. Can't we just forget it?' She knew as soon as she spoke the words that they were preposterous. Why hadn't she thought this through? How could she have been so stupid, so incredibly stupid? No wonder Elliot was looking at her as if she had two heads. She had spoilt everything. 'It was a mistake. My mistake. I'm sorry.'

Her utter dejection cut through Elliot's anger. The feisty, sensual woman who had sparred with him, teased him, flirted with him, aroused him and satisfied him beyond anything he had ever known was fled. 'Deborah, I don't know what it is going on in that clever head of yours, but—'

'Nothing. It is nothing, save that I am sorry that you seem to have misunderstood—that I have not made myself clear. Please don't let this spoil things between us, Elliot. I want us to be friends.'

'Cannot friends be lovers?'

'No! No, I can't. It was Bella. I wish now that I had not told you about her,' Deborah said wretchedly.

'For God's sake, I wasn't making love to Bella!' Elliot exclaimed in exasperation.

'Yes, but, Elliot, that's exactly what you were doing.'

He stared at her in silence, quite unable to formulate any meaningful answer to this *non sequitur*. Snatching his coat from the floor, Elliot dragged it on and made for the door. 'I assure you, *I* was under no illusions about who I was making love to. You told me only this afternoon that the time had come for you to stop hiding behind Bella. Are you absolutely sure that is the case? I would think hard about that, if I were you.'

'I am not the only one hiding,' Deborah threw at him, but Elliot closed the door to the bedchamber, making a point of not slamming it. She listened to the sound of his boots on the stairs. The parlour door creaked open as he went in search of his hat and gloves. She heard the sound of the latch on the front door being lifted. There was a pause, as if he was waiting for something, then the soft thud of the door closing and the house was silent.

Deborah curled up into a ball and huddled under the sheets. They smelled of Elliot. And sex. She smelled of Elliot and sex. Despite the misery of his departure, her body still throbbed with satisfaction. It was like a battle which they had both won. The sheer elation of their coupling was so very different to the sense of subjection, latterly the degradation which she had endured in the marital bed with Jeremy. Elliot made her feel powerful. Or was that Bella?

What did it matter? Elliot was gone and Deborah was bereft. He would never understand. She barely understood herself. It had seemed so right to tell him about Bella; she had been so sure she was seeing things clearly for the first time. She would forget all about the past. The future would be filled with new writing, new friends. And Elliot.

Deborah buried her head under the feather pillow.

The very idea of an Elliott-less future made her feel sick. Whichever way she looked at it, it was a colourless wasteland of a place. She couldn't bear it.

She would not have to! She would not! When he thought about it, Elliot would surely understand about Bella. Things between them would go back to how they had been. She would forget all about this afternoon. They both would. *Wouldn't they?*

Deborah groaned. She did not want Elliot to forget, any more than she really wanted to believe that he had been making love to Bella. Had she been hiding? Was she hiding still? She beat her fists on the mattress, furious at her own contrariness. What the devil was going on in her head? She couldn't want him. She couldn't let him see how much she wanted him. She *didn't* want him. It was Bella, not Deborah, and Bella was no more.

Sitting up, she hurled the pillow across the room. *'Devil take it!'* Deborah dropped her head into her hands. She was not in love with Elliot. She could not possibly be in love with him, she *couldn't*. It would be fatal.

Chapter Ten

Elliot sent Alex his excuses as soon as he returned home. Now he sat in his study, staring at the parcel of books sitting on his desk, strangely reluctant to cut the string. What was stopping him? He poured himself a glass of Madeira and stared at that instead. His mind was such a tangle of thoughts, he had no idea how to begin to unravel them. Taking a sip of the wine, he made a face and put it down.

I am not the only one hiding. He had a horrible suspicion that there were uncomfortable truths lurking somewhere under that last remark of hers, but he wasn't at all sure he was ready to confront them. What the hell had happened, there in her bedchamber, afterwards? He racked his brains, but could think of nothing he had said or done. His offer to spend the night had been the trigger, but why?

Why had he offered anyway? He hated to spend the night with his *chères-amies*. He took a sip of the Madeira and made a face. *Chère-amie* no more fitted his idea of Deborah than mistress. *Affaire* seemed such a temporary word. He had always liked that about it. Before.

Elliot picked up his paper knife and cut through the string. Two books, unbound and uncut, lay before him. *Arsenic* and *Wolfsbane.* Deadly poisons. Deadly Nightshade. Deborah. This afternoon, the revelation of her authorship had been exciting. Tonight, he wondered what his reading would tell him about her marriage. Bella wreaked revenge so that her creator could endure the mess she had made of her life. What mess?

He stared at the frontispiece of the first book. He was afraid. He didn't want to pity her. He didn't want to think ill of her. He wanted…

Elliot swore, then took a deep draught of his wine. He didn't know what the hell he wanted any more. With a sigh, he took his knife and began to cut the pages.

He read both books, one after the other, sitting up late by the library fire in his dressing gown. Like the novel Lizzie had lent him, these were *risqué,* funny and savage. Now that he knew she had penned them, he could detect Deborah's caustic wit in almost every paragraph. Her talent was undeniable; the stories were exceedingly well written. That way of hers, of sketching a character in two or three brief sentences, transferred brilliantly to the page. No wonder the books were popular.

He found them—unsettling. He could not at first understand why this was so, for the knowledge that Deborah had written this scene, her pen had described that act, her mind had conjured this twist in the plot, distracted him. His imagination moved seamlessly from Bella to Deborah to Bella.

Elliot frowned. He had been so carried away, he hadn't really thought about the extent to which Deborah had been transformed, in talking about Bella. To the extent where she had forgotten herself, confused herself with her own creation, the woman she said was everything she was not. Bella was Deborah's secret weapon. Did she really believe that? And why?

What the *hell* had gone on in her marriage? Elliot cursed. How many times had he asked himself that? Whatever it was, he had to admire her for the way she had kicked back. No matter how skewed she was emotionally, Bella Donna was a masterful instrument for revenge. But revenge for what?

The clock on the mantel chimed four in the morning. She wasn't going to tell him and he had to know. Elliot's stomach rumbled. He'd missed dinner. He'd call on Lizzie in the morning, he decided, making his way down the back stairs to the kitchen. Knowing his sister, she would already have done some digging. In her own way, she was every bit as devious as he was. There was ham and cheese in the larder. Some rather stale bread went into the frying pan with several eggs. He wolfed all of it down at the scrubbed table, his mind flying in all sorts of different directions, while all the time, at the centre, was Deborah.

I'm not the only one hiding. What *had* she meant by that? He was not hiding behind the Peacock, was he?

Hiding from what? Elliot pushed back his chair and stretched, rolling his shoulders. This afternoon had been so—just so! He grinned. Perfect. Utterly fantastic, just as he had known it would be. It wasn't just the act itself, it was her. The way she talked and teased and challenged him. The way she made him feel. The way she got inside his head and his skin. What it had felt like, being inside her. Joined in body, in mind.

God Almighty, it was as well no one could hear his thoughts! Elliot cast his plate, fork and knife into the basin by the pump beside the dirty skillet. He hadn't thought about the Peacock in weeks, but perhaps it was time for another outing?

He tested himself for the familiar sense of excitement, but found none. He could not tell Deborah, obviously. She would worry. Not that she had a right to worry. Not that he felt himself accountable. But he wouldn't tell her. Because she *would* worry.

I am not the only one hiding. Dammit, why wouldn't it go away? A stupid remark, flung at him merely to hurt him, that was all. What did he care? Elliot picked up the lamp, and made his way back up to the study. He had a housebreaking to arrange.

By dawn, Elliot had done most of the planning and could no longer keep his eyes open. He dragged himself up to bed and slept soundly for five hours. A bath, a shave, a change of clothes, and he was at his sister's house not long after noon, only to discover she was gone out for the day with her mother-in-law and not expected back until after dinner.

He thought of calling in Hans Town, but was loath to do so until he had spoken to Lizzie. Yesterday he had been hurt by Deborah's refusal even to consider an *affaire*. Today, he was inclined to agree with her. He did not want an *affaire*. What, then, did he want? Why did he no longer want what he had? *Was he hiding?*

Out of habit, Elliot sought respite and clarity in exercise. An hour spent in his shirt sleeves and stockinged feet, thumping hell out of the huge punch bag which swung from a hook in Jackson's sparring room, helped. There was something soporific and at the same time liberating about the thwack of his fist on leather scarred with the thwacks of many hundreds of fists. It was like beating down his own resistance.

Bella was Deborah's revenge on her husband. The Peacock was his revenge for Henry. *That* parallel was obvious enough. Deborah had captured Henry's spirit so well in her book, reading her words had reminded him of the Henry who laughed and broke the rules, who was infuriating as well as funny, as foolish sometimes as he was brave. The real Henry, not the crazed creature who had taken up residence in that fetid wreck of a body before he died. The real Henry, who had loved life above all. Was he done with extracting revenge for Henry's death, as Deborah was done with avenging her marriage?

But the Peacock had not been born just for Henry. Elliot needed him. What would Elliot do without him?

He was no politician, but he was a first-class *agent provocateur*. An agitator, who could make politicians act. Was there such a thing? Could he be such a thing? Would it be enough? Whether or not he would miss the excitement of his night-time escapades, tonight would tell. Whether or not something else could replace them...

The punch bag caught Elliot a glancing blow in the midriff as he stood stock still in the sparring room. Something else already had. Someone else. Elliot dropped his head against the leather bag. 'Bloody hell, not that,' he muttered. 'Surely not that?'

Suddenly aware that he was in the middle of Jackson's salon talking to a leather bag filled with sand, he straightened up and looked around, but attention was focused on a sparring match. Elliot groaned. He couldn't be. Dear God, he couldn't be—*could* he?

Why did he have to choose someone so complicated? Not that he'd chosen her. In fact, he'd gone out of his way *not* to choose her. And not that he was, he told himself as he doused his torso in cold water. Not that. Most definitely not that.

For the second day in a row, Elliot returned home in a daze. Slopping wine into a glass, which he then placed on a side table and completely forgot, he slumped down on to the chair in front of his desk. Wasn't it supposed to make you happy? Weren't you supposed to feel like you were walking on air or some such balderdash? Henry, who liked to think of himself as handy with his fives, had once described a mill he'd seen on leave, just before the Battle of Trafalgar. John Gully, unknown and untested, had gone more than sixty rounds before the champion, known as the Game Chicken, had knocked him out. Henry described Gully's bloody visage in gory detail. Elliot thought now that he knew just how the man must have felt. Surely this couldn't be love?

There, he'd let the word loose and the sky hadn't fallen down. Remembering his wine, Elliot retrieved it and took a cautious sip. It tasted the same. Wasn't the world supposed to look different, somehow? 'What do I know?' he said aloud. Putting his glass down on the mantelpiece, he stared at his reflection in the mirror. Hair in disarray. His neckcloth lopsided. Was there a light in his eyes, a sparkle even? Elliot laughed. 'Damned if I can tell!'

Disconsolately, he returned to his desk and retrieved the file from its secret drawer. It was such an easy job, he had no need of any recce. He'd do it tonight. That would tell him something, surely? He looked at his drawings, scanned his notes, waiting for the familiar sense of excitement, but nothing happened.

He remembered the last time. Deborah's clutching that damned dog, trying to stifle her laughter. The sheer exhilaration of their escape, the reckless gallop, the thud of their horses' hooves, the steam of their breath in the cold air, the *frisson* of awareness, knowing she was there at his side. And afterwards in the boathouse...

And yesterday, in her bed. And before that, all the other days. That strange squeezing in his chest when he looked at her—there, he could admit to that now.

The stupid things he saved up to tell her. The things she knew about him that no one else knew. Did all this, then, amount to love? And if it did, even if it did, what did it mean, what could it mean, when she was so patently still living under the cloud of her past?

A soft tap on the door roused him from the mire that this question enveloped him in. 'Mrs Murray called,' his batman said. 'She has returned earlier than expected and asks if you wish to join her for dinner. Her husband and her mother-in-law will not be with her, she said to tell you.'

Elliot grinned. 'That is most fortuitous.' It wasn't as if he'd be picking the lock on the house in Berkeley Square any time before midnight. 'I'll wear the black coat and the grey pantaloons,' he told his man. 'I shall most likely go on to my club. Tell the servants not to wait up.'

Knowing full well that his master never visited his club, his batman gave him a knowing look. 'You need have no fear, I shall make sure you are not seen.'

Quite taken aback by this remark, Elliot could only stare as the servant left the room. He picked up the file on his lap, gave it another quick glance, then cast it on the flames of the fire. It seemed Alex Murray wasn't the only man with suspicions. He'd better make damn sure this next act didn't turn into his final one, if that was the case!

It was a close call. The kind of close call Elliot would have relished, back in the old days. Back in the days before Deborah. He was careless, quite distracted by what Lizzie had told him of Jeremy Napier over dinner, and did not check the rooms on the third floor, or he would have spotted the light shining through the gap at the bottom of the door. The general, whose conscience was not as clean as Elliot believed, was prone to nightmares, and had become a most reluctant sleeper. As the Peacock's pick slid the last tumbler on the safe's lock home, a creaking in the hallway outside alerted him.

The old man who peered around the door of the dining room wore only a nightshirt and a cap. He was frailer than Elliot remembered. His bare feet made him look vulnerable. Though he had no option but to ambush him, covering his toothless mouth with a muffler to stop him from crying out, the ropes he used to bind his victim to the chair were loosely tied. Still, he could easily have completed his task, but the contrast between the brash, muscular general Elliot remembered and the scrawny man who flailed weakly at his bonds was too much. Henry would never have approved such a conquest. Elliot had better uses for his energies. The thirst for revenge, which had flourished like a weed inside him for years, was already wilting. Now it began to shrivel. He closed the safe without retrieving what he had come for, taking care to keep his face out of the old man's line of sight. The peacock feather remained tucked inside his pocket.

The night was warm, a light cover of cloud covering the sky as Elliot made his way along Mount Street. It was late enough to be early. There was no one about to disturb his thoughts, only the echo of his footsteps to accompany him. Deborah was right. He had been hiding, but he did not need to any more. The Peacock had served his purpose. Like Bella, he would die. And Elliot—Elliot had no desire whatsoever to risk dying with him.

He touched the feather in his pocket. The last one. Perhaps he would keep it as a memento. As the dawn began to filter through the clouds, he turned homewards. He did love Deborah. He *was* in love with her. It was so obvious, he should be laughing at himself for being so blind. There wasn't any other explanation for what he felt. There wasn't any other he wanted now either. He loved her and he was pretty certain that she loved him. If he could only persuade her to let go of the past.

Could he? Would she? His steps faltered. What Lizzie had told him was not common knowledge, but, according to her, it was accepted fact in Jeremy's circles. Deborah had been married for seven years. She must surely know the truth? Yet if she did, why was she so determined to assume so much of the blame for the failure of her marriage? No, it was impossible that she did not know the truth. He simply needed to persuade her that neither shame nor blame attached to her. Why could she not see that for herself?

As he made his way slowly home, his brow furrowed, Elliot veered between anger and pity. The utter misery of two people bound in such a marriage was almost beyond contemplating. Their vows had sentenced them to a lifetime of failure. Sixteen years in the army, where a blind eye was turned to men who took their comforts where they could, had taught him that there were some men as irrevocably inclined to men as he was to women. Unlike many of his fellow officers, Elliot was confident enough in his own sexuality neither to judge nor to feel threatened. Under any other circumstances, what Lizzie had told him of Jeremy would have been of no import.

Save that Jeremy had been married to Deborah. His pretending to love Deborah, marrying her for her money, was bad enough, but to have used her in such a calculating way—no, Elliot could not forgive that. Not that it mattered. What mattered was Deborah, who seemed unable to forgive herself for her husband's rejection. He couldn't understand it.

Deborah had said that she was done with the past, but it was patently untrue. What if she was never done? What then? An abyss opened up under his feet as he contemplated this possibility. Elliot clenched his fists. There could be no more hiding for either of them. He would make her see that. Failure was simply not an option.

Deborah was working—or trying to work—about as successfully as she had tried sleeping, telling herself not to worry and attempting to stop reliving that afternoon of love-making. The page in front of her was not blank, but covered in a hotchpotch of squiggles, blots, tearstains and—she noticed with dismay—Elliot's name. She couldn't stop thinking about him. Thinking about him led to remembering every kiss, every look, every touch. The ecstatic quiver and clutch of her muscles around him as he entered her. The soaring high of her climaxes. The bliss of skin on skin. The scent of him on her. Remembering made the jolt back down to reality so much harder. It made the panic, that he was gone for ever, that she had ruined all, so much more difficult to quell.

She picked up her pen again and stared blindly at the page. She wished he would call. She was not ready to face him. She was terrified he would not call. She wanted—she wanted—she wanted—the one thing she could not have. That much was constant.

A knock on the door made her jump. Leaping to her feet, her stomach a seething mass of nerves, Deborah looked down quickly at her ink-stained pinafore. A glance at her reflection in the hall mirror confirmed the worst. She had a blob of ink on her cheek and her hair looked as if she'd had some sort of fight to the death with curl papers.

Elliot on the other hand looked very Elliot-ish, she thought as she opened the door. His coat was dark blue, not one she had seen him wearing before. His waistcoat was grey, as were his pantaloons. His cravat was more elaborately tied than usual, with a sapphire pin winking discreetly in the folds. She stared up at him wordlessly, caught in the memory of him without any clothes, in her bed, his face taut with desire as she took him into her mouth. Her face flamed.

'May I come in?'

Too embarrassed to meet his eye, Deborah held the door wide and let him precede her into the parlour.

'You've been working,' Elliot said.

Deborah quickly snatched up the smudged, wasted bundle of papers and held them defensively to her chest. Her hands were shaking. He had perfectly good clothes on, she didn't need to keep thinking about what was underneath. 'I wasn't expecting you,' she said, her voice an odd combination of breathless and harsh. It was true and it was a lie. Like everything these days, or so it sometimes felt.

Despite having spent the rest of the night rehearsing every variation on the scene which was about to unfold, Elliot was still lacking a battle plan. He tried in vain to quell the unaccustomed panic which knotted his stomach. The last time he had seen her, Deborah had been naked, flushed from their love-making. Here, in this very room, it had started. The teasing. The kissing. The touching. Their eyes met and Deborah looked away quickly. She was blushing. He was—just thinking about it, and he was—dammit, he shouldn't be thinking about it!

Elliot made to sit down, realised Deborah was still standing, and propped himself up against the mantel instead. His mind went blank. He had a thousand things to say and he couldn't think of one. He nodded at the papers she was holding against her like a shield. 'Bella's final curtain, I take it,' he said. She thrust the bundle into a drawer. 'I read two of your other books,' he told her.

Deborah dropped into her seat at the fireside. 'Which ones?'

Taking his cue from her, Elliot, too, sat down. '*Arsenic* and *Wolfsbane*.'

Were they going to just sit here and make polite conversation about her books? What else was she expecting? 'Did you like them?' Deborah asked. Her voice sounded desperate. She had to calm down.

Elliot nodded. 'It was strange, reading them and knowing that you wrote them. I can see why they are so popular; you are very talented.'

'But you did not like them?'

'Oh, I did. They are clever and exciting and—sad.'

Deborah winced. 'They are supposed to be witty. No one has ever described them as sad, to my knowledge.'

'I have the advantage of knowing the author. I doubt anyone else would see Bella as I do,' Elliot said.

It was the gentle way he spoke, which made the tears clog her throat. Deborah swallowed convulsively. 'How—how do you see Bella?' she asked eventually.

She was as pale as she had been flushed a few moments ago. She looked as if she were bracing herself for a blow. Elliot's heart did its squeezing thing. He hated seeing her like this. 'Bella,' he said, choosing his words with care, 'she doesn't let herself be defeated, does she? But she doesn't win either. She is so intent on playing men at their own games, she doesn't know how to be a woman. That's what is sad.'

Deborah sat slowly back into her chair. 'Oh.'

'I wish you would tell me about it,' Elliot said. 'I wish you would trust me.'

'For God's sake, Elliot, don't you know more than enough already? I can't. I can't talk about it. It's over, Jeremy is dead and buried, surely that's all that matters?'

He got to his feet and pulled her from her chair, holding her tight. 'It's over, but it's not buried. It's still there, hurting you.'

'I still feel so small sometimes,' she whispered. 'When I was married, I used to feel I was shrinking. I used to want to be so small no one could see me.' Deborah drew a shaky breath. It hurt so much, remembering the ghostlike figure she had become. She hated the idea of showing herself thus to Elliot, but she realised now, with a leaden heart, that if she did not he would never understand, and if he did not understand it would always be there between them, a barrier to any sort of friendship. And she so desperately needed any sort of friendship, for she could have nothing else.

'You're right,' she said finally. It was an agony, suffocating the love which had only just put out the first green shoots, but it would be much, much more painful for her to let it bloom. These last two nights, pacing her chamber, she had tried so hard to talk herself out of the truth and failed miserably. She loved him so much. She knew what she had to do, but she so much wished she did not have to. 'You're right,' she said again.

That determined little nod she gave was his undoing. 'I love you so much,' Elliot blurted out. Stark, and to the point, and utterly true. The relief of it. He took the shock on her face as surprise. 'Deborah, I love you,' Elliot said, warming to the task. 'I've never said it before, not to anyone. I've never wanted to, but I think I could get very used to saying it to you. I love you.'

'Elliot!' Deborah stared at him, aghast. The words she most longed to hear, which she had not thought for a moment to hear, for just a few wonderful seconds made her heart soar. Then plummet. 'Oh, Elliot.'

He caught her hand again. 'I know. I know that it's sudden, it's a shock to me, too, but I know it's right. I won't change my mind. I'm absolutely sure, I couldn't be more sure. I know that your marriage still haunts you, but—'

Deborah yanked her hand free. 'Elliot, you have to stop! It doesn't just haunt me, I can't escape it.'

'You can. I can help you. I *know,* you see—'

'You can't help me,' she interrupted, wringing her hands in anguish. 'I wish you could, but you can't, and I can't let you try. I would fail you in the end. Elliot, I could never make you happy.'

'I can't be happy without you.'

'Oh, please, don't say that.' Deborah dug her nails into her palms. 'Listen to me. You need to listen to me. I had no idea that you felt—but it will pass, I know it will pass,' she said fervently, the words she had recited over and over in the night to give her courage, though they failed to convince her. 'You just need to listen.'

Her voice had a feverish quality that worried him. He wanted to pull her into his arms, to kiss away the frown which scarred her brow, to tell her it would be all right, but everything about her—her rigid stance, the clenched fists, the tight white face—warned him against such action. He had waited so long for her to trust him, but it felt all wrong, more like an end than a beginning. He wanted to tell her that he knew. He wanted to smooth the path to her confession, but the very fact that she was finding it so difficult kept him mute. Could Lizzie have been misinformed? Was there some other dark secret he knew nothing about? The optimism which had lightened his step since last night scuttled off like a frightened rabbit. It took all his resolution to remain calm, but he managed to sit down, to cross his ankles in an appearance of negligence. 'I'm listening. Tell me. Take your time.'

'Yes. Yes, I must tell you.' Deborah took a turn around the room, then straightened her shoulders and resumed her seat. 'You know that my marriage to Jeremy wasn't happy. I told you he married me for my money, but that wasn't the only reason. His family are an old and revered one. They pride themselves on having the line passed down through direct heirs. Jeremy needed a son. So when I came along with my fortune and my bloody great wide-eyed innocence, I made it so easy for him. I was so desperate to be loved, you see.'

Her voice began to break, but when Elliot got up to comfort her, she motioned him away. 'No. Stay there. I can't talk if you touch me and I need to explain.'

Elliot sat back down again, feeling as if he were preparing for a battle in which his forces were vastly outnumbered. Was she going to tell him about Jeremy or not? Deborah was twisting his handkerchief round her fingers, but she seemed calmer. Ominously determined. 'Go on,' Elliot said, trying to sound encouraging.

'It was a disaster, right from the wedding night. Jeremy couldn't—he found me repulsive. He—we did not manage to consummate the marriage for some time, and when we did it was a—a painful experience for both of us. I didn't know any better. He could not—when he came to me—which he did at first, as often as he could bear it, for his desire for a son was even stronger than his disgust of me. It was always in the dark. I was not to touch him. I was always—he made me—with my back to him. And he was—he wasn't like you.'

She was blushing deeply, concentrating on her fingers, his handkerchief, but determined to finish, no matter how embarrassing. 'It was awful, but it was my fault. I knew that, I knew that I was just not the sort of woman who could—and the more I worried about it the worse it got. One night I tried. Those books—I wasn't reading them for Bella that first time. I thought if I could—so I—I can't tell you what I did, but it failed. He hit me then, for the first and only time, and I hated him. That's when Bella Donna was born. Poor Jeremy, he was every bit as destroyed by the whole farcical performance as I was. I hated him, but I could not blame him. It was my fault.'

'Your fault!' Unable to contain his outrage, Elliot leapt to his feet.

'Don't be angry, Elliot. I've been angry for years and

it doesn't help. It was wrong of him, I know it was, but if I'd been a better woman, maybe we—I don't know. He tried, you know, in the beginning, he did try to love me, and God knows, so too did I try, but I simply wasn't good enough.'

Staggered by her ignorance, Elliot dragged his fingers through his hair. 'I can't believe—you really didn't know? You had no idea?' He took a deep breath, forcing his fists to unclench. Another deep breath. 'Deborah, it wasn't your fault. My God, I still can't believe—all those years and he didn't tell you. I can't believe no one told you. Kinsail—he must have known.' He took an agitated turn around the room, struggling to find the words. 'You really didn't know?'

'Known what? Elliot, what didn't I know?'

Elliot took another deep breath. Her face, utterly bewildered, nearly set his temper flaring again, but he managed to damp it down. She didn't know. She really didn't know. All those books she had written and she didn't know. It was unbelievable.

'Elliot, you're frightening me. *What* didn't I know?'

'About Jeremy.' He sat down abruptly. He needed to let go of his anger. She had been deceived. It was done. What mattered was explaining. And understanding. He needed to help her. He could help her. He could. Elliot laced his hands together in an unconscious reflection of Deborah's. 'You were right about one thing. Jeremy needed a wife, but not for the reasons you think. Or not only for those.' He sat forwards, leaning his elbows on his knees. 'Look, I want you to know that I haven't been spying on you or sniffing around your past. I wanted you to tell me yourself, but when I realised how I felt about you, I needed to know, so I asked Lizzie. Jeremy was a—a…' Elliot struggled to find the right words.

'Deborah,' he said delicately, 'the fact is that your husband preferred men to women. Not just as friends, but in every way. He'd been having an *affaire* with another man. These—these relationships, they are not uncommon, but your husband and his lover were not discreet. The Kinsails obviously put pressure on Jeremy to avoid scandal. I remember you told me how proud your husband was of his heritage. I'm sorry.'

Deborah's pale face turned ashen. 'What do you mean?'

'He married you to protect his name. He used you.' Elliot's hands clenched into fists again as his sympathy for Jeremy's undoubted plight warred with the man's perfidy. 'If only he had confided in you. If he had had the guts to tell you. But to blame you as he obviously did, for failing… To make you think that you were the problem—' He broke off. 'Sorry. That's not helping, I know.'

Deborah was shaking. 'Do you mean that Jeremy—are you saying that my husband—the man who married me—that he loved men?' She shook her head, her expression a heart-wrenching mixture of incomprehension and hurt. 'He wouldn't have—not even Jeremy would have lied to me about such a thing. Someone would have told me, surely? They would not all have—have colluded over such a thing.'

'Deborah, they probably all assumed that you knew.'

'But I didn't,' she said slowly. 'I didn't know. Did Jacob—do you mean that Jacob knew?' Her voice choked. 'He did. Of course he did. All this time. And Margaret, his wife? Surely she did not…'

Elliot's nails dug into the flesh of his palms. 'I don't know,' he said grimly. 'It doesn't matter a damn.'

Deborah clutched at her chair. There was a rushing noise in her ears. 'But it does. Why did no one tell me?' She clutched at her face now. Her fingers were icy. 'All these years, all the things I did to…' She shuddered. 'Oh God.'

'Deborah, it doesn't matter.' Elliot tried to pull her into his arms, but she pulled away.

'Doesn't matter?' She looked at him incredulously. 'Have you any idea of the humiliation that I suffered? To say nothing of the guilt. How could I not have known? How could I have been so *bloody* stupid? Dammit, only the other day I was talking about moving out from the shadows of the past.'

Her voice had an edge of hysteria to it. She was shaking, her teeth were actually chattering, but when Elliot tried again to touch her, she pushed him away. 'Deborah, I love you. Please, listen to me…'

'How can you love me? How could you possibly love me? I'm a dupe. Even the servants must have been laughing at me.'

This was going badly wrong. Elliot tugged ineffectually at his neckcloth. Deborah had retreated so far into herself he doubted he could reach her. All his confidence, the joy of discovering himself in love, was being shred into little pieces in the face of such misery. 'Deborah, I love you,' Elliot said, clinging to the one certainty. 'I really love you. I've never said that before. I've never had the least desire to think it, never mind say it. I love you, and it's not going to go away, what I feel. You could feel it, too, if you would just let go. If you would just believe in yourself a little.'

'Believe in myself?' Deborah exclaimed. 'Seven years I was married and my husband could not bring himself to trust me. For seven years, and two more since I was widowed, not a single soul has thought enough of me to tell me what seems to have been common knowledge.'

'Deborah, Lizzie did not say…'

'What kind of person does that make me,' Deborah swept on, 'that my own husband lied to me about something so—so fundamental? What on earth is there to believe in, save an ability to bring misery to all those I love?'

He needed an answer, but all he could think about, seeing her distraught face, was that he wanted to make it all go away, make it all unsaid. Yet where would that leave them save back at the beginning with it all to say again? Never in his life had he wanted something so much as to take away her pain and never in his life had something seemed so utterly unattainable. Elliot tried to rally himself, to remind himself of the old saying that love could conquer all, but he never did have much faith in old adages. He loved her, his heart was aching with love for her, but even if he could make her listen, make her believe what he felt, what difference would it make? He had thought his revelation would clear the path to a happy future. Instead, he seemed to have placed an insurmountable object in their way. His dejection was all the deeper for the height from which he had fallen.

Elliot picked up his hat and gloves. His feet felt weighted to the ground, his actions felt as if they were happening in slow motion. Already, it seemed as if Deborah was far away, out of his reach. 'I love you,' he said, his voice cracking on the words he believed he was saying for the last time, 'that won't ever change, but until *you* do, then there is no point in my saying any more.' He waited, but she made no move, said no word. He left.

Chapter Eleven

For more than a week, Deborah struggled to come to terms which what had happened, but every time she tried to reconcile her heart and her head, she failed. The truth, stark and terrifying, took stronger and more resolute root the more she tried to shift it. It hurt because it was so painfully clear, like the sun reflected on snow. She was in love with Elliot.

She was in love and had never been so utterly and completely miserable in her life. It tormented her, this love, which she would never be able to tell him. She tormented herself, crying over the sentimental romances she had so formerly despised, deriving small consolation by constructing alternative, unhappy-ever-after endings. She lost hours gazing into space, dreaming up rose-bowered cottages in which she and Elliot could live happily ever after, even though she hated cottages and the notion of Elliot spending the rest of his life contentedly tending their garden made her laugh. Bitterly. In the park, she gazed enviously at couples strolling arm in arm, inventing falsehoods to explain every little sign of affection. If she could not be happy, why then should anyone else?

But such hostility, such railing at the unfairness of it all, such resentment and vitriol, was exhausting and pointless. Weariness and depressions seized her then and finally, in the void created by lethargy, her spirit began to fight its way back. She loved Elliot. She loved him with her blood and bones as well as her heart. Her love for him made a flimsy edifice of what she thought had been love for Jeremy. Her husband had been right. She'd been in love with the idea of love, no more.

Poor Jeremy. If only she could have understood his turmoil, perhaps she would have made him a better wife. If only he could have told her, trusted her with his secret, perhaps then…

Perhaps then what, exactly? Deborah hauled herself out of bed, where she had been languishing, and sat in front of the mirror. 'Honestly,' she said to her wan reflection, 'what do you think you could have done, if you had known? It wouldn't have made him love you.'

There. It was a fact. Elliot was right. There was nothing she could have done to make Jeremy love her.

'I am not a failure.' She tested the words out in no more than a whisper, but they lacked conviction. Because she *had* failed, hadn't she? She had not realised what everyone else had known. Her not knowing had made it impossible for her to console Jeremy. Had, in fact, forced Jeremy into prolonging his attempts to…

Pity enveloped her, followed by guilt. She could have

helped him, consoled him, made his life a little less miserable, if only she had known. But she hadn't known. He hadn't trusted her. Deborah straightened her shoulders and resumed her study of her reflection. 'It wasn't my fault,' she said, and this time her words sounded like the truth. 'I didn't fail, because he made it impossible for me to succeed.'

Jeremy had been ashamed. His repeated failures had made him more ashamed. She could see that. Deborah gave a little nod. 'Yes, I can see that. But he should have told me.' Another little nod. 'It wasn't my fault.' Convincing. 'I am not a failure.' More convincing.

Elliot didn't think she was a failure. 'Elliot,' Deborah said his name, just for the pleasure of it, and smiled. She loved him. For the first time, this gave her a warm glow. The kind of warm glow that she had, until that point, decided was an invention of the Minerva Press. 'I love him.' Utter conviction. Her reflection softened. She took a deep breath. 'And Elliot—Elliot loves me,' she said tremulously. Her smile became positively foolish. Her warm glow spread.

He loved her. She loved him. She was not a failure. It was not her fault. Was it too late? Deborah turned her back on her reflection, her face set in determined lines. The best things were worth fighting for. Elliot was the best thing ever to happen to her, but how—what could she do to persuade him that she had changed her mind? *Had* she changed her mind? All these years of thinking herself unattractive, undesirable, unwomanly—could she put them behind her? She couldn't be sure, but she could try. Weren't some things worth taking a chance on?

'Oh God, not just a chance, but the biggest gamble of my life.' Deborah paced the floor of her bedchamber, her bare feet icy on the boards. She couldn't risk hurting Elliot. She couldn't bear to hurt Elliot. But if Elliot truly did love her as he said, if he felt what she felt, had she not hurt him already? What was worse, taking a chance or not taking a chance?

Stupid question.

It was dawn before she lit upon the solution. The symmetry of it made her smile again. A beginning where it had all begun, except this time there would be two of them committing the crime. It was seditious and daring, it was illegal and it had the added attraction that by breaking the law they would be offending one of Jeremy's closest conspirators beyond any hope of forgiveness. Deborah thumped her fist into her open palm. It was perfect. Her smile faded. If only Elliot could be persuaded.

'He loves me. I love him. There is no question of failure,' she told her mirror confidently. Then she threw on her clothes and made haste down to her parlour. She had plans to make.

Elliot returned home dejected, having waved Lizzie, Alex and their entourage off on their journey north. Their obvious domestic bliss was like a dose of particularly disgusting medicine, except it did him no good.

He told himself that time would heal. Another of those old adages he had no faith in.

Though he had been angry and hurt by Deborah's rejection, he had been sustained, for the first few days, by the hope that she would change her mind. She would see, once she'd had time to think over what he had said, that he was right. She would realise that she loved him as he loved her, and that alone would be enough to change her. But days passed without a word, and his confidence waned. His nights were fraught. When he slept he dreamt, horrible dreams of running, running, and never reaching his destination. He was always losing things in his dreams, too. Packing them in a portmanteau, then discovering that he had not packed them after all. Leaving his valise somewhere, forgetting where. Putting things in the wrong pocket. Leaving them carelessly for someone else to steal. Nothing valuable, never the same things, but the loss was gut-wrenching.

He woke sweating, panting, his heart racing. Despair swamped him. Deborah did not come. Time and again, he set out to persuade her, but each time he changed direction. Having waited all his life to fall in love, he would not compromise it. Instead, he would focus on his future. There was unrest brewing in the country. With help, it could spread. The army had taught him how to lead. The Government had taught the Peacock how to break rules. He simply had to find a way to combine both talents to good effect. He would work out a role for himself. He would find a purpose. It would be enough. Sometimes, he almost believed it. He made plans, lots of plans, sure that one or several of them would be the thing which made him want to get out of bed in the morning.

He sat down by the empty grate, and was wondering how he was to fill the rest of the day when his servant brought him a note which had been delivered by hand. The familiar, untidy scrawl set his heart thudding. Elliot broke the seal.

It is set for tomorrow morning, he read, then paused, frowning. His own words, more or less, he remembered them clearly. The note he had written to Deborah that first time, when they broke into the house in Grosvenor Square. Not exactly what he was expecting, but then Deborah never did anything expected.

I will call for you at nine o'clock. Nine in the morning? What was she planning?

Bring your usual accessories. Daylight robbery?

If you do not wish to take part in this last assignment, send word by the boy. No signature. Elliot turned the single sheet over, but it was blank. Succinct and to the point. What point? For the first time in days, he found himself smiling. The point was that they would be together. He could hope. He could allow himself to hope.

'Will there be any reply, sir, only the boy is waiting?'

'No. Give him a sixpence and send him on his way,' Elliot said, unable to keep from grinning at his batman. *It is set for tomorrow morning.* Whatever *it* was, it was something.

He was waiting on the steps at fifteen minutes to nine. With still five minutes to go before the hour, Elliot had persuaded himself that she was not coming. He ran his fingers through his hair. The effect was to make it look considerably wilder. It needed cutting. He checked his pocket watch for the tenth time, giving it a shake, certain that it had stopped. He was upon the point of setting out for Hans Town on foot when a post-chaise pulled up in front of him and the door opened.

She was wearing her man's clothing. Breeches and boots. Greatcoat. Hat pulled down over her hair. Her smile, in the gloomy light of the carriage, was tremulous. 'You're here,' Deborah said foolishly, unable to say more because just seeing him made her breathless.

Elliot climbed into the chaise and sat down beside her. 'You're here,' he said, equally foolish, equally breathless. The carriage jolted over the cobblestones.

'Did you bring…?'

From the large pocket of his greatcoat, Elliot drew out his box of picks, his wrench. And the peacock feather.

The initial thrill of seeing him had receded. Deborah began to twist at one of the large brass buttons on her greatcoat.

Elliot took her hand, forcing her to relinquish her hold on the button, which she had already loosened. 'I've missed you,' he said.

Her fingers fluttered in his grip. 'I've missed you, too,' she whispered. She risked a glance up at him. His smile was only just perceptible, but it was there. Enough to give her courage. Enough to give her hope. 'Elliot…'

'Deborah?'

She sighed. 'I had a speech, but I don't think I can say it.' She took off her hat, and threw it on to the bench opposite. Then she gave one of her little nods. 'Elliot, I love you.'

He had hoped, from the moment he had read her note, he had hoped that she would be willing to consider the possibility, but he had not allowed himself to dream that she would say it. Just like that. Elliot was dumbfounded.

'I said, I love you.'

'Say it again.'

'I love you, Elliot.'

He tugged at his neckcloth. 'Are you sure?'

Deborah gave a funny little laugh. 'You think I'd be saying it if I was not?' She pressed a quick kiss to the back of his hand. 'I don't blame you for being sceptical.'

'Not sceptical, just scared, if you must know,' Elliot said, too afraid to consider prevaricating. 'I don't think I could bear it if you found you were wrong.'

She had never seen his face so stripped bare. The simple honesty of what he said, even more than his declaration over a week ago, made her realise the depths of his love for her. Almost she told him that she didn't deserve him, realising just in time that what mattered was that he believed she did. 'I know I love you, Elliot,' she said fervently, 'it's the thing I'm most certain of in the world. I promise.' She pressed another kiss on to his hand, then held it tight against her breast, then spoke in a rush, all the things she had planned so carefully tumbling out at once. 'You were right. About Jeremy.

About it not being my fault. About my hiding behind Bella. You were right about all of it, only it was such a shock. It took me days to be able to think straight. I knew I loved you, you see, from before—before we made love—but I thought it was impossible. Only after what you told me, I realised that I could make it possible if I wanted it enough, and I do, Elliot, I want it more than anything. You. Us. Only you have to understand, there are bound to be times when I think I'm not good enough. It's a hard habit to overcome, but what I'm trying to say is, that I want to try. I want to be happy, and I can't be happy without you, and that's worth trying for, isn't it? If it's not too late?'

'Too late?' Elliot tucked her hair behind her ear. Relief was already turning into something he thought might be happiness, spreading like fingers of sunshine from the inside out. 'It could never be too late. I love you. Didn't I tell you that's not going to change?' He swept her into his arms, pulling her across the bench of the carriage and kissing her ruthlessly. 'I love you,' he said, breathing heavily some moments, later. 'You have no idea how much.'

'I do. I do, Elliot. I have every idea.' Deborah clutched at his shoulders, pressing herself into the reassuringly solid bulk of him, kissing him back, deep passionate kisses, desperate, needy kisses. She ached with love for him. Her fingers twined in his hair, roamed restlessly down his back, under his coat, fumbling with the buttons of his waistcoat. Kisses were not enough. She needed him. All of him. Now.

Except that she had a plan, she remembered belatedly as the post-chaise jolted around a bend in the road and began to pick up speed, throwing them both hard back against the squabs. Elliot looked out of the dusty window, surprised to discover that they had left the city far behind. 'Where are we going?'

'Back to where it began. And ended,' Deborah said.

Elliot pulled her into his arms again. 'I'm not much in the mood for riddles. What I'm in the mood for involves you and me and a bed,' he said, slipping his hand under her coat and cupping her breast.

'That is the plan, sort of,' Deborah said, though she was having serious doubts about her ability to wait until then. His thumb was circling her nipple. She couldn't think and she needed to think. With a huge effort, she struggled free of his embrace. 'An hour, not much longer,' she said.

'An hour!' Elliot looked out of the window again. The countryside looked vaguely familiar. He turned back to Deborah, narrowing his eyes. 'Back to where it began, and ended?'

She nodded.

Her eyes were sparkling, that mixture of daring and excitement that sent the blood rushing to his groin. Elliot bit down on his smile. 'Please don't tell me that you plan to break into Kinsail Manor in the middle of the day?'

She nodded again.

'Am I to fall off the drainpipe and into your arms?'

'No.' Deborah began to pluck at the button of her

greatcoat again. 'We are going to make love. In my bed. In the daylight.' The button came away in her fingers. She stared at it in some surprise, before tucking it away in her pocket. 'I don't want there to be any ghosts to come between us,' she said. 'I want you to know I mean it. I love you.'

Elliot couldn't help it, he laughed. 'And you intend to prove it by breaking into your dead husband's home and making love on your marriage bed? That is the most outrageous, outlandish, subversive and utterly perfect plan I have ever heard of in my life. How could I ever doubt you, after this? And if I have to dangle on the end of a hangman's noose, I will take comfort in knowing that you are by my side.'

'Don't be silly, Elliot, they are not actually in residence.'

'That, my love, I had deduced for myself.'

'So you'll do it?'

'I will do anything you ask, provided you kiss me.'

'I don't think I will ever tire of kissing you.'

'Prove it,' Elliot said huskily, as his lips claimed hers.

They left the post-chaise at the Cross Keys, a mile from Kinsail Manor, and completed the journey on foot. It was hot; the sun beamed down from the pale blue summer sky, making their greatcoats look decidedly out of place. Deborah's step was almost a skip as they approached the huge portico which fronted the manor. She could not stop smiling.

'Are you sure the place is empty?' Elliot asked, surveying the shuttered windows doubtfully. 'There must be a skeleton staff in charge?'

'Mrs Chambers, the housekeeper. And she visits her niece on a Wednesday. The rest are either in London or have been paid off.' Deborah grinned. 'Don't worry, I've checked it all most meticulously. I have, after all, been trained by the master.'

'Then let us get on with it,' Elliot said.

'There is no need to hurry. I've told you, Mrs Chambers—'

'I don't give a damn about Mrs Chambers, and there is every need to hurry. I have a burning need to see you naked, my love,' Elliot said wickedly.

'Oh.'

'Precisely.'

The recent loss of his precious blue diamond had not been enough to overcome Lord Kinsail's inherent miserliness. No new bolts had been fitted to protect his property. Picking the two ancient locks which protected the kitchen door was a simple task which Elliot said disparagingly was quite beneath the Peacock.

The house was cold, unmistakably empty. Deborah led the way through the cavernous kitchens, noting without surprise that the ancient range had still not been replaced. The stone stairs which led through the baize door into the main hall were still treacherous. She paused, looking around her, waiting for the ghosts to grab her, but felt only a wild elation, a growing sense of certainty.

Telling Elliot to wait, she went hastily into the dining

room, retrieving two of the best crystal glasses from the cupboard. Their footsteps echoed on the wooden staircase as they made their way up to the first floor. The master suite was in the east wing. Two doors. Jacob slept in Jeremy's room, she knew that from previous visits, but Cousin Margaret occupied another, in the west wing. The mistress's chamber, in which Deborah had spent almost every night of her marriage, was no longer used.

She paused outside the door. Her mouth was dry. Her hand hovered over the intricate brass handle.

'Deborah, you don't have to...'

'I want to.' She threw the door back and stepped over the threshold. Placing the glasses along with a small bundle on the dressing table, she opened the shutters, filling the room with light. Dust motes danced in the air. The room smelt stuffy, stale, but she could detect no scent of either failure or misery. Hauling the holland covers which shrouded the bed on to the floor, she looked around her, trying to summon up the past, but it eluded her. Here was the bed. There was the connecting door. But the woman who had been Jeremy's wife was not present.

Turning to Elliot, Deborah smiled. 'Now we can make our beginning.' Wrapping her arms around his neck, she stood on tiptoe. 'Make love to me, Elliot. To me. To Deborah. Not to Bella. Make love to me now,' she whispered, then kissed him.

He kissed her back. Slowly. Lovingly. Then deeply and passionately. The kisses that had begun in the post-chaise blossomed in the sunlit room. They kissed and kissed and kissed, then kisses were not enough. Coats, waistcoats and shirts were cast off, scattered across the room as they kissed.

Deborah sank on to the bed and Elliot removed first her boots and breeches then his own. He cupped her breasts, sucking deep on one nipple, then the other, sending white-hot heat down, pooling in her belly. Her hands roamed over his back, his chest, his stomach. They fell back on to the mattress, kissing, touching, stroking. His fingers traced fire in a path along the tender flesh of her thighs. She touched him, shivering with anticipation as she wrapped her fingers around his shaft, potent and thick.

He sank his fingers into her, making her gasp. She could feel herself tightening, clenching. She wanted him inside her, wanted it with a primal urgency that should be shocking, but was exciting. 'Elliot,' she said, closing her eyes, trying to cling to the edge, 'Elliot, I don't think I can wait.'

She felt the rumble of his laughter as he pulled her on top of him. 'That makes two of us.' His eyes were ablaze. He lifted her on to him, guided her down and she moaned harshly as he slid into her, high inside her. Already, she could feel the spiralling. He bucked under her and she clutched at his chest, her hair trailing over his face. He lifted her, slid her back down again on to him and she cried out at the wonder of it, thrust with him this time and again, harder, higher each time until her climax swept her away. The clenching of her muscles around him sent him over the edge and pulsing into her.

Deborah collapsed on to his chest, warmed by the sun, heated by their passion, breathing hard. 'Elliot,' she said, pressing hot, fluttering kisses to his mouth.

'Deborah,' he said, mirroring her action.

'I used to feel so empty, here,' she said, looking round. 'Now I feel—filled.'

Beneath her, Elliot chuckled. 'I hope so.'

'That's not what I meant,' she said, though her eyes were dancing.

He rolled her over, pinning her beneath him. 'Complete. That's what you meant.'

She blinked away a sudden tear. She had cried enough tears here. 'That's exactly what I meant. But there's just one thing missing.' Wriggling out from under him, she quickly untied the bundle she had brought with her and grabbed the crystal glasses. 'It will be warm, I hope you don't mind,' she said, holding the champagne bottle aloft.

'I must congratulate you on your plan,' Elliot replied, taking the bottle from her and popping the cork. 'You seem to have thought of everything.' He handed her a glass. 'To us.'

'To us,' Deborah said. She smiled at him, Bella's wicked smile, but she was under no illusions. It was Deborah who smiled it. 'I sincerely hope that after today, I shall be the only woman you will drink champagne with. Naked, in the middle of the day.'

Elliot took her glass from her and placed it on the

bedside table. 'I can promise you more than that,' he said. 'You, my love, will be the first and only woman that I will drink champagne from. Naked or otherwise. Day or night.'

'What do you mean?'

He tipped her on to her back and straddled her. 'Let me show you,' he said. The contents of his glass made her gasp as he tipped them on to her. Then his lips began to lap the wine from her skin, licking down the valley between her breasts, sipping from the dip of her belly and down.

The sun had moved round to the west wing of the Manor by the time they finished the champagne. 'They'll realise someone has been here,' Elliot said, tying a careless knot in his neckcloth, watching Deborah arrange the empty bottle and glasses neatly on the side table.

'I want him to know and I want them to know it was us,' she said, picking up the parcel from the dressing table. From it she produced a book. *Hemlock*. She laid it in the centre of the bed. On top of it she placed an antique wedding ring. 'Now Jacob will know that I know, he will know who wrote Bella's stories, and he will be far too embarrassed to do anything about any of it,' she said. 'This is where Bella was born, it feels only right that I leave her here.'

Elliot stared down at the book and the ring and the bed. Then he reached into his coat pocket and took out the last feather, laying it on top of the book, weighting it with the ring. 'In that case, it feels only right that the Peacock should die with her.' He pulled Deborah into his arms and kissed her tenderly. 'You are the most extraordinary woman I have ever met.'

Deborah emerged from his embrace ruffled and heated. 'You know,' she said, casting a final look around the room, 'I think I'm beginning to believe you.'

* * * * *

REQUEST YOUR FREE BOOKS!

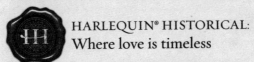

HARLEQUIN® HISTORICAL:
Where love is timeless

2 FREE NOVELS PLUS 2 **FREE GIFTS!**

YES! Please send me 2 FREE Harlequin® Historical novels and my 2 FREE gifts (gifts are worth about $10). After receiving them, if I don't wish to receive any more books, I can return the shipping statement marked "cancel." If I don't cancel, I will receive 6 brand-new novels every month and be billed just $5.19 per book in the U.S. or $5.74 per book in Canada. That's a savings of at least 17% off the cover price! It's quite a bargain! Shipping and handling is just 50¢ per book in the U.S. and 75¢ per book in Canada.* I understand that accepting the 2 free books and gifts places me under no obligation to buy anything. I can always return a shipment and cancel at any time. Even if I never buy another book, the two free books and gifts are mine to keep forever.

246/349 HDN FEQQ

Name _____ (PLEASE PRINT) _____

Address _____ Apt. # _____

City _____ State/Prov. _____ Zip/Postal Code _____

Signature (if under 18, a parent or guardian must sign) _____

Mail to the **Reader Service:**
IN U.S.A.: P.O. Box 1867, Buffalo, NY 14240-1867
IN CANADA: P.O. Box 609, Fort Erie, Ontario L2A 5X3

Not valid for current subscribers to Harlequin Historical books.

Want to try two free books from another line?
Call 1-800-873-8635 or visit www.ReaderService.com.

* Terms and prices subject to change without notice. Prices do not include applicable taxes. Sales tax applicable in N.Y. Canadian residents will be charged applicable taxes. Offer not valid in Quebec. This offer is limited to one order per household. All orders subject to credit approval. Credit or debit balances in a customer's account(s) may be offset by any other outstanding balance owed by or to the customer. Please allow 4 to 6 weeks for delivery. Offer available while quantities last.

Your Privacy—The Reader Service is committed to protecting your privacy. Our Privacy Policy is available online at www.ReaderService.com or upon request from the Reader Service.

We make a portion of our mailing list available to reputable third parties that offer products we believe may interest you. If you prefer that we not exchange your name with third parties, or if you wish to clarify or modify your communication preferences, please visit us at www.ReaderService.com/consumerschoice or write to us at Reader Service Preference Service, P.O. Box 9062, Buffalo, NY 14269. Include your complete name and address.

HH11B

HARLEQUIN® HISTORICAL:
Where love is timeless

A deliciously sinful and mischievously witty
new trilogy from

BRONWYN SCOTT

Rakes Beyond Redemption

Too wicked for polite society...

They're the men society mamas warn their daughters about...
and the men innocent debutantes find
scandalously irresistible!

Can these notorious rakes be tamed?

Find out this September!

HOW TO DISGRACE A LADY
Available September 2012

HOW TO RUIN A REPUTATION
Available October 2012

HOW TO SIN SUCCESSFULLY
Available November 2012